IRREPLACEABLE

IN A SMALL TOWN

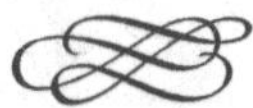

ALIE GARNETT

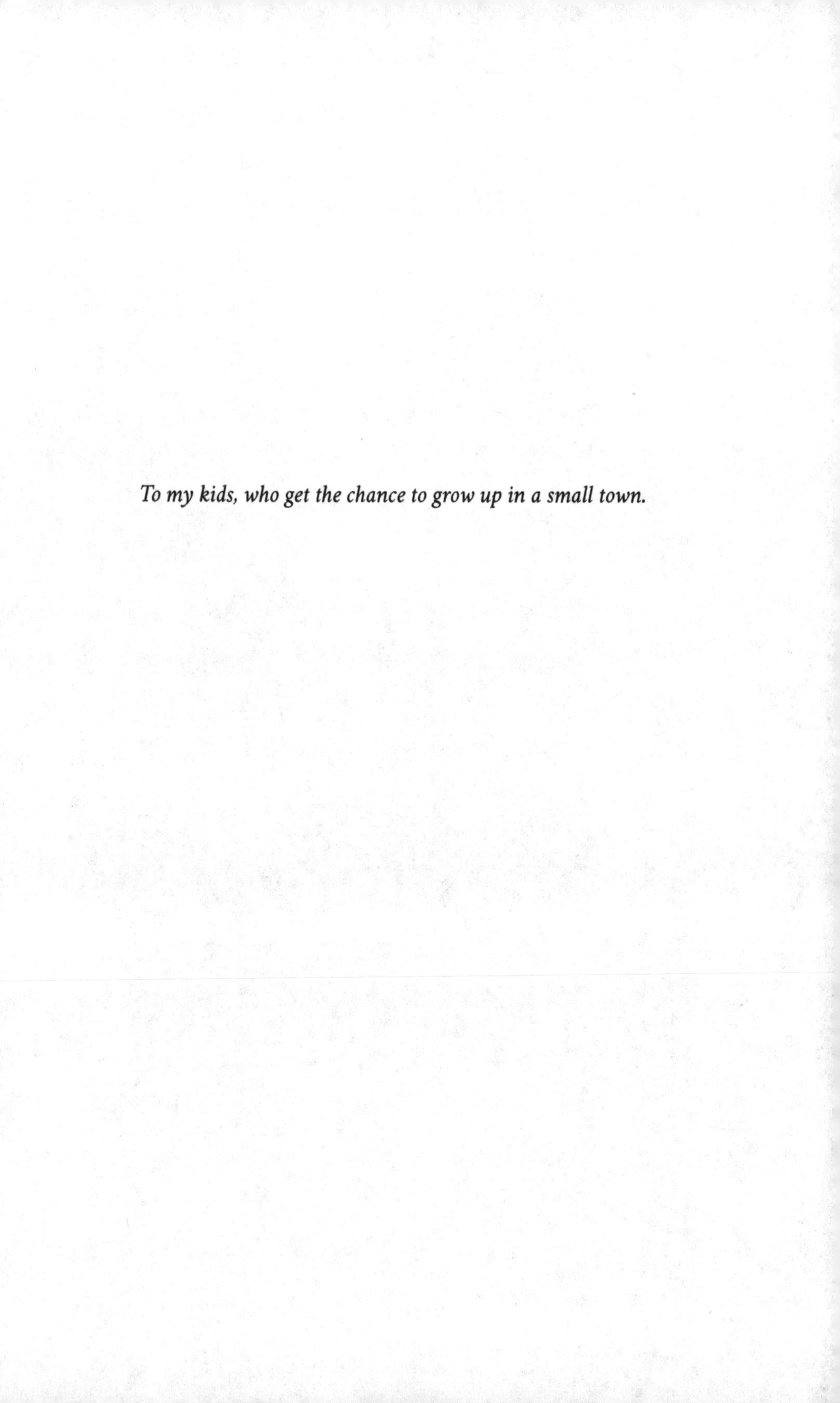

To my kids, who get the chance to grow up in a small town.

NOTE FROM THE AUTHOR

If you have been engrossed in Landstad, North Dakota, you know that Mia and Rafferty have been circling each other for months, maybe years. Which is why their story starts around the same time as Ruth and Anderson's. So when their story starts, we go back in time. As a bonus, you get to go back to the important events in Landstad over the last year or so.

***

PS: If this is the first book you are reading of the series, please please please, just go back and start at the beginning. You will not regret it.

Love, Alie

CHAPTER 1

Winter

Mia Lawson was being dumped.

This wasn't the first time, and it obviously wasn't going to be the last time.

In fact, she even saw this one coming. For over a month, not that she was pushing to end it, because then she would be single ... again.

And what was worse than being in a dead-end relationship with Damion "bald at thirty" Paulson? Being single after you were dumped by Damion "asked his cousin to prom and got turned down" Paulson!

Not that she wasn't used to being single. She was twenty-nine, and her longest relationship had been six months, and that was years ago. Sadly, that guy had dumped her, too.

"... and I think we want different things, Mia." Damion was still talking even is she wasn't listening to him.

In reality, she was expecting him to dump her via text or ghost her like the last guy from Norden last summer. But not this guy. No. He did it in person while she was working. In front of people. Not that Bill and Carl cared one whit about her love life, but Rafferty Brooks was behind Damion "cries during Disney movies" Paulson, all ears. He was probably reveling in her embarrassment.

"What do you think I want?" glaring at him her arms were crossed and her eye was twitching. She hated when it did that!

Mia wasn't deep. Her wants were simple: she wanted to be married with kids, and she wanted it the day before yesterday. Mia Lawson was the kind of girl who a good man dated through high school and proposed to at prom after their first magical time together, married her one hot summer night a few months later, and by the time the snow started to fly that fall, had her knocked up with the first of two perfect kids and one accident that came along a few years later. That one was also perfect.

Then they would enjoy living in the small town they had been raised in, enjoying the little things, like the fall festival, Christmas festival, Fourth of July parade, and everything else that happened in this one-horse town. Oh, and their Christmas cards would have been the talk of the town. Simply gorgeous.

Was that asking too much? Apparently, it was because that wasn't what she got. Not even close. Instead, she was still here and still single ten years later. She had lost her virginity to the wrong guy on prom night. Had waited that entire hot summer for him to call afterward. That never happened. By the time the snow flew, she had forced herself to move on, to give up completely on him. Admit she had been used.

And all those festivals? She went alone. Every damn year.

Mostly because she dated jerks. Case in point, the one in front of her. The one who didn't walk away as she stared him down.

"Ahm, I just … You know …" the idiot stammered, unable to actually admit what he had been up to.

"You know what I want, Damion? I want a boyfriend who isn't drooling after some chick from seven miles away in Norden. What's her name? Sally? Sidney? Sylvia?" Mia tapped her finger against her temple as if she was really trying to remember. She knew the answer. It was, after all, her job to know what was happening around the area. She served the food, and her patrons gave her all the information they thought she needed—as well as the information she *didn't* want.

"Donna," the man actually admitted. He was making this too easy.

"Donna Farley, you mean. Donna 'I'm not divorced from my fourth husband' Farley, Damion? Or is it Donna 'I cheated on my last four husbands' Farley, Damion? Or is it Donna 'I have an STD' Farley?"

Mia had only learned that one this morning, but it was nice information to have right now. At the time, she had only been relieved that their relationship hadn't gone beyond a few kisses, mostly because he wasn't exactly a good kisser. Wet, very wet.

"She doesn't have an STD." Damion defended his new love. Not once had he defended her when they were together.

"You're right, of course, Damion," Mia said, her eyes twitching again. "She has two. Do you want me to name them? In front of Bill and Carl over there and Rafferty back there. Oh, and there is your aunt Candy and her sister, you're mom, in the back. Hi, ladies." She actually looked at the empty booth, which caused him to look that way. So maybe he wasn't the one, and maybe she knew that a long time ago. But the pickings were slim in Landstad, ND. Sometimes you had scrap the bottle of the pail.

Without spotting his mom, his eyes swung back to her. "Mia, be reasonable."

"There is no reasonable, Damion. How long have you been seeing her?" She tapped the order pad with her pen as she waited on the answer.

"Not long." His eyes were on the uneaten plate of food in front of him that was getting cold.

"Before or after Christmas? Did you go see her family for the holiday, or did she have to tell her mother that you were busy on Christmas? Did she have to tell her mother that you couldn't get time off from work? When everyone knows you're a government employee and don't even work on Christmas Day?"

Mia had spent the entire holiday making excuses as to why her new man wasn't there. Why he was too busy to spend the day with her. At the time, she had thought it was her five sisters that might have scared him off. Since everyone knew they were hard to take as a group. Then she started to hear things. A lot of things.

"I went to her place that day," Damien confirmed, something his own sister had admitted last week. Because his sister already knew it was over, and Mia wondered if Damion had asked his sister to break up with her for him. Mia wasn't letting that happen.

"Surprise surprise. I would assume it's her bed you've been sleeping in because it hasn't been mine. Which is alright since you probably have more than one STD by now." Mia made sure to say it loud enough for the entire café to hear and secretly wished Bill and Carl were talkers. But she had long since realized they only talked to each other.

The fact that she and Damion hadn't actually slept together might be the reason he had jumped into Donna Farley's bed so quickly. But she wasn't ready to make that move with him. After all, a girl had to be picky about that sort of thing. Which was turning out to be smart, very smart.

"Damion, I think it's time to go." Rafferty Brooks was suddenly on his feet and grabbing Damion's shoulder, pulling him from his stool. Of course, Rafferty would try and protect his fellow man.

"I'm not done eating." The man pointed to the nearly full roast beef meal and mashed potato he'd thought was worth dying over. A meal she was sure he thought he wouldn't have to pay for since, when he ordered, they were still dating.

Before Damion even moved, Mia dismissed him and focused on Rafferty Brooks instead. "Let the man eat, Rafferty. He's right; we're done. Three months of my life for nothing. Nothing."

Before she even thought about what she was doing, she grabbed Damion's plate from in front of him as he stabbed at another piece of roast. The man barely had time to look up before the plate landed on his head, food side down. The plate had even slid from his head to the floor before his large glass of milk followed the path of the plate.

Her only hope was that it splattered on Rafferty—he always deserved to be splattered. Today his suit was the gray one she had always liked. He looked good in gray. She hated that he looked good in everything.

When she told them to leave—or one of them, and really, she didn't know which one—she grabbed a pie plate in each hand. Rafferty headed for the door, but Damion was still in shock and covered in mashed potatoes and gravy, sitting on the stool.

Reminding herself to have Rafferty's bill ready for tomorrow because he hadn't paid, the door closed behind him. He could run, but she knew where to find him. She always did.

Damion's bill was also due. "Get out of here, Damion. Before I do something I'll regret."

"You don't regret this?" He pointed to his head.

"I will never regret that. In fact, I'm proud of that. I'll regret giving you a black eye, though." She grabbed the counter to control herself from going over that very edge.

Damion finally got a clue and jumped up, heading for the door. Grabbing his coat from the coat rack as he went. Before she could stop herself, she threw two small glass pie plates at the man's retreating form. Both hit their mark but didn't do anything other than make the man yelp as he rushed out the front door, the bells tinkling as it slammed closed behind him.

Watching him nearly run to his truck through the glass windows, she once again wondered what she had ever seen in the man. He was right; they wanted different things. They wanted different people.

As the door closed, she took a deep, calming breath before turning to smile over at the old men who were looking at her. Neither said anything about what had happened, which was a good thing because both had full plates in front of them and she didn't know if she could control herself yet..

Shaking her head, she surveyed the mess she had caused. And what a mess it was. Sadly, her life was in even worse shape. She was trapped in this town with nobody who loved her and nobody she wanted to love her. She needed out. Now.

CHAPTER 2

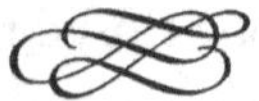

MIA LAWSON WAS BEING DUMPED, right in the middle of her own café in front of at least half a dozen people. It was a train wreck, and Rafferty Brooks couldn't look away. Because this train wreck was sure to turn into a train explosion.

As she started to hurdle food at the man, Rafferty barely got far enough away to not get covered himself. He quickly looked over himself, trying to find any chunks or splashes of anything he was sure Mia had secretly wanted him also covered in. Seeing her eyes look him up and down, he knew she was disappointed he got away unscathed.

"Get out," she said in a low voice, her hands reaching for the plastic-covered pies sitting on the counter.

Rafferty knew it was time to leave, but Damion wasn't as smart and started to argue with her. Grabbing his coat from the booth he had been sitting in, he was almost out the door when Damion wasn't only hit with a blueberry pie, but also the award-winning apple.

Once outside, the cold hit Rafferty, and he quickly pulled on his coat. Now what to do? He had gone to the café to get away from his dad and the bomb that was dropped on him today. The bomb wasn't a surprise in itself, just that it was happening already.

This morning he had shown up to work, a job he'd had for years selling insurance alongside his dad. His dad showing up had never been a good thing, but today, his dad was actually happy to be there. Well, for a few minutes, at least. Because Howard Brooks was retiring as of today. No warning, no planning, just done.

On top of that, Howard had sold the building he had owned since before Rafferty had even been born. Rafferty had thought he would work at the place forever … until his dad sold it. According to Howard, he had gotten an offer he couldn't turn down. And it seemed he couldn't have run it by his son and successor before making the deal.

Now his whole future looked hazy. A few years ago, he had joined his dad's insurance agency in hopes of getting to know the man who hadn't done much to be close to his only son over the years. It hadn't worked, and today, Rafferty was reminded that his father was still a jerk.

Not that working with his dad had been the only reason he came home. He missed the town he had been raised in. He missed knowing everyone in the café when he went in. He missed the Fourth of July parade where so many people showed up just to watch that the town's population raise by ten-fold for a few hours. He missed that he could walk through the entire town and name the people in every house for the past twenty years. So, he came back, and he stayed.

Standing on the sidewalk on Main Street, the cold was seeping into his body as he debated what to do next. What he should do is go home and spend the day deciding what to do with the rest of his life.

Only the realization that Mia Lawson was single again had him rooted to the spot. Not that the woman had ever had a long-term man in her life; most were short flings, and a lot were nonstarters. But she was fun and popular, and it was a matter of time before she found the one, or the one she would settle for.

With his work life in shambles, he decided that he could try and get his love life in order. Suddenly, he thought he knew the way. He would get a friend of a friend to talk him up a bit, making him look good. Maybe convince Mia he was someone to take out for a test drive and kick the tires. Buy?

His friend Anderson Miles's personal assistant and Mia had recently turned into close friends during the last few weeks. Not that they didn't know each other before. They went to high school together and had both lived in town for years. As had Rafferty.

But the woman hated Rafferty. Hated. She had a long list of reasons why, and she wasn't afraid to remind him of them. Or at least she would if she didn't spend all her time ignoring him.

Angel Johnson's name was actually Ruth Kennedy now, but she was always Angel in school. She became a Kennedy when her mom married when she was fourteen. He liked to think of Ruth with her old name. It suited her better. The woman was born with white hair and pale blue eyes. She actually looked like an Angel, and now she acted like one, but in high school, the name didn't fit her at all. Back then, she was known for getting into trouble and getting too handsy with her boyfriend.

The worst part about Angel's hatred of him was that he truly loved her. He kind of always had. They had a connection from the beginning. He must have met her on the first day of kindergarten if not earlier—it was a small town, and they were the same age. They connected that year when she was, of course, chosen as the angel in the kindergarten school play, where he was a shepherd and had to stare at the angel for almost the entire two hours. Why he was the only one who noticed that she was going to fall, he didn't know. Why he thought he would be able to catch her, he didn't know either. They both ended up breaking their arms, and then they had actually been friends of sort the entire time they were in school.

Just friends, too. He had never been sexually attracted to Angel. By the time he realized what sex really was, she was already dating Franky Berg, and she dated him from the time they were twelve until he dumped her during college. Almost as soon as that relationship was over for her, she learned the secret her mom had been keeping from her for eighteen years: who her dad really was. That information is what had turned them into supposed enemies. He and Angel shared a dad.

Angel was the product of his dad's fifteen-year affair with Sara Johnson. To this day, he had yet to acknowledge her as his daughter in any way. Sara had been the one to tell Rafferty, not his father. It was Sara who had asked him to be tested to see if he and Angel shared the same blood type. The woman was desperate and would do anything for her daughter. Sure enough, they did, and then came more tests. That was when he had found out Angel had actually lost function of her kidneys and needed a transplant.

Today he had one kidney, and she had the other. She owed him, and he was about to ask for payment. Mia was worth far more than a kidney to him.

Rafferty walked across the street without looking for traffic. Traffic would stop for him; it was Landstad. Of course, there was no traffic to speak of since it was freezing outside.

Pushing through the door, Ruth was sitting at her desk and seemed happy until the moment she saw him. Then she was as cold as it was outside.

"Anderson, your friend is here," she announced in her best angry personal assistant voice.

Anderson quickly came out to her office area. "Rafferty, what can I do for you today? Come into my office. My personal assistant has some issues with you." He was trying to get him away from Ruth as fast as possible.

It almost made Rafferty laugh. His friend was suddenly smitten with his personal assistant, which for the past few weeks had been fun to watch and even more fun to tease the man about. Ruth had been working for Anderson for years, and now suddenly he was interested.

Rafferty looked over at Ruth, who was staring intently at her computer. "I want to talk with her for a minute."

"Nothing to say to you, Brooks." Ruth turned and was now shuffling through the papers on her desk, making a point not to look at him.

He grabbed a visitor chair, pulled it to the front of her desk, and plopped down in it. "I need you to talk to Mia for me. Talk me up."

"No, I don't want any of my friends talking to you. They deserve better." She didn't look up at him, but he kept staring at her anyway, which caused her to start blushing. She always blushed easily, and he liked to see that hadn't changed.

"You owe me, Angel," he mumbled quietly, hoping Anderson wasn't paying attention.

Standing up, she looked down at him with anger. "And this is what you want? Mia Lawson? What happens when you need a liver?" Her voice was just as quiet.

"I hear yours is getting quite the workout at book club." Their gazes didn't break as he got to his feet, the smile gone.

"Not nearly as much as yours always has," she countered, but he knew she had no idea. She never went out for fun. She was too much of a homebody for that.

"Could you just talk to her?" he asked, nicer now. Anger wasn't going to get him anything.

"No. If she wants to talk to you, she will. She knows you as much as I do." She picked up the pile of papers.

Which was exactly why he needed someone else to talk to her. They had too much of a past. It wasn't even all that had happened in the last few years. He had messed things up badly long before he came back to Landstad.

"Come on, Angel." He begged.

"No, you can lord it over my head some more. It's nice when you drag it out like this. I would hate for that to stop." Whispering so Anderson didn't hear, Ruth sat down and turned her back on him. Only to stare at the wall, not even pretending to be doing anything productive.

Leaning against the door jam, Anderson folded his arms, his face set in slight annoyance. "Come into my office, Rafferty. She said no."

Rafferty shrugged in defeat. His work life was done, and his love life was done. Now he had nothing to keep him in town, which meant he would have to give up on Mia forever. But maybe it was for the best. Ruth was right—if Mia had wanted him, she knew where he was. She'd never wanted him.

In Anderson's office, he sat heavily in the chair across from his friend. "Dad just sold the building our office is in. Someone offered him way more than it was worth, and he took it."

"So now you have rent. I rent this place. It's not bad, and you don't have to worry about taxes and upkeep. When something breaks, you just call the management company, and it gets fixed." Anderson tried to make it sound like it wasn't the end of the world.

"No, they want us out. They doubled the average rent price in the area. Dad is retiring, but I need the office. I don't want to leave town, but I might have to," Rafferty admitted. There was no way he could afford the rent. Any rent, really. His dad wasn't as well-liked in town as Anderson. So far less successful.

"Maybe somewhere else in town?" Anderson suggested.

"No luck. They own almost all the open rental space in town." Rafferty leaned back and rubbed his eyes hard.

What he hadn't realized until today was that for being a small town that should be having issues with keeping renters and finding buyers, Landstad was the complete opposite. The town was thriving for some reason. There were only a few homes and no businesses for sale in town, and it had been that way for years now.

"I rent from M Johnson Inc., and I haven't had any issues." Anderson leaned toward him across the desk.

"That's who bought the building. We've been there since before I was even born, and now we are going to have to move. Or I am," Rafferty said, trying not to sound as depressed as he felt about it.

"Well, if your dad is really retiring, maybe you want to join me over here," Anderson suggested from out of nowhere.

Ruth rushed into the room as if she had been listening to them, which he was sure she had been. Her hands were on her hips, and her voice unwavering as she stated, "No way is he working here. I'll be out that door if he comes in it. I won't spend my days with him."

"Ruth, it was just an idea." Anderson turned his attention to Ruth.

Rafferty could tell that he didn't like that he had upset Ruth. He appreciated how much the man was into the woman. She had it for him just as badly, but for a lot longer.

"We could be co-workers, Angel. It would be fun. You, me, and Andy, a trio of insurance fun," Rafferty couldn't help himself from teasing her.

"I'll quit. In fact, why don't you just think about how my quitting would affect you because I'm leaving right now. Have a good weekend!" she yelled through the door at them as she walked out into the cold.

Anderson panicked at the woman leaving without her jacket on. It was, after all, freezing outside. Rafferty wasn't too worried about her. Within seconds of her angry exit, she'd be home in her apartment right above them.

Her retreat meant she wouldn't help him. And without Ruth, he had no way of convincing Mia of anything. There was no way she would give him the time of day without someone else's encouragement. He had to get Ruth to help him. She was his only hope.

CHAPTER 3

Mia knew everyone in town felt sorry for her when Betty said she could clean up the mess of Damion 'walked to class until the eighth grade by his mom' Paulson. Betty never volunteered to clean anything, and since she came with the place when Mia bought it, she was sure Betty had never cleaned before.

But after the pitiful dumping that Mia got, Betty was willing to do it. Which meant it was worse than Mia had thought. Much worse.

Betty enveloped her into a tight hug with too much menthol and too much old lady boob for Mia's liking, but she accepted it. Because her life was in the crapper.

"You go see your mama, baby. She will make you feel better," the woman stated in her 'pack a day since time began' gravelly voice.

The only answer Mia could give her was a nod as she headed for the back of the café and her jacket. No way was she going to her mother's, though. Her mom thought Damion was her last chance to catch a decent man. There were so few of those around.

Pulling on her jacket, she headed out the door. After a decade of working at the café and a few of those owning it, she didn't bring anything but her coat with her anymore. Her purse was left at home because it was just a building away, and she never needed it here.

The bitter cold assaulted her as she walked out the back door and shoved her hands into her coat pockets. She had forgotten her mittens this morning, and she was paying for it now. Hurrying, Mia headed for her apartment, where she would spend the rest of the day on the couch with a good bottle of whiskey and a good movie or two. Which was all way better than dating Damion "scared of rabbits" Paulson.

Coming up the alley, she saw there was almost nobody on Main Street this afternoon. It seemed the temperatures were keeping people from being out and about, which was fine by her. Across the street, she could see Ruth Kennedy sitting at her desk in front of the big insurance office window.

The woman was looking the other direction, so Mia didn't wave. Sometimes when she was looking out, Mia would wave, and Ruth would sometimes wave back—more often in the last few weeks since they had started a book club together. Before that, it was more hit and miss, but mostly miss and ignore.

Admittedly, Ruth had been one of the original members, her and Tess Thorn, who was the president of the bank. But Mia had found her way in by providing a location and encouraging everyone to keep coming back, even when the location changed to Ruth's apartment. Mia would've loved to have had it at the café forever, except the booze flowed too freely for her little café. Due to the city council being old busy bodies, the location had to be moved before the town discovered what made the club so much fun.

There were six members in all since Mia had forced her cousin to go. Mostly because she didn't know Tess well and what she knew of Ruth wasn't very encouraging for her to stay a member. Mandy Nordskov was loved by everyone, and nobody would kick her out of a book club, or her cousin who had kindly invited her to join.

The other two were quite a bit younger, and Mia was sure that neither would return to another meeting since they spent their lives avoiding each other. But Hazel May and Natalie Beckett kept coming back week after week. Sure, they said nothing to each other, but Mia was convinced they would work things out one day. It was her goal, so she knew it would happen.

Walking in front of the clinic between the café and her apartment, she saw her cousin sitting at the reception desk. The town was too cheap to actually hire someone to fill that spot, so Mandy had to be the receptionist and nurse practitioner all in one. So far, Mandy had been at the job for a few weeks and had time for it all, but Mia was encouraging everyone she knew to go to the clinic. A successful clinic made a healthy, happy town.

Pushing her way into the clinic, she wanted to say it was because she wanted to talk to her cousin, but it was because it was too cold to go on without a little stop to warm-up. The hot air hit her, and she breathed deeply for the first time since she left the café.

Mandy's blonde head came up from looking at the computer and smiled at her. "Business or pleasure?"

"Is a checkup business or pleasure?" Mia demanded. Neither were actually very descriptive of what could happen in this place.

Mandy's blue eyes went to the computer, and she started to type. "Do you have an appointment?"

"No, I don't have good enough insurance to make appointments. Appointments are for those with fancy insurance. My insurance only covers me asking my cousin hypotheticals over Sunday dinner." Mia leaned against the counter and loved that her cousin laughed at her joke. Okay, maybe a joke, but mostly real.

But Mia knew Mandy hadn't been overly happy to move back to her hometown. Mia hadn't pushed for details because she was happy Mandy had moved back. Mandy was one of four siblings, and only her brother lived in town until Mandy had found her apartment. The other sisters were off living in the big city. Well, two different big cities. It was the same for Mia's sisters. Of the six of them, only two still lived in Landstad, and Kipling was only there because she was in high school. Since she was a senior, Mia knew she would soon be gone as well.

For now, she was enjoying having Mandy here, and she lived right above the clinic. That made her Mia's next-door neighbor. It was nice having family so close.

"Aren't you supposed to be working?" Mandy asked with a raised eyebrow.

"Aren't you?" Mia countered.

"You, my dear, stepped into my workplace. Not the other way around." Mandy grinned.

"Want to play doctor?" Mia teased her.

"Nurse practitioner, and I don't play doctor." Mandy always pointed out that she wasn't a doctor, but she was as close as they got around here. And everyone who knew her loved her. "So, why are you off so early?"

"Damion dumped me." She pouted as she slumped into a hard plastic chair.

Mandy looked at her in confusion. "Didn't you dump him like a month ago?"

"I was thinking about it, but then decided to keep him through the holidays. That was a mistake. He'd been cheating on me for weeks, which I was willing to overlook in order to have a man to point at during the holidays. Except he didn't even show up for either holiday. And he was 'busy' on New Year's. A complete bust."

"Are we still talking about Damion Paulson? Shorter than average and with that oddly shaped head?" Mandy mimicked the shape against her own head with her hands.

"Yes, and he cheated on me. Me! Would you cheat on this?" She waved her hands over her jacket-covered body.

"In that jacket? Nobody. That jacket is amazing," Amanda said sarcastically.

"Is it because it's pink? I'm a woman; I can wear a pink jacket." Looking down at it, she knew it was far from the latest style. And maybe it did make her look like she was four. But she had thought she had been pulling it off.

"You look like you're six, Mia." Amanda chuckled.

"It's cute and makes me look young. And it was on sale."

"Young, like a toddler. How big of a sale?"

She shrugged. "Very!"

"Your mom bought it for you, didn't she?"

"Wrong! She bought it for Kipling, but she wouldn't wear it. Mine was falling apart, and it fits." She really only needed one jacket, but maybe she should look for a different one when winter ends, and the winter sales begin.

"Why would you take it if an eighteen-year-old won't wear it?" Mandy questioned.

"Eighteen-year-olds are fickle creatures. And a free jacket is a free jacket. I also got a sweet pair of boots in matching pink if you're so interested in colors. I didn't wear them today because it didn't snow. But you just wait." Not that she was going to mention that the tennis shoes on her feet were actually a shade lighter than the jacket itself and matching boots, and she had purchased them herself. What can she say? She was a girly girl at heart. The jacket being pink hadn't been the worst part of it, that had been the extra fluffiness.

"Your mom guilted you into taking these, didn't she?"

"Have you seen my mom's eyes, Mandy? You cannot say no to that woman!" Which was a lie; Mia said no all the time. But the woman had a shopping problem that sometimes came in handy for her oldest daughter, whose café took all her shopping time without giving her much in way of shopping money.

"They are the same as my mom's, and I have no issue with it," Mandy stated. In fact, they were the same ones Mandy herself had. Sadly, they weren't the eyes Mia ended up with. What she wouldn't do to have those amazing baby blues for herself.

Narrowing her eyes at her cousin, Mia said, "You're cold, Mandy. She's your mom."

Mandy gave her the same look back. "You let your mom get away with way too much."

"I'm all she has—everyone else moved away. And we all know Kipling isn't coming back once she graduates from college. Not to mention that I haven't given her any grandkids yet, and I'm telling you, I have to give her *something*. And now Damion has dumped me, so again I have no prospects. I'm a spinster and shall remain alone until I die." Mia sighed and looked at the ceiling to keep the tears at bay. Her life sucked.

"You're just being too picky, Mia."

"Does Damion 'lives with his mother' Paulson scream picky to you, Mandy? Damion 'hates walnuts' Paulson is scraping the bottom of the available men barrel within a hundred miles, Mandy."

"He hates walnuts?" her cousin asked, as if that was of any importance at all.

"Yes, and you know they are the best nut available. His loss. Me and walnuts!"

"You are walnuts, Mia," Mandy accused with a smirk.

"Thank you, because they're the best. And I know you were making a dig at me, but I don't care. Want to watch a movie tonight? I just happen to have a frozen pizza that I know you love waiting in my freezer."

"You mean the type of pizza you love?" Mandy raised an eyebrow in question.

"Maybe," Mia admitted. She figured everyone liked what she liked since everyone loved her specials at the café.

"Can't anyway. I have plans to meet up with a few friends in Grand Forks." Mandy looked at the clock on the computer since there wasn't one in the waiting room. Nobody needed to know the time when they were out there. Instantly, she started shutting down the computer.

"Cancel," Mia whined. Why was everyone abandoning her suddenly?

"No." Mandy jumped up from her chair and shrugged off her white jacket, hanging it on a hook behind where she had been sitting.

"For me?" She gave her best pathetic smile.

"How about tomorrow?" Mandy suggested, and she grabbed her jacket from the same set of hooks and shrugged it on. The jacket was in a nice black, and Mia knew from the logo it was expensive.

Not that Mia was jealous.

"Fine, but you pick up a pizza for yourself, then. I can't stock everything we both like." She followed her cousin out the door. It seemed once Mandy was done at the office, she was done. No hours of cleaning for her to do like at the café.

"Deal," Amanda agreed and waved as she walked to her car in the other direction.

The weather hadn't warmed up one bit since she had gone into the office, but it was a good thing it was only a few more feet to her apartment stairs door.

Talking to her cousin had improved her mood for a few minutes, but once she hit her apartment, she was back to being the woman Damion "let's split the bill every time" Paulson dumped. The only thing that could fix that was ice cream, and luckily Mia had a lot of that.

CHAPTER 4

DRAINING the glass of beer in front of him, Rafferty set it down and waved at the bartender for another. He and his friend Anderson had come to the bar after Rafferty had let Anderson in on his personal assistant's deepest, darkest secrets. Well, not the darkest maybe, but for some reason, she had never told her boss that she lived above the office they worked in.

Angel was going to be pissed at him when she found out Anderson knew. In truth, he had no idea Anderson didn't know the woman lived upstairs. She had lived up there for more than a dozen years now—where did he think she lived? Didn't they talk during all those hours they spent together?

Anderson had offered him a place to land, a job and a work place. But it was Angel who would get in the way of that. She was Anderson's personal assistant and would walk away if Anderson hired Rafferty. He knew she would, too, and her job was all she had. She had never married, never moved, barely drove, and went to her mother's every weekend. Her life outside of that building was nonexistent. He wouldn't take that away from her. She was his sister.

So here he was, nursing a beer, trying to figure out his future when the door to the bar burst open, and Angel and Mia tumbled in from the frigid night and landed in a heap on the floor. Mia yelled out their drink order to the bartender as they got up and stumbled to a table. Her purple hair was all he could see for a moment, then he instantly replaced it with the chestnut it actually was in his mind.

He could feel the moment they both noticed him. The daggers that were sent his way were a little more painful than usual. *Just ignore them*, he thought, but then he decided he had to take another shot at Mia today. You can't catch a fish if you're not fishing.

Motioning to Paul behind the bar, he took the glasses over to the women. Setting them down as Mia was on the phone texting, he turned his attention to Ruth. "And I thought you were against favors, Angel."

"Rafferty, just leave them alone. Ruth is going to throw her drink at you." Anderson pushed Rafferty back to the bar and relative safety.

Back on his stool, he chatted about something with Anderson for a while, not taking his eyes off the woman. Silently, he just watched Mia, who was drinking her drink and talking animatedly about something. Or anything; it was Mia.

When the outside door opened again, bringing with it a swirl of cold air, a woman walked in. Rafferty recognized the bank president, Tess Thorn, immediately. She was dressed like this was downtown Minneapolis instead of a hole in the wall in the middle of North Dakota. Mia called out to her as if they were friends, and she acknowledged her but stopped at the bar on the other side of Anderson to order a drink.

When she got her drink and sat with Mia and Ruth, Anderson said quietly, "Looks like the book club is having a midweek meeting."

"Book club?" Rafferty had heard that they were friends suddenly, but not why. It made sense—Mia and Angel had never been in the same circles, bit lately they were talking a lot more than they used to.

"These three and three others get together ever few weeks to talk about books and drink," Anderson filled him in.

He noticed that Mia was drinking more than she probably should be, but Anderson kept bringing the table more rounds, and she just kept drinking them. Not that her friends weren't matching her drink for drink.

Rafferty ordered another beer as Tess from the bank went to the other end of the bar. He watched as she spoke quietly with a man sitting there after she ordered. He knew that man's face but couldn't remember his name. He was a few years older than Rafferty and wasn't one of his customers. He was probably Anderson's customer—the joys of having only two insurance companies in town. The man was drinking some mixed drink, and she ordered him another, as well as four whiskeys for the table. Paul poured the drinks and gave them to her. Paul set the drink in front of him, but the man pushed it away with anger. Rafferty had no idea what the woman's expression was because she was turned away from him, but she took the glass and drank it in one go. Setting the empty glass on the bar, she grabbed the other four with ease and went back to her table.

Turning to see who the drinks were for, he watched her hand them all to Mia, who already had four empty glasses in front of her. When had she had time to finish them all? He had been watching her. His last count had been two empty, two full.

Her back stiff, he watched her pick up one of the glasses and drink it almost to the end. After setting it down, she put her hands in the air in surrender and started to laugh. The bar was now too full and too loud for him to hear the laugh, but he knew what it sounded like. It was a laugh he was always able to pick up in a crowd. No matter the size.

To his shock, the banker took all four glasses of alcohol and drank them one after another. Even the last bit that Mia hadn't finished. When she added the glasses to Mia's stack, he figured out how Mia had drunk so many so fast. Apparently, the banker lady could hold her liquor and everyone else's.

Soon after her impressive shot line, Tess stood up and said goodbye to the girls and walked out of the bar. Rafferty watched her to see if she was too drunk to make it to her apartment, but she was walking straighter than he could right now.

The two remaining women talked for a long time, and both looked to be having fun. Their earlier animosity was completely gone today. A few of Mia's friends came in, but Mia just waved at them, continuing to talk to Angel. Soon Heather started to hang on to Anderson—she had been trying to get him since word got out about his break-up. He had shown no interest, but she still tried.

With his view blocked, he almost missed one of Mia's friends go to the table and talk to Mia. But since he couldn't see Mia, he watched Angel glance from Mia to her friend to the bar and then back. The dejected expression on her face made him stand up. To do what? Defend his sister? Against what?

He watched her quickly stand up and then stop dead. Rushing to her, he grabbed her around the waist, making her sit back in the booth. She was wasted. "Are you okay, Angel? You know you can't drink like that."

"I'm fine. Get away from me, Rafferty," she told him through gritted teeth. Pushing him away, she got up and he watched her walk out the door. To his surprise, Anderson ran out the door after her. Maybe it wasn't that big of a surprise since he had done the same thing earlier today. Rafferty knew Ruth was in good hands.

Eyes still on the door, he slid into the booth across from Mia. It took her a moment to realize it was him. Her friend had gone back to her friends, and Mia was alone.

"Are you as drunk as Angel is?" Rafferty knew she was more than buzzed now.

"Nope, I'm good," she stated without a snide comment, most definitely drunk.

"Your friend can handle her liquor." Rafferty slid farther into the booth since she wasn't fighting him.

"Angel? No, she can't." Mia looked behind her at the door.

"The other one, Tess." He laughed at her expression.

"You keep away from her. She's my friend, not yours." Her words were slurred as she tried to be stern and giggle at the same time. "God, she can put them back. She drank as much as me in one sitting. Maybe more, I lost count."

"More," he confirmed, loving her giggles.

"Where is Angel? She was just here." Mia looked around the room.

"Gone She went home. Anderson made sure she got there." Rafferty smiled at her expression. Her expressions were very exaggerated when she drank.

"She likes him, but don't tell anyone," she whispered loudly. "She's his secretary."

"I know. I think he likes her too," Rafferty whispered back to her.

Her eyes widened, and she put her hand to her mouth in shock. "She's his secretary," she said again.

"He's her boss." Rafferty went with her on it.

"Do you think they make out in the office?" She giggled.

"No, they are very professional there."

"Yes, yes profes … professssion … prof … I can't say that word anymore."

"It's a hard one." He couldn't believe how her eyes were sparkling with excitement and wonder.

"Do you want to know a secret?" she whispered loudly again as she looked around to see if anyone was around them.

"Yes." He wanted to know all her secrets.

"I'm moving before the new year. This is my last year in Landstad, North Dakota." Her eyes darted from side to side as she said it as if someone was listening to her.

With a sinking heart, he asked, "Where are you going?"

"Don't know yet. Somewhere big and busy and where everybody doesn't know my business."

"Maybe I'll make you stay. Make you see that this is the town for you," Rafferty professed. He was sure she wouldn't remember any of this come morning anyway.

"Not going to work. This town is no fun. I want to live somewhere fun and exciting." She was slurring more of the words.

"I think I should get you home." Getting up, he reached a hand out to her. She grabbed it, and he pulled her to her feet.

Without a word, he kept her hand in his and led her out of the bar, down the street for a block, and into the building where she lived. How long he had known where she lived, he didn't know, but it seemed like one of the first things he had found out when he moved back to town.

Mia was the one who got away. They were never on the same page. Now he wanted to stay here forever, and she was ready to bolt. Pulling her up the stairs into the hallway, he asked what door was hers. She dropped his hand and reached into her pocket and pulled out a key, opening the door on the end.

The door swung open on the tiny apartment with a small kitchen, a small living room, and two bedrooms. But beyond the size, it was decorated as only Mia could. Bold colors, and old furniture that had been painted or had slipcovers on them.

When they had made it in the door, she put her key on the table and shut the door behind them. Kicking off her shoes, she grabbed his hand and started to pull him toward the bedroom. "Now I'm going to have sex with you, Rafferty Brooks."

Following, he wondered when she was going to pass out. She had to be close. He would see how far he could get before that happened. Not that he would actually have sex with her in this condition, but he would make out with her forever like this.

The bedroom was cozy and comfortable, just like the Mia he knew was under that purple hair. She had let go of his hand and was in the process of stripping out of her clothes. He kicked off his shoes and shrugged out of his jacket and tie, opening the first few buttons of his shirt. By the time he was getting to the last button she was on him, ripping the shirt open.

Buttons flying across the room.

Laughing as he fell back on the bed, taking her with him, he rolled her on her back so that he was above her. That's when he noticed she was completely naked underneath him. When had she had time to get everything off? Reaching between them, she caressed his cock through layers of clothing.

His thoughts stopped as she pulled his head to hers and kissed him. Her tongue was in his mouth before he could process it. She was in charge of this. She tasted the same as she had at sixteen, and it had taken him years to forget that taste. But tonight it all came rushing back. She held his head as she deepened the kiss even more. Their breaths were ragged, and they couldn't get enough of each other.

As the kiss grew heated, he took her breasts in his hands, not letting himself miss this opportunity. They were perfect. Pulling his lips from hers, she whimpered a little until the whimper turned into a moan as he took a nipple deep in his mouth and suckled it, circling it with his tongue, loving it. Then he turned to the other and did the same thing.

He let his hands roam over her body, trying to imprint every dip and curve in his memory. Her body writhed under his caress.

"Touch me, Raff," she begged as her hips surged up, welcoming his touch.

Suckling her breasts, his fingers slid over her mound and across her core, causing a groan to escape. His fingers continued circling her clit, which caused her hands to fist into the quilt on the bed and her breathing to turn heavy. Her body writhed beneath his hands, and when she came, she called his name in the mostly dark room.

Smiling, he slid his hand back to her hip, caressing the smooth skin as she brought herself back to earth. He wondered if she was still drunk or if she had recovered her faculties enough to have sex with him. That answer came when he looked at her face; though she was smiling, she was also passed out. Mia had come in his hand, then proceeded to pass out cold.

Getting up, he pulled the blanket back and put her in the bed with her head on the pillow. Covering her beautiful body was hard, but she would get cold in the chilly winter night if he didn't. Going through her apartment, he found some aspirin and filled a glass of water, and placed them on the nightstand next to her bed. Everything would be ready for the morning when she woke up.

With a chuckle, he went to the kitchen and wrote a note and brought it back to the bedroom, placing it under the glass of water. He took out his wallet, grabbed a condom package, and opened it. He placed the empty package by the glass on top of the paper also. Taking the condom into the bathroom, he unrolled it and looked around the room. Finding a container of hair gel, he squirted a little into the condom and took it back to the room. Casually, he tossed it on the floor near the bed.

Leaning down, he kissed her forehead and ran his hand over her purple hair, then kissed her forehead again. Because he could.

"Good night, Mia. I'm going to spend the next eleven months making damn sure that you want to stay here forever." he promised as he headed out the door. He knew she would be pissed at him, but he couldn't stop himself from the prank.

CHAPTER 5

IN THE WEEKS THAT FOLLOWED, book club had actually taken shape, different from the original. It had been the third meeting at Ruth's great apartment where Natalie had suggested they record their conversation and turn them into a podcast. This week was going to be the first one they recorded. Mia was a little nervous, but also a little excited.

Since the night she got wasted at the bar, she had avoided Rafferty as best she could. He still came into the café more days than not. But she had avoided talking to him completely. Even if he sat in her area in the café, she had the other waitresses take his table, or she just took off for lunch then.

So far, he hadn't said anything about what had happened that night. And to her mortification, she had no idea what she had done. Based on the evidence around the room, they'd had sex. Even her body said they had sex, but her mind couldn't remember it. Just a few images of stripping out of her clothes, kissing him when she was naked, and the feeling of coming while looking into his smiling blue eyes. Then nothing.

But today she was going to kick him right out of her mind. The temperature had hit the big zero, and there was going to be a party. For years, when the temperature finally warmed up to above zero, Joe Jordan had a bomb fire to celebrate. Winter was far from over, but they had gotten past the coldest days, and that was worth a party.

With excitement, she hurried over to the insurance office. Ruth would love the party, she was sure of it. Shoving into the office and barreling out of the cold, she felt something was up. There was something going on, but her friend was pouring coffee and Anderson was just talking to her. Looked like nothing, but it felt like a lot. Maybe Ruth and Anderson needed to go to this party even more than her.

"Mia," Ruth exclaimed, greeting her a little too excitedly.

"Hey guys, what's going on?"

"Nothing, just getting more coffee. Anderson said it was snowing," her friend said in a rush.

"It's snowing, all right. It's supposed to snow most of the night," Mia said. Weather. The filler of all conversations in this town. Don't know what to say? Talk about the weather. There was always weather happening, and everyone had their opinion about it.

"I think I heard that also," Ruth replied and seemed unable to stop staring at Anderson as he left the front of the office and go back to his desk without a word, leaving the women to their conversations.

"The temperature hit zero today. You know what that means," Mia hinted.

"The cold snap is over?" Ruth questioned in confusion.

"No, silly. Joe Jordan's party is tonight," she said, because everyone knew about the party. Or at least they should.

Ruth shook her head. "I don't know Joe Jordan."

"You don't have to know him. You can just go to the party," Mia assured her.

"I don't know. I don't like parties," Ruth admitted, and Mia knew it, but she also knew that Ruth needed to get out sometimes.

"You had fun at the bar a few weeks ago; it will be like that." *But it will definitely not end like that*, Mia thought. She was staying away from a certain person for the rest of her life.

"I had fun, yes, but a party is different." It wasn't, but Ruth hadn't been to enough parties to know that.

"What if I get Anderson to come. Then will you go?" Mia wasn't above bribery.

"He won't go, so then I won't have to go." Ruth smiled at her

"Are you coming, Anderson?" Mia asked from Ruth's office space. He was lost in thought, and his head popped up at his name.

"Where?" he asked, his eyes on Ruth and not her.

"Were you not paying attention at all?" Mia walked into his office. "Joe Jordan is having his annual 'over the donut' party tonight. Are you going?"

"Never heard of it." He shook his head as if to clear it.

"She didn't either. Do you two not live in this town? Every year, the first day the temps hit zero again for the first time, Joe Jordan has a bonfire to celebrate. Today we hit the mark, and tonight is the party." Mia sat herself down in his guest chair. She needed him to agree so that Ruth would go out.

"I don't know who Joe Jordan is," Anderson said. The same thing as Ruth.

Now she had to repeat that conversation, so she didn't have to go alone.

"You don't have to. Come on, Anderson. We need a ride; my car isn't starting." Mia had no idea if her car was starting or not. It had been a few weeks since she had needed to drive. She assumed she would have trouble when she finally decided to start it so it wasn't a lie exactly.

"You need a designated driver?" He leaned back in his chair.

She shook her head in denial. "Not really, but my car is out. And if Ruth goes, she doesn't have a car, so we are in need of wheels."

He asked Ruth, "Are you going?"

"I don't know." Ruth bit her lip.

"Come on, you two. Come to the party with me. I don't want to go alone." If she didn't go to the party, she would stay at home and watch TV by herself, thinking about what had happened with Rafferty for another night.

"You are never alone in a crowd, especially not one in Landstad," Anderson said.

"I won't leave your sides. I promise to spend my whole night with you two. And I'm not drinking too much. I'm done with drinking until I pass out." Mia wasn't getting drunk again for years.

"If Ruth goes, I'll drive you." Anderson turned to the woman in question, and so did Mia.

Ruth only gave a slight nod that she was willing to go with them. Excitement flooded Mia as they planned the evening. She needed a night out.

An hour later Anderson picked them up outside Ruth's apartment, and the drive to the party was short. It was already in full swing when they got there, and the sun had barely set. The cold air around them and the snow under their feet was barely noticeable with the huge fire burning at the center of so many people. Mia talked to everyone as she, Ruth, and Anderson wandered through the crowds.

Chatting and drinking as she went, Mia remembered how much she loved these things. Just spending time with people she knew, nothing special. At one point, she stopped and looked around and just smiled at all the people who would show up at a party they didn't know about twelve hours before. Landstad had some positives.

Mia turned to Ruth and Anderson. "Isn't this great?"

"You go have fun, Mia. You don't have to babysit me." Ruth looked a little panicky to Mia; maybe it was time to get her home.

"I'm not babysitting you, silly. I'm partying with you." Mia finished her beer and pulled another from her coat pocket. Was this number three or four? She couldn't remember. Maybe she shouldn't open it. *No more getting drunk, Mia*, she told herself. This was the new Mia.

Just one more, she decided, and opened the bottle. Taking a drink, someone put their arms around her. Even though she had a nice buzz going on, she knew it was Rafferty. Her body always knew when it was Rafferty.

His warm lips were touching her cold ear as he whispered, "Are you drunk enough to fuck me yet?"

Pushing him away from her, she calmly handed her beer to Anderson. Then she turned on the little weasel. His face registered that he wasn't ready for an actual physical fight, but she was.

With all the anger from the last few weeks, months, and years over Rafferty Brooks, she wound back to punch him. As she swung, he must have seen it coming because he dodged her, and she fell into the cold snow. Not ready to stop yet, she wrapped her arms around his legs, and he fell to the ground. Trying to grab him around the neck with her mitten-clad hands, she could see he was laughing at her, which made her even madder at him.

Just as she was getting the advantage over him, she felt someone pulling her off. Anderson held her away from Rafferty, who was still laughing on the ground.

"Never speak to me again. Never!" she yelled so he could hear, along with everyone else at the party.

"I think it's time to head home," Anderson said as he pulled Mia toward the parking area.

To Mia's surprise, Ruth drove Anderson's truck back to town. She didn't think the other woman could drive. Or she knew she could, just it happened so rarely that she always forgot. Ruth didn't have a car, and her step-father or mom always picked her up for the weekends she spent with them. Mia knew Ruth had a sports car, but she rarely saw it. She just parked it outside the insurance office a few days a year.

On the drive, Mia was talking too much, but she couldn't stop. When she was buzzed, she liked to talk, and she would talk about anything with anyone. Usually, she didn't remember much about the chats.

All too soon, town came into view, and then they were downtown. Sweetly, Anderson opened her door for her and escorted her to her apartment door. He was so nice. Why couldn't she have accidentally slept with him? Why Rafferty?

Once in her apartment, she shed all her layers of clothes and took a long hot shower—the night had been so cold. Clean and warm, she put on a tank top and the panties she would sleep in. Adding her bathrobe, she headed to the living room and plopped down on the couch, leaving the lights off.

So far, she wasn't tired yet. She knew that 5:00 a.m. would come way too soon, as it always did, but she didn't want to sleep yet. Flipping through the channels on the TV, she found a movie she loved and pulled a blanket off the back of the couch, snuggling in to get lost in someone else's problems.

The movie was about halfway through when someone knocked on her door. Looking at her phone, she saw it was almost midnight. *Shoot*, she thought. She needed to get to sleep. She needed to be up to open the café in just a few hours.

Another knock came. Maybe it was Ruth to talk about what was happening with Anderson.

Happy to talk to her friend, she swung open the door and swore.

"Hello to you too, Mia." Rafferty was leaning against the door jam.

"Get out of here, Rafferty." She swung the door closed again. In his face.

Catching it with his foot, Rafferty walked into her apartment, already taking off his jacket, and hanging it on her coat tree in the corner as if he was welcome. "I just wanted to make sure you made it home all right."

"I did. You can leave now." She flopped back onto the couch trying to ignore him.

Pulling the blanket back over her and snuggling back into the warm spot she had left, she turned her attention back to the TV. After a second, she pushed her feet out so that she was took up the entire couch. Rafferty had walked over to the couch and was looking down at her.

Leaning over her, he grabbed her pillow out from under her head, and she sat up a little. Angrily, she grabbed at the pillow he had taken. While she was distracted, he sat down where her pillow had been. Then he put the pillow on his lap. Gently, he laid her head back to where it was.

"Just watch your movie, Mia." He brushed her hair with his hand to get it out of her face.

Ignoring him, she concentrated on the TV, not on his body pressed against the back of her head. Not about his hand still caressing her hair. Letting herself relax and enjoy the movie, she fell asleep within minutes.

CHAPTER 6

RAFFERTY DIDN'T KNOW when it happened, but by the time the credits rolled on the movie, he knew she was fast asleep. Earlier, when she had answered the door, he was sure she had been sleeping. Which might explain how she had let her guard down enough to let him inside.

When he had made it back to town, he had driven by her place, and when there had been no lights on in her apartment, he had to make sure she was home and not stuck in the ditch or lost. Though she had been drinking at the bonfire, he didn't think she was too drunk to pass out but drunk enough not to drive. And drunk enough that he was worried about her.

He had noticed her right away at the bonfire, but he always noticed her right away wherever they were. No matter the location or the size of the crowd, she was always who he looked for and found. Since the night out at the bar, she had been avoiding him. Well, she wasn't talking to him, but every time he saw her, she was looking his way.

After an hour at the party, he couldn't help but talk to her, to touch her. All he had wanted to do was slip his arms around her and kiss her again, but he had opened his mouth and stepped in it. Before he knew it, she was attacking him. And he was loving it. Mia was a feisty fighter, and to have that feistiness in his arms was amazing.

He had actually been about to kiss the fury away when Anderson had pulled her off of him. He still wondered what she would've done if he had kissed her. Would she have fought harder or kissed him back? With Mia, he never knew.

Running his hand over the now paler purple hair, he noticed it had faded in the last few weeks from when they were in the bar. Though the color was weird, it was soft and silky, and it made him never want to stop touching it. Up close, he could see her real hair color coming though, a rich brown that made her hazel eyes look brown. The purple made them look more of a gray.

He could spend the night like this, with her head on his lap, but he knew Mia would be stiff and sore, which would make being on her feet the next day miserable. Carefully, he slid out from under her and went into her room. Pulling back her covers, he looked around the room and smiled. He saw her personality in every corner. Fun and homey.

Returning to the living room, he picked her up in his arms. He had heard her complain about the extra weight that she carried, but she was still easy to lift. Laying her gently on the bed, he slid the robe she was wearing off her shoulders. Underneath, she wore just a white tank top and pink lace panties. The material of the tank top was so thin that he could see her breasts, leaving nothing to the imagination.

Lifting the blanket over her sexy body, he paused to take one more look. swearing quietly in regret he ran a thumb over one of her nipples, only to be rewarded when it pebbled, and she moaned in her sleep. His cock twitched at the sound, and he swore again as he pulled the covers to her chin.

She mumbled something as he went to shut off the light in the bathroom she had left on. Then he once again got her a glass of water and two aspirin, and put them on the bedside table. Taking her phone, he opened it—she hadn't set a password—and turned on her alarm for five am, since she had to open the café at six. He hoped she only needed an hour to get ready.

Kissing her forehead, he was about to leave when he turned back to her. Pulling a condom packet out of his wallet, he ripped it open and put the wrapper next to the water glass. This time he didn't do anything to the condom, just dropped it on the carpet, still tightly rolled. She loved a good practical joke.

Smiling, he kissed her forehead again. Because he could.

On his way out of the apartment, he turned off the TV. Shutting her door behind him, he chuckled. Once again, she was going to be so pissed at him. Maybe it would end in her attacking him again. He could only hope.

CHAPTER 7

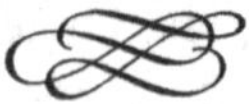

ONCE AGAIN, she was trapped in Landstad North Dakota on Valentine's Day. The only thing positive about it was that it was her last one in this place. Next year, she would be in Grand Forks or maybe Fargo. Anywhere but here.

Also, once again, the café was serving meat loaf. Sure, it was shaped like a heart, but it was still meat loaf. Same thing every year, yet people always ordered it and made comments like they had never seen meat shaped like a heart before in their lives.

Since her café windows faced the town's only flower shop, or actually the drug store that sold flowers, so she had spent the day watching men go in and come out from the place. Bouquets and bouquets of flowers walked out. She saw men she knew and men she had never seen before. But none of the flowers were for her, because once again, she had no one on the most romantic day of the year. This year, she hadn't even tried, though she wasn't going to tell that to her mom.

What she did have was the same old customers who came in every day. Sat at the same places and ordered the same thing. Bringing another order of the special from the kitchen, she straightened her red sweater and watched Anderson come in through the door. He wasn't wearing a coat, even though the temperatures were bitter today. But the walk across the street was short.

"Happy Valentine's Day, Anderson. Do you have big plans for Ruth tonight?" Mia asked about her friend. It was their first holiday as a couple. Her heart instantly sank at his surprised expression. "By that reaction, I see you have no plans. Did you forget? You can't forget; it's Ruth."

Ruth hadn't had a date on Valentine's Day for way longer than Mia. She was a little mad that Anderson had forgotten. Writing their orders down—she didn't have to ask with these two—she sent it to the kitchen for her cook and leaned on the counter.

"I forgot," he admitted, sitting heavily on a stool.

"Anderson, it's your first Valentine's Day as a couple. This is big. Did you get her anything at all? Ordered something online maybe?" Mia asked.

"No," he said sheepishly.

Mia glared at him. "No card? No flowers? No nothing?"

"I forgot," he reminded her.

"What are we going to get her? In Landstad today?" Her mind ran through all the places he could get her something, but nothing seemed right for her friend. Not on the first one. flowers wouldn't cut it.

"I don't know. I messed up, again," he admitted, his eyes downcast and dejected.

"Again?" she pressed. This wasn't sounding good.

This morning when she had woken up, she had been happy to know that at least Ruth would have a good Valentine's Day. Now she was beginning to think nobody in this entire town was having a good Valentine's Day and that they should have just cancelled the holiday altogether. It would be for the good of the town.

"I hurt her feelings this morning." He didn't really tell her anything.

"How about giving her a day off? She was saying she doesn't get a lot of alone time lately. I think she kind of misses being alone. You can still see her in the evening, but she can spend the day doing what Ruth does," Mia said, getting a little excited as she talked. Ruth had been a virtual hermit up until a few months ago. Whatever she had done to keep herself busy all that time, Mia didn't know.

"I'll think about it. Thanks." He took the boxes containing their lunches.

Watching as he walked out the door and across the freezing cold street, she hoped he would figure something out to make Ruth's day special. The cook called her name, and she took the plates to the diners at the end of the room in the last booth. Regulars. Both excited about the meatloaf.

As she walked back to the front, the café door opened and Rafferty walked in, carrying a balloon and a brown paper bag. The balloon was red and said, "love" in big letters.

He sat down at the counter, and Mia went to him in annoyance, asking, "What can I get you, Rafferty?"

She needed him out of here as soon as possible. Him and his damn balloon. Her holiday was already bad, he was only going to make it worse.

"Nothing for me today, though the special is tempting." He licked his lips, and she had a sudden flashback to those very lips on her nipple. She had a love-hate relationship with those flashbacks.

"What are you doing here?" She crossed her arms and ignored the tingle that had shot straight to her core.

"I got you something for the holiday." He handed her the bag and the balloon.

Taking it, she looked at him skeptically. "Why?"

"Just being a good lover.. Thought you would need it," he said and winked at her.

Looking around, she lowered her voice and hissed, "What is it?"

Rafferty shook his head and whispered back, "Maybe you should open it at home. It's kind of private."

At his words, she slowly opened the bag and peered inside. It was a pregnancy test. Quickly closing the bag, she leaned close to him and whispered, "What the hell, Rafferty?"

"I was just thinking that it got a little heated last time, and we might have forgotten something important. I don't know if you remember; you were a little drunk." He was smiling as he said it, like it was no big deal that they kept having sex when she was drunk.

"You took advantage of me when I was drunk, again." Hissing quietly, she glared at him as she tried to make the bag as small as possible and hand it back to him.

"You were all over me, Mia. It's not my fault you can't keep your hands off me." Holding up his hands and not taking the bag, he pushed away from the counter and headed to the door. Opening it, he turned, smiling and saying loudly, "Call me when you know."

Seething with anger, she pulled the balloon down and, with her pen, popped it, which drew everyone's attention. Smiling at her customers, she wrapped the deflated balloon around the bag and threw it all in the garbage. He was such a liar. Nothing happened that night. She distinctly remembered falling asleep watching a movie. No way she woke up, had sex, and fell back asleep and didn't remember it happening. There was no way.

Or was there a little way? She had been drinking, and she knew how she got when drunk. Horny. Would she have slept with Rafferty again? Wasn't one drunken hook-up enough?

Mia was contemplating giving up alcohol completely, cold turkey. Because lately, every time she drank, she slept with Rafferty, then couldn't remember a thing the next morning. Every. Stupid. Time.

Biting her lip in annoyance, because she couldn't just go into the drug store and buy another one, not with every man for miles around buying flowers today, and now, she was questioning everything. She was about to grab the test from the garbage when Anderson ran into the café. "Have you seen Ruth?"

"No, she's probably at home." Mia forgot about the test and the possible pregnancy, suddenly thinking about her friend instead.

Anderson looked back out at the street at her apartment door. "I checked. She's not there."

"I haven't seen her mom come get her, she couldn't have gone far," Mia said, though she hadn't been paying attention to that. After all, she was all-consumed with her pregnancy scare right now. Ruth's whereabouts was the last thing on her mind. Her eyes darted to the garbage.

"Can you call me if you see her?" Anderson begged her.

"Did you do something? Did she realize you had forgotten about Valentine's Day?" She kicked the garbage out of her line of site. She needed to focus on Ruth right now.

"No, my ex called when I was getting lunch. Ruth answered. She said something, but I have no idea what." He looked so worried and concerned. If Mia hadn't known he was in love with Ruth before this, she knew now. Lucky Ruth; she got a good one. Not an annoying playboy like Rafferty!

"I'll call if I see her. She's most likely up there," Mia assured him, but he probably didn't hear her because he was out the door before she finished speaking. Shaking her head, she wondered what really happened. She knew she would find out eventually, she always did.

After Anderson had left, she forced herself to walk away from the garbage and the test it contained, only to spend the rest of her shift thinking about the test in the garbage. Should she take it? Was she even late? By her calculations, she wasn't even late yet. But if they had unprotected sex, maybe she should take it to make sure. Nosy Jackie at the drug store wouldn't even have to know.

Better to know than not.

So as she left for the day, she grabbed the balloon-wrapped test from the garbage and hurried down two buildings to her apartment. Letting herself in she quickly, she discarded the balloon and paper bag. Taking it test straight into the bathroom, she read the directions. Staring, she realized she would have to take it in the morning. That was hours away.

Leaving it on the shelf in her bathroom, she threw herself on the couch. What was she going to do if she was carrying Rafferty's baby? First, she would beat him within an inch of his life; she didn't want a baby now, and she *never* wanted his baby.

After changing into yoga pants and a sweatshirt, she spent the rest of the day and evening watching movies on TV. Most were from her high school years, so she loved them all. And they were able to take her mind off the test waiting in her bathroom for her to pass or fail in the morning just like high school. She hated tests.

As midnight neared, she knew she had to go to bed. It was never going to be morning if she didn't sleep. And worse, her day at the café would be awful with no sleep. Turning off the TV and the light in the living room, she looked out the window and saw Ruth's light on in her apartment, and she even saw movement. She grabbed her phone to text Anderson like she promised, but then decided no. If Ruth wanted alone time, she was going to let Ruth have her space. Anderson would find her soon enough.

Climbing into bed, she snuggled into her covers and hoped morning would bring joy instead of terror. Her sleep was fitful and full of dreams of crying babies and disappointed parents. She woke up almost every hour from a nightmare, until at four, she finally just got up to take the test.

The small prayer to the lord above for a negative result was answered. She wasn't pregnant. And as penance, she decided that she would never drink again; unless Rafferty wasn't around, then she could drink like a fish. Cold-turkey seemed harsh after all.

CHAPTER 8

Spring

Now that Ruth knew everything he did, Rafferty was able to let the ever present exhaustion overtake him. He had been up all night. It was just before 8:00 a.m., and all he wanted to do was drive the three short blocks to his house and sack out. And ignore all the calls that were sure to start coming in.

Early this morning, he had said goodbye to his father. Today, he could stop trying to prove himself to the man who never felt his son was worth anything. Rafferty had worked alongside him for years, and he still didn't trust him—he was always double-checking his work. Pointing out the finest errors or flaws. It had been that way his entire life.

When he was young, his dad had no time for his only child. By the time Rafferty had gotten to high school, no matter what the accomplishment, it was just short of enough for his dad. If he hadn't really wanted to be back in his hometown, he would never put up with the old man.

But now he was gone. Heart attack. Which was crazy since the man didn't even have one. Proof of that was Ruth, who had been ignored by the father they had shared her entire life. Worst of which was that she was sick when they were kids, and his father hadn't bothered to try and help. It was like he had wanted her to die. That he probably did made Rafferty hate him even more.

Through the slushy, melting snow, he was almost to his pickup when he ran right into someone coming out of the post office. Grabbing the person around the waist so that they would not fall to the ground, he heard the grumbling of Mia Lawson. Of course, Mia.

"What the heck, Rafferty?" Her "heck" almost made him smile. She could swear a blue streak when she wanted. But today, it was "heck."

"Sorry," was all he could muster as he let her go, continuing on his way.

She must have followed him because he heard her from close behind him say. "What's wrong?"

Leave it to Mia to know something was wrong with him. At this early hour word couldn't have gotten out about his dad, though he was sure Mia would've been one of the first to know.

"Just leave me alone, Mia."

"I won't until you tell me what is wrong." She was following him. For weeks since the bomb fire, she had been avoiding him, and now she was following him?

Stopping suddenly, he was surprised when she ran right into him; she had been that close. He turned to her as she mumbled apologies about running into him. "My dad died this morning."

To his surprise, she threw her arms around him in a tight hug. "I'm sorry. Was it sudden? Of course, it was sudden, I just saw him yesterday. Are you okay? Of course not, look at you."

"Do you have any questions you don't know the answer to? I just want to go home now." Rafferty just held her, not able to let her warm, comforting body go. At that moment, he knew he didn't need to get home. He just needed to keep holding Mia.

"You can't be alone. Your mom is still in Fargo, right? Does she know?" Mia asked, a tear in her eye. Was she sad because his dad was dead or because he was in pain? He couldn't say.

"Yes, Fargo. Yes, I called her. She didn't care too much." He answered her next question before she could even answer it. The couple had been separated for years now, why they hadn't divorced he didn't know. Right now, he didn't care.

"You can't be alone. Do you want to watch movies with me?" She took his hand and started pulling him down the street.

"Movies?" His feet stayed planted on the sidewalk, not moving.

"They take my mind off things." She gave him a weak smile.

Pulling her tight against him into a hug, he whispered, "Yes. Take my mind off this."

Expecting her to stop hugging him, he was surprised when she just stood there, holding him. This was exactly what he needed. Mia Lawson.

The morning traffic was starting to get busier. He was starting to feel that people were watching, so he reluctantly pulled out of her arms, knowing she didn't want to be talked about . But still, he kept a hold of her hand, unable to let go. "Your place or mine?"

"Mine. I don't need to see you're sex den." She winked playfully at him, though her eyes were still watery.

That made him smile, a real smile, only for Mia. They walked across the street to her apartment, still hand in hand. "My sex den gets you excited."

"You're sex den disgusts me." She wrinkled her nose as they went up the stairs.

"Makes you so hot," he countered as she opened her apartment door.

"Do I look hot, Rafferty?"

At her words, he grabbed her arm and pulled her into him. He just hugged her and whispered into her ear, "You always look hot, Mia."

This time, she pushed out of his arms as fast as he had pulled her into them. Stomping across the apartment, she seethed, "I invited you over to take your mind off your dad, not have sex with you."

"Okay," was all he said as he walked into her apartment and shut the door behind him. Taking off his jacket and shoes, he realized she had vanished from the main area of the apartment, so he went looking for her. The bedroom door wasn't completely closed, and he peeked inside. He watched as she changed out of the black jeans she wore to the restaurant and into sweatpants. She didn't notice him watching. He felt like a pervert but couldn't stop himself.

When she turned and opened a drawer of her dresser, he quickly went back to the living room and sat on the couch to wait for her. Leaning back and putting his feet on the coffee table, he looked at the ceiling. He had so much to do today, but he didn't want to do any of it. All he wanted to do was let the world go by and spend today with Mia. She would make him feel better just being there.

At the sound of her bedroom door opening, he turned and watched her walk across the floor. An orange Landstad Tigers sweatshirt had been added to the black sweatpants. Her hair was still red from Valentine's Day, though it was dull, and her roots were showing now. What color would she choose next? He hoped it would be back to her chestnut brown. He missed it.

Plopping down on the couch, she grabbed the remote near his feet. "What do you want to watch?"

"Anything. You choose." He was still watching her as she flipped quickly through channels.

"How about this one?" She pointed at the screen.

Not bothering to look he agreed, "That one's good."

Turning to him, she put the remote down and curled her feet under her. "Why were you downtown this morning? Were you going to work?"

"No, I just needed to do something." He closed his eyes. His first stop in town this morning was to tell Ruth. She deserved to know.

"Really? Just something. Did you at least get it done?" Mia questioned sarcastically.

"Yes, I did." He smiled at her, knowing she wanted to know everything. She was a gossip and prided herself on knowing everything that went on in town.

"Do you want something to drink?" she asked, thankfully dropping the subject.

"No, I'm good." He didn't want her to get up.

"Did you have something at Angel's then?" she questioned.

"No, I wasn't there very long," he answered before he could stop himself.

"I knew it! You talked to Angel this morning. Why did you have to talk to her?" She was leaning toward him, and her hands were on his arm. "What does Howard have to do with her?"

"Nothing, Mia. Drop it." He sat up.

"Oh my God! That's it, isn't it? That's the big secret between you two. Howard's her dad, too. I should have figured that out. Why hadn't I figured that out? You don't really look alike." Mia's hazel eyes were leaning toward green today and were as big as saucers as she looked at him. Her hands were still on his arm.

"Angel doesn't want people knowing," was all he said through his teeth.

"I won't tell anyone. I swear." She pulled her hands away and leaned back on the arm of the couch.

"Pinky swear." He held out his hand.

"Pinky swear!" Mia grabbed his pinky with hers. "I won't tell anyone. Ever. Have you always known? Do you have holidays together?"

"No, and of course not. We both found out when we were eighteen. When Angel got really sick." He didn't let go of her pinky, just lowered his hand that now was still connected to hers on her leg.

"I remember her being sick. I don't know how bad it was. Maybe not many people around here did since we never thought about it when she wasn't sick anymore." Mia had been a senior that year and was now feeling like she was a bit self-centered.

"She almost died. Well, she would've if her mom hadn't called me," Rafferty explained.

"You talked to the dragon?" Mia questioned in awe. Ruth's mom had earned the nickname early during their growing-up years.

"Yes, she called and asked if I would see if I would be compatible to give Angel a kidney. Hers were done." Her kidneys had been failing most of her life at that point. She had barely graduated from high school because she had missed so many days.

Mia sat up and grabbed his hand in hers. "Were you?"

Smiling at her, he admitted, "I only have one now."

"Ruth Kennedy has your kidney? But she hates you," Mia said in awe.

"She doesn't hate me. She hates Howard. I'm just guilty by association." At least that was how Rafferty had always seen it, and she had every right to hate their father. The man had never acknowledged her as his child, even when he was still sleeping with her mother. Add to that Ruth had always had kidney issues, and he had never once been tested to see if he could give her the kidney she needed. The man had died with two healthy ones. Since it was Rafferty who had been able to donate one, his father would've probably been just as compatible as he had been.

"I can see it now." Mia leaned back into the cushions. "You treat her like the big brother you are."

"I do not."

"Yes, you do. A few months ago, when she almost passed out at the bar? You're such a great brother." Mia smiled at him and squeezed his hand.

"I don't think so. Just a friend. But more of a friend to her boyfriend." Which was sometimes awkward when Anderson got all gushy about his girlfriend—which he tended to do more and more lately.

"Are you an overprotective brother? Anderson is practically living with her."

Since Valentine's Day, the two had been nearly inseparable. Only on book club night did he really get to spend any time with his friend, and that was usually only for the hours the club was meeting. Not that Rafferty could blame him. If he could spend all his time with Mia, he would.

"No, she's happy with him. I'm glad she found him. Hopefully, he won't mess it up."

"Don't you think she might mess it up?" Mia asked, leaning back on the couch, away from him.

"My sister doesn't mess up, Mia." He laughed, and it felt good to be happy again. To be with Mia.

"You're right. Ruth is so Ruth. Anderson is going to mess that one up." Mia smiled and turned to the TV that was showing some movie he hadn't paid attention to. When a commercial came on, she turned back to him, "Can I see your scar?"

"What? You want me naked?" He laughed at her expression of surprise.

"No, just the scar. I don't remember you having one," she said, then bit her lip at her words.

"Are you having trouble remembering all the times you have seen me naked? I should be hurt."

She let go of his hand to punch him in the arm.

With a laugh, he pulled his shirt from his pants and unzipped them. He loved that all her attention turned to him taking off his pants. So much so that he wished all her attention wasn't on just his pants. Showing her the scar, he almost groaned when she touched it, her soft fingers hot on his skin.

"When did you have it done?" Her eyes were still on his skin and the faint scar.

"April, the year after I graduated." Rafferty knew what she was thinking the moment he said it.

Pulling her hand away, she leaned back again and looked at him. "That's when we … you know." Blushing, she didn't go on. She didn't have to.

He remembered every moment of that April night, had dreamed of it many times over the years. He wished he hadn't messed everything up so badly afterward.

"You mean when we made mad, passionate love, Mia?" He teased her, though it was how he had thought about it over the years. Love.

"No, I mean the night we fumbled our way through mediocre sex." She punched him in the shoulder again.

Zipping his pants, he said, "Yep. I went for the surgery the next day."

"Why didn't you say that? You could've called."

He knew they should have talked about this years ago."I really thought I would be fine in a day or two. But instead, it took weeks. And by that time, everyone knew you hated me. I did try and talk to you, but you weren't interested." Rafferty watched her reaction as he spoke. He knew he had messed up back then, and that was the reason she hated him today.

"Is that some sort of apology?" Mia demanded.

"Yes. I'm sorry I never called, Mia. I was busy saving my sister's life." He took her hand and pulled her to him.

"I guess you had a good reason. But you're still the most annoying person I know," she said as she settled in beside him on the couch, his arm around her shoulder.

"At least you love me," he said and kissed her red hair.

"Dream on, Rafferty Brooks, and watch the movie. You'll like this one, there's a near sex scene." She settled in closer, and he grabbed a blanket from the back of the couch and pulled it over them. Once it had been arranged, he turned to the TV. But the action on screen was nothing compared to how her body pressed to his was making him feel. All he wanted to do was pull her onto his lap so he could kiss her.

Instead, he just sat next to her. He wasn't pushing anything, not anymore. He had moved too fast for her before, but now he was letting her take the lead. She would be the one taking their relationship to every next step. So today, he was going to enjoy sitting with her, getting lost in movies and not thinking about his father, his mother or a future without Mia in it.

CHAPTER 9

Summer

I⟶T HAD BEEN a few months since his dad had died, and so much in Rafferty's life had changed. Instead of working alone after the older man's sudden death, he had been offered a position at Anderson's insurance agency.

The offer had actually sent Anderson and Ruth's relationship into a tailspin for a while. His sister had actually done something nobody in town ever expected her to do: she moved out of town. Just for a month to avoid Anderson, who she had been convinced was leaving town and her in the dust. But Anderson had quickly realized he couldn't take Ruth away from Landstad and that he didn't want to leave either.

While she was gone, Mia had kept him informed on her, and if Anderson had asked, Rafferty would've told him how to find her. But he never asked, and Rafferty didn't tell him.

During that time, he started working with Anderson, and he had found out how different working with Anderson was than with his dad. And even though Anderson was his boss, he treated him ten times better than his father ever had. Now he enjoyed going to work every day.

Just when he was getting used to working with Anderson, the man had won his sister back, and Rafferty's life had changed again. But not in the way he thought it would. He thought Anderson would fire him the moment Ruth was back in his life, but instead, they had just moved the office back to the building Rafferty had always worked in. It was bigger and had two office spaces, whereas Anderson's office only had one.

It was possible because Ruth had been the one who bought the building. Not just his dad's building, but dozens in town. In fact, she was the biggest landholder in Landstad city limits.

If that hadn't been shocking enough, he had found out that she was also a writer, churning out books in her spare time for years. It was because of her writing that she could buy the buildings.

So far, he hadn't been able to read the books she had written; after all, reading sex scenes that came from his sister's head didn't seem right. Even the covers made him nervous. There was a lot of cleavage happening on those.

With her writing and her rental business, she had taken over Anderson's office. As far as Rafferty could tell, she was happy. Happy with her work and happy with Anderson. Rafferty had never seen her this happy. He liked to see her that way.

The only thing that really didn't change was Mia—she still hated him. Maybe not hate, but close. He still saw her every day or two in the café, but they never really talked. Not since his dad had died. And somehow, whatever fun they had during that day had been forgotten, replaced by the same anger she always had for him.

The only conversation they had was when she asked him to bid on her friend Tess Thorn at the Red River Flood Funding Auction that she organized. Her friend was the bank president and not well-liked in the community, and Mia had been nervous that she wouldn't get bid on, and her friend would feel bad.

Mia had reluctantly agreed to go on a date with him if he bid on her friend. But only if he won. So, when the time came, he bid on the woman. Maybe some financial advice would be something he could use anyway. But to his surprise someone else started bidding on her also. In the beginning, Rafferty had been willing to go to $500 on her. It was for charity and for Mia. When that number was surpassed, he continued until it hit $1000 since he would also get financial advice *and* a date with Mia for the money it would be worth it. After that point, he kept bidding to see how high this guy would go. When the number hit $2000, he stopped, he couldn't afford to win at that point.

So he didn't get his date with Mia, but he did get a big hug from her. Which was enough for the effort, but he really wanted that date. When he asked anyway, she said no.

But today, he would finally get the date he had been waiting for. Well, not a date exactly, just a day with her. Anderson had invited him on a trail ride with him and Ruth and their friends. Tess and her new boyfriend, Math, the man Rafferty had bid against on her, was going to be there. And of course, Mia.

But Mia was pissed that he was there. Apparently, she hadn't been told he was going, and she wasn't happy to see him. Or that she would have to ride with him since there were only three machines. The hushed words between the women meant that Ruth and Tess were well aware of Mia's anger.

Today, Mia was in jeans and a Landstad Tiger's orange sweatshirt a few sizes too big that hid her glorious curves, from her great breasts to her round hips. Today, her hair was also orange to match the shirt. Well, they didn't actually match. They were two different shades of orange. Turning, she caught him looking and glared at him, then stomped over to him.

"Let's get this over with." She climbed on the machine that Rafferty was standing next to.

"At least try to have fun," he asked as he climbed on in front of her.

"Hard to do with you here," she hissed into his ear.

Starting the engine, he hit the gas, and the machine jerked forward, forcing her to grab on to him tighter to not fall off. So, her body was pressed nicely to his as the others headed down the path into the woods on Math's property.

Slowly, her hand slid over his body as one pressed against his stomach and one pressed against his chest as she held on to him. Feeling her breasts pressed into his back, and her lower body pressed to his butt, he could barely concentrate on driving.

Soon enough, her hold loosened as she became more relaxed on the ride. Her hands were now resting on his hips, but her body was still pressed to his. The landscape was hillier than he had expected, and in some low spots, there was water. The longer the ride the more low spots, more water.

Turning his head, he said to her above the sound of the machine, "Do you want to get dirty or stay clean?"

Her laughter rang in his ears as she admitted, "Dirty, of course."

Her arms tightened around him as he sped up and went through the next puddle at a higher speed, and the splashing water almost got them. The next was the same, so he held back a little so the other two couples could get farther in front of them he could get their speed up some. At the third puddle, he accelerated and hit the puddle enough to send muddy water high into the air and right on top of them.

He was worried she was going to be mad since her body had tensed when the mud had fallen onto them, but to his surprise, she just laughed. So he did it again, and by the time they caught up with the group, both were soaking wet and muddy. The other two couples didn't have a speck of mud on them.

As the ride continued, Mia encouraged him from behind to hit every puddle. By the time the three couples stopped for a rest by the river, Rafferty needed to wipe the mud from his face. But it was worth it to see Mia smiling and happy.

"How did nobody else get dirty out there?" Rafferty asked the group after the machines were shut off, and they could have a conversation without yelling.

Mia grabbed him around the waist and swung off the machine as she answered him. "Because their girlfriends would kill them if they got dirty."

"You got that right," Ruth said as Anderson helped her off their machine. Before he set her on the ground, he kissed her.

Mia ignored the couple and said, "You know, when you asked me to come on this trail ride, I expected mud to fly."

"I didn't know that," Tess said. "I just thought it would be fun to get away for a day. With friends."

"It will be fun. Except for the whole Rafferty thing." She waved her hand in his direction. It seemed her anger hadn't completely diminished.

"You mean the guy who took you mud-running? When no one else would have?" Ruth asked Mia.

"That might be him," Mia murmured behind him.

He was looking at the river they were parked by. It was almost not a river, since if he took a running leap, he could get over it, but it was still a river. It was a beautiful spot, and Rafferty was glad Math had picked it. Though he didn't know Math Nordskov very well, Anderson did. And the girls were all part of their book club, so they got along. His sole purpose of being here was to be with Mia. It had been a while since he got any alone time with her.

Turning, he saw Mia and the other women were sitting on a fallen log, probably left there for that purpose. They were chatting about something, and Math and Anderson were off looking at something in the woods. With no interest in the fauna, he wandered over to the women.

"So, Mia, what's happening in town?" he asked. She was the town gossip. Except he noticed when it came to the book club, she didn't talk about them at all to others. He liked that she was loyal to her friends.

"Let's see." She leaned back and looked up at him. "There's this jerk of an insurance guy who keeps showing up at places I am."

"Mia!" Ruth yelled at her.

"Okay, I'm sorry, Rafferty." Blushing, she looked away. "We were talking about the Baker house. It's for sale. I was just asking Ruth if she was going to buy it."

"Are you going to?" Rafferty asked her. After all, Ruth was loaded and liked to buy property in Landstad.

"I haven't decided yet," Ruth said, then she looked over at Anderson. "I mean, we haven't decided yet. It needs a lot of work. I don't know if we want to take on a project. And I like living downtown."

"If it were me, I would buy it in a heartbeat!" Mia exclaimed, wiping mud from her neck. "I have always wanted a house on The Hill."

Rafferty looked at her. Her excitement was showing, and it was charming. Almost as charming as calling the street just one block off Main Street "The Hill." There was no hill, and there had never been one. In fact, it was a lower street than Main Street was. When he biked it as a kid, he realized that. But what it did have was six large old houses, most in need of repair. Well, there were five now since one had been torn down a few years before.

"Really? There's a hill? In Landstad?" Tess asked in confusion.

"No, not an actual hill, maybe a rise. But anyway, I have always loved those houses. The Baker one was my favorite. It was painted all kinds of colors before they repainted it white the last time. It always looked amazing from the outside. You should buy it, Ruth. It would be perfect for all your little Andersons." Mia turned to her friend in excitement.

"I don't know if we are having any little Andersons, and I love it downtown. You should get it," Ruth told Mia, even if downtown and work would only be a block away.

"I can't afford it. I'm only a waitress!" Mia exclaimed.

"You have owned that café for years," Rafferty reminded her. She always downplayed her owning the café. She had owned it for years and wasn't even thirty yet. She should be proud of what she had accomplished so far in her life. Instead, she always just told people she was a waitress.

"Doesn't mean I make much money. Definitely not enough for a house on The Hill," she told him, making the area of town sound far more important than it was.

Looking at her orange hair, Rafferty decided he would have to look at the house of Mia's dreams one day soon. Probably this week. He himself couldn't tell the five remaining from the one that was gone. But for Mia, he was suddenly very interested. Until right now, he had no idea that just a house could make her so excited.

As the men came back, they joined in the conversation, and it turned to who had lived in the houses on The Hill over the years. Since the three who had grown up in town were almost all the same age, they couldn't remember back too far, but the recent history gave them enough to talk about.

Soon they were heading back to their cars. Again, Rafferty and Mia were in the back, but Rafferty let Mia drive. Her eyes had lit up at the prospect, and he wondered if he had made a mistake.

But it hadn't been a mistake. Not only had he been able to wrap his arms around her, but she spent the entire time talking to him. No real conversation, but excited words and questions about what they should do. Mostly, they just let the group get ahead of them to see how wet they could get. And they got wet and dirty.

When they finally made it to Math's yard, the other four had already crawled off their machines. And when Ruth had seen Mia, she stated that the orange-haired woman wasn't allowed in her new SUV. To Rafferty's delight, he had to take her home.

They said their goodbyes and headed back to town. Of course, this meant his pickup's interior would be covered in mud, but he got to spend a few more minutes with Mia, so it was a price he was willing to pay. And the Mia he was bringing home was happy and seemed to forget her anger at him.

At her door, he watched her jump out of the cab. Climbing out, he rushed around to follow her. She was already at her door when he caught her. Following her into the stairwell, they stood at the small landing that held three mailboxes, though he was sure there were only two apartments.

"I had fun today," he said, because the day had been nearly perfect. All it was missing was spending the rest of the day with her.

"It did turn out to be pretty fun. Even if they are all sticks in the mud."

"I think we're the muddy ones." Rafferty smiled at her.

"You definitely are," she said, leaning against the wall behind her.

"You need a mirror." He had been itching to touch her hair all day, so he ran his hand over the orange hair with flecks of mud in it. Some were more chunks than flecks.

"Are you flirting with me, Rafferty?" she asked, then licked her lips.

"Do you want me to?" He watched her tongue.

"Yes," she whispered breathlessly, then quickly said, "No."

He lowered his lips to hers, "Let's go with yes."

As his lips finally touched her soft ones, he wondered why it always took months for him to kiss her again. Deepening the kiss, he pulled her soft, wet body to him. Her hands went around his neck and held on to him. God, she felt so good in his arms.

The room suddenly echoed with the sound of Taylor Swift singing about New York. Mia pushed away from him and dug in her pocket, pulling out her phone. "Mandy," was all she said.

Turning away, she headed up the stairs, talking to her cousin. He watched until she made it to the top of the landing, then she was gone.

Leaning against the wall she had just been leaning against, he cursed her cousin. If she hadn't called, he might have been able to follow her up the stairs and maybe into the shower. Stomping out the door and into the sun, he wished it would just rain to match his mood.

CHAPTER 10

WELL, that didn't go as expected. As the personal attendant to the bride, Mia had been in charge of getting the bride to the altar. But instead, she had shoved the woman out of the church window in the pouring rain to avoid the altar. And she would do it again if asked, or if the bride was as jittery as this one had been. Cold feet didn't even begin to explain what had happened.

It had been close to three hours since Natalie, the bride, had left, and most of the church was empty. A bridesmaid was still lingering, and the groom was talking to her. Maybe a little too close. Not that it mattered anyway—the wedding was off, and so was the relationship. The groom could do anything he wanted.

Upstairs, she knew her friend Hazel was talking to the pastor somewhere, so Mia was glad something good might have come from the failed wedding. Hazel had been avoiding the man for weeks, but Mia knew there was something there. This was maybe just the kick in the pants they needed.

Which was why she was avoiding leaving the basement, staying in the little room in the back of the basement where the bride had gotten ready and escaped from.

Pouring herself another paper glass of whiskey she had brought

60

with her, in case the bride needed encouragement, she wondered how she was getting home since the bride took her Jeep. Well, maybe that wasn't really an issue. She lived four blocks away, but it was still raining out.

Once the smiling bridesmaid and groom left, she could clean the rest of the basement and be on her way, but the two were in no hurry to leave. But then again, neither was Mia. All she was going to do was go home—she wasn't up for the reception that was still taking place.

At least her dad could celebrate his daughter not getting married. Based on his reaction when she had told him Natalie had left, she knew he would be celebrating today. It seemed not many people were upset the wedding was off, not even the groom.

The door opened, and Rafferty stuck his head in the room. Seeing her, he smiled. Then he slipped into the room and shut the door behind him. Today he was wearing gray slacks and a light blue dress shirt, and he looked far too good, as usual.

Since the trail ride, she hadn't seen much of him. Well, she saw him in all the usual places, but nothing more. Not that she was going out as much as before. She was beginning to think she was turning into the town's new hermit since Ruth was going out far more than she was these days.

Every time she saw Rafferty, she knew she had to forgive him. He had a good reason for ghosting her so many years ago: his sister needed him. But as much as she wanted to believe he had planned to call her, to see her, all it would've taken was a single phone call. Such a simple thing for him to do, and yet it never happened.

"I was beginning to wonder if you went out the window as well," he said in reference to the bride's departure.

"Nope, just waiting for the groom to finally make his move on his sister and leave." She lifted her glass to toast the people still in the basement.

"She's probably not his sister. I think the other two are," Rafferty said.

Natalie's bridesmaids were the groom's two sisters and a friend.

"You believe what you want, Rafferty Brooks. I'll believe what I want." She stayed on the table.

He easily walked over and jumped on the table beside her, picked up the bottle of whiskey, looked at it, and set it down again. "Can anyone join this party?"

"As long as you're not in the wedding party, except Natalie." She flattened her pink dress against her legs as she spoke.

"How did you get her out that window?" He pointed to the small window behind them.

"Everybody fits out that window. I have been in and out of it more than the regular door." Mia laughed at herself. This had been the church she had attended her entire life. And since her mother was a devout woman, her six girls spent most Sunday mornings here. So, this was like a second home to her. There was no place in the church she hadn't been.

"I bet you have. Are you going to get married here one day?" Taking the glass from her, he took a drink, then handed it back to her.

"Of course. And I won't go out the window, either. I won't say yes unless I'm truly in love. And the guy has to look at me like Anderson looks at Angel," she said wistfully.

"I haven't noticed. How does Anderson look at Angel?" He bumped her shoulder with his.

"Like he would die if she left him again. Like she's the reason he's alive." She took a sip of the whiskey.

"Oh, that look. He pulls it off."

"That's what I want," she whispered, more to herself than to him.

"I hope you get it one day." Rafferty took her glass and finished the last bit of alcohol left.

Grabbing it back, she filled it with more from the bottle beside her. "Do you think Anderson will marry her?"

"Oh yeah, I can't believe he hasn't yet. I think it's her mom. She wants big and catholic, and that's not Angel. I see them having a small, private ceremony." Rafferty tried to take the glass again, but Mia held it up far enough away from him that he couldn't reach it.

"Me too." Grinning, she continued to hold up the glass.

"I like them." He pulled her arm until she let him take the glass from her.

"Do you think the groom is going to have sex with his sister today?" She looked at the door beyond them.

"Probably. I would if my bride left me." Rafferty bumped her shoulder.

"I know your sister," she whispered in surprise at his answer.

"It was a joke. Nice hair." This week she had chosen a subtle auburn, more like a natural color than a flamboyant one, but she was in a wedding this week.

"Thanks. Natalie didn't want crazy today. And she gets her way for one day. Tomorrow will be a different story." She giggled and covered her mouth—she might be getting drunk.

"Maybe you should just keep it like this for a while. It's gorgeous." He reached out and touched the shoulder-length, slightly curly bob.

Trying not to react to him touching her hair, she took another drink. It had taken her two months to get over him kissing her after the trail ride, and it had only been a month and a half since it happened. But she didn't need Rafferty Brooks in her life now; she was almost over the last time.

"We'll see." Half of her was planning her next color change for later today and the other half suddenly wanted to stay this color forever. Rafferty liked it.

They sat in silence, watching the door in front of them, and silently drank. Every once in a while, he would bump her shoulder with his. Or bump her knee with his.

Jumping from the table, Rafferty pulled out his phone and looked through it for a minute. Then to her surprise, he started to play a slow Taylor Swift song. Gently, he took her hand, helping her off the table. "Dance with me, Mia."

Going willingly into his arms, she rested her head on his shoulder. "Dancing is for the reception."

Wanting to stay away from Rafferty and doing it were two completely different things. Tonight, she was going to give in to him. Tonight, she wanted to be in his arms.

"Let's call this the reception then," he whispered into her hair.

"Reception then," she repeated.

As the song ended, she tried to pull out of his comfortable warm arms, but he held fast, and the same song came back on again. So she stayed. The song played on repeat for so long, she was caught up in the fuzzy haze of alcohol, the tingly lightheadedness of being in Rafferty's arms, and the imagery of the song that when he kissed her, she kissed him back. It was love, Taylor said so, and Taylor knows about these things.

CHAPTER 11

Rafferty knew the moment she passed out. Was it because she was in his arms, and they were dancing? No. It was because he was kissing her when it happened. What an ego boost. Now he was left holding up a limp body in the basement of an empty church.

If Mia hadn't been passed out, she would've loved it; in fact, she would've been the first person he would have called for help if she wasn't the drunk person. Grabbing his phone, he shut off the song. He was happy he picked the right song for the event. It had been glorious to have her in his arms, even if it had been for two songs when she was drunk. Though he had to admit, he didn't think she was pass-out drunk until she actually passed out.

Shifting her easily, he picked her up into his arms. With her there, he grabbed the nearly empty whiskey bottle and left her little room. He couldn't get the image of her out of his mind: She was getting ready for her wedding. She was in a tight white dress, and her hair was the brown she used to have when she was younger. And, of course, she was happy to be marrying him.

Wait. Did he even want to marry her? He wanted to think that the idea was so farfetched it had never crossed his mind. That he hadn't sat in that church waiting for the wedding that didn't happen, imagining him and Mia in front of the church, promising forever in front of everyone they knew.

When he left the little room, he was relieved that the groom and bridesmaid were gone, along with everyone else. So nobody saw him carrying the passed-out woman through the church. Rafferty chuckled at Mia's insistence that the groom and the bridesmaid were related to each other. Only Mia would even think that.

He was successful in getting her out of the church, across the parking lot, and past puddles and mud. Though now the sun was shining, it hadn't erased the evidence of the downpour that had happened just hours before.

Getting her into his car was a challenge, as she was dead weight, but after a few minutes, he had her buckled in. Turning on the car, he cranked the air conditioning—he had to go back into the church, and he couldn't leave her in a hot car.

That set, he went back in to see if anyone was still around. He didn't want to leave the building unlocked, and he didn't have a key to lock it.

To his surprise, he found the pastor still in his office. Knocking on the door frame, he stated, "I think I'm the last one still here."

The man looked up at him and smiled before saying, "Okay. Good."

"Do you get a lot of weddings that fall apart?" Rafferty wanted to know.

"More fall apart during the first year than the few minutes before."

"Then it's good that she bolted today." Rafferty didn't know why he was still talking to the man, but he hadn't been to a wedding where the couple ended up not getting married before.

"Yes. I don't know your name, but I've seen you around town," the pastor stated.

"Rafferty Brooks. I sell insurance in town," he said, in case the man was looking for insurance. You never know.

"Nice to meet you, Rafferty. I'm Pastor Ruston Abbott. You must be a friend of the bride?" he asked, probably because the groom wasn't from town, and the bride was.

"Mostly a friend of a friend of the bride. I kind of crashed," he said sheepishly.

"It was a good one to crash." Ruston smiled at him.

"It was. A runaway bride. Well, I'm going, so you can lock up." Because Rafferty had a drunk Mia to put to bed.

"Thanks, Rafferty," the pastor said as Rafferty went back to his car and to his drunk friend of the bride.

The drive to her place was so short, it was almost not worth the hassle of getting her into his car earlier. It was only a few blocks, and he probably could've carried her. Probably should have carried her. Would've loved to carry her in his arms as far as needed. Except then they would've been the talk of the town, and Mia would hate him anew.

Once he had wrestled her out of the car and up the stairs to her apartment, he was glad he hadn't carried her all the way. She wasn't heavy, but she *was* dead weight.

Once in her bedroom, he laid her on her bed, and she sat straight up and started to fight her way out of her dress. Where was this person when he was trying to get her out of his pickup? The one who can undress while passed out?

Helping her as best he could, they got the dress off, but she almost choked him when she grabbed his tie and pulled it as hard as she could. He had no idea what she thought it was, but she wouldn't let go. Loosening it, he took it off. Then he got to gaze at her glorious breasts that hadn't been in a bra this entire time. While he was appreciating them, she had removed her panties. Rafferty smiled as he pulled the covers over her body.

Yup, she was still a brunette under all that hair dye.

Once again, he got out some aspirin and a glass of water, and put them on the night stand. He knew she was still holding his tie, so he left it. He could pick it up another time, when she wasn't holding on to it with everything she had.

Picking up her dress, he found a hanger in her closet and hung it up—no need for it to be wrinkled. He wanted to see her in it again. She looked amazing, and now he knew she didn't wear a bra with it.

Closing the door behind him, he wasn't as happy as he usually was when he left her drunk in bed. Today, he wanted her sober and in bed. Today, he had crashed the wedding in hopes of getting Mia to dance with him at the reception. He was happy he got his dance, but he wanted her sober.

He was tired of her being drunk every time he got close to her. Though she was a fun drunk, she was also fun sober.

CHAPTER 12

Fall

After handing a meat loaf special to her mom and a ham dinner to her aunt Dolly, Mia sat down next to her mom, Dotty. These two came in a few times a week and were always fun. They got along so well for women in their sixties, but they had lived such parallel lives that it was no surprise. Both had married in their early twenties and stayed in the same town they had been raised in. Both had a bucket of kids, six for her mom and four for her aunt, and at almost the same time. Though Dolly's were all older then Dotty's, Mia and her cousin Julia were the same age. Mia was the first born, and Julia the baby of her family.

But for as long as Mia could remember, the families were in each other's pockets. From holidays to birthday parties to school functions, the Lawson and Nordskov families were there. Though the two sisters were originally Haans girls, nobody thought of them as that anymore. But nobody could miss that they were sisters.

"How is Mia?" Aunt Dolly asked like every week.

"Mia's good," Mia answered, like every week.

"How is the waitress shortage?" her mom asked.

"I've got it covered now. I hired two more and have one more I might hire if one doesn't work out." She was always having trouble getting and keeping waitresses—nobody wanted to be a waitress these days.

"That's good," Dotty said.

This was actually the same conversation the sisters always had with her, but she enjoyed them getting along. It was hard on everyone when they started to fight, as all sisters do. Mia was an expert on sisters—she had five little ones.

In her pocket, her phone made a noise, signaling she had a text. Excusing herself, she pulled it out as she walked back to the kitchen area. It was from Ruth at the rental office, formerly the insurance office across the street.

SOS. Ruth

Sliding it into her pocket, she turned to the other two waitresses working today and told them to take over. Of course, it was only her mom and aunt in the restaurant. Hurrying over to them, she told them she had to run over and see Ruth. They didn't ask any questions, they never did.

Tossing her order pad at Kelly behind the counter, she hurried across the street. So far, it wasn't too cold for a mid-October day. Sure, it was chilly, but not cold enough for a full-blown jacket. You just needed a sweatshirt or sweater to ward off this cold. She didn't skip the jacket because she was still wearing the pink one since she hadn't found anything to her liking when spring brought winter clothes sales.

Pushing her way into the rental office, she found herself missing the insurance office it used to be. With Anderson in the back office, and Ruth right her at the window. Ruth ready for conversation at a moment's notice. Now she was busy in the back office, writing most of the time since the rental office was basically only open if you had an appointment.

Today Ruth was in the back office when she came in, looking the same as she always had. Well, happier now than she used to be, now she had Anderson and the ability to do what she loved all day long: write books.

"You wanted to see me?" Mia said from the doorway. This was the first SOS she had ever received, so she didn't know if it was good or bad.

"Could you close the door, Mia?" Ruth stated calmly.

Mia closed the door and walked over to the chair Ruth had on the other side of her desk. Then, as usual, she looked at all the black blinking boxes that lined the shelves behind her friend. What any of them did was beyond Mia, but Ruth knew what they all did. All those black boxes kept Ruth's computers running and connected to the world. Anderson teased her about her network sometimes when Mia was around, but she knew he was impressed that she was an expert. Enough so that she maintained his internet connection at his insurance office as well.

"What's the emergency?" Mia asked.

"First, I want to know if you can get a few days off?" Ruth asked cryptically.

"What days?" Mia leaned on the desk with her elbows and rested her chin on her hands, looking closely at her nervous friend.

"The rest of the day today, tomorrow, and maybe the next one," Ruth stated.

"So, today and Friday. I get the weekend off this week. I think I can swing it." Smiling, she rescheduled in her head. She knew two of her waitresses would fill in for her, no questions asked.

"Good," was all Ruth said.

"Why?" Mia wanted to know..

"I want you to come with me and Anderson to Las Vegas We're getting married." Ruth grinned as she said it.

Mia knew her mouth was wide open in shock. Ruth and Las Vegas seemed like oil and water, but Mia really wanted to see them together just the same, "Why?"

"Because I think I'm pregnant, and no way am I having a baby without being married. I'm not making my mother's mistakes."

Which made perfect sense Ruth had been raised by a single mom with no man in the picture for most of her life. Though she and Mia hadn't been friends, Mia knew life hadn't always been easy for Ruth.

"You're getting married, like, today?" Mia asked in confusion.

Ruth shook her head. "Tomorrow."

"When do we leave? Will I get time for some shows? Some gambling?" Mia jumped up and started to pace, starting to pack in her mind.

"The plane leaves in three hours, so we have to leave soon. I only need you sometime tomorrow, and we'll know more when we get there. The rest of the time is yours. But ..." Ruth stopped shifting the stack of papers on her desk.

Mia turned quickly—there was always a but. "But?"

"Anderson is asking Rafferty to go as well." Ruth bit her lip.

Rafferty. Of course, Rafferty. She had been avoiding him since the wedding—the "not wedding." Once again, she had woken up hung over and naked after spending time with him. Once again, she couldn't remember anything. Had they had sex? Had they had sex in a church? Had they used protection? There was no evidence of it this time. The last thing she remembered was kissing him while dancing at the church, then nothing. But she'd woken up in her own bed.

So far, he hadn't said anything, and she was never going to ask him about it. So, she had no idea what had happened. All she knew was that she had his tie wrapped around her hands when she woke up. Bondage? Was she even into bondage? She had no idea!

"He's my brother, Mia, and Anderson's best friend. There's no way Anderson would want his own brother here, so can you put up with Rafferty for me?"

Mia looked at one of her best friends, who chosen her over all her other friends for this. "I can do it for you. But you owe me. Big time."

Ruth jumped up and hugged her. "Thank you, Mia! Now go get packed, and don't tell anyone. We want to keep it secret until we get back."

"Okay."

With only an hour, Mia ended up not having a lot of time to pack. She got the restaurant organized for her to be gone for a few days and then threw some stuff in a bag, grabbing as much cash as she could find for gambling, and her currently empty travel credit card. She rarely got to travel. After changing into more Vegas-appropriate attire —a yellow sundress—she was ready.

Climbing into the back seat next to Ruth, she wished she'd had time to color her hair. It was supposed to be platinum blonde, but the black it had been before had actually made it so close to her natural color that she usually just stared at it when she looked at herself. It had been years since she had brown hair. But the bleaching had done some damage, and she couldn't fix it for a while. So she was stuck for a few weeks with the brown.

"Is everyone ready?" Anderson asked from the driver's seat.

"You bet! So excited that in a few hours, I'll be betting on anything and everything." She laughed in excitement, which seemed catchy because everyone laughed with her as they headed out of town.

Since she was next to Ruth, they chatted the entire way to Grand Forks to catch the plane. She hadn't even noticed Rafferty was there except she could hear his voice, but he was in front of her, so she could only see the back of his head. He was easy to ignore this way.

It was even easier on the plane, because those seats were way bigger. There he was still right in front of her next to Anderson, but she couldn't hear or see him.

"So, I've come up with my payment for putting up with your family on this vacation," Mia said to Ruth, who was sitting by the window, looking out at the ground far below.

"What would that be?" Ruth turned to her and asked.

"Godmother to your first born." Mia pointed at her stomach and grinned.

"Really? Because I bet I can tell you who Anderson will pick as godfather then." Ruth pointed to the seat in front of Mia. The one Rafferty was in.

"But you don't need a godfather. I'm enough of a godmother that your baby will never even know there are other families not like ours out there, two godparent families," she stated boldly, because she was losing her dream. So far, not one of her sisters had picked her either. What was it about her that nobody wanted her to be a godparent to their children?

Ruth stared at her in confusion for a moment before she shook her head. "Nope, you will have to share. We want two people."

"What if I'm married?" Mia asked. She could swing it. She would just have to double down on her efforts. And since effort hadn't been being put forth in a long time, it would be easy.

"So, in less than nine months, you'll not only fall in love, but be married?" Ruth's perfect eyebrow went up in question.

"You doubt me and my abilities?" Mia said more confidently than she felt.

"Just a little. You're waiting for your true love, and he might not show up in the next few months."

"Maybe I already know him, like you and Anderson."

"And who would that be?"

"I don't know yet. Maybe when I move to Grand Forks, I'll meet my neighbor, and it'll be true love. Like in a romance book. Do you know anything about those?" Mia asked, knowing that Ruth had written more than a dozen books on the topic. Mia had read all her books since she'd found out about Ruth's big secret. And that exact scenario had been in not one, but three of her books.

Ruth just rolled her eyes. "But you can't leave anymore, Mia. I'm having a baby, and Tess will have her baby any day now. You can't leave."

"But it's my destiny, Ruth."

"No, it's not. You're a Landstad Tiger, through and through." Ruth argued, a Tiger was the not only the school mascot, but the nickname for a Landstad High graduate who chose to live in Landstad long after they could have left.

"I can be a Tiger from afar." It was true; she wasn't going to cut her ties with the town. After all, she did love it there. Just not every day, day in and day out.

"Nobody is a Tiger from afar." Ruth shook her head.

"Then I'll be the first." She tried to convince Ruth … and herself.

"I'll let it go for now," Ruth said, then took out a paper from her purse. "So, last night Anderson found this on line. I think this is the place."

Taking the paper from her hand, it was for a cute little wedding chapel that looked like an actual church. Stopping, Mia looked at her. "Last night? You gave me an hour to get ready!"

"Sorry. We were just going to go alone, but Rafferty found out and insisted he had to go. So, I decided to bring you."

"You at least made a good choice. Anderson didn't." She looked at the back of the seat in front of her, it was the first time she made it sound like she didn't want Rafferty there.

"So, we're going to swing by the place today when we get in, and then get married tomorrow," Ruth explained, taking the paper back and folding it up again.

"Why not today? Why wait?" Mia questioned. There was no way she would be able to wait.

"Because tomorrow is the anniversary of when Anderson took over the insurance office from Frank. When we met." Ruth got a dreamy look in her eyes, making Mia wonder if that was the true reason behind the wedding and not the baby excuse.

Mia giggled, "You're so romantic I thought you were knocked up?"

Ruth shrugged. "I am. It just happened that I realized right as this was coming up. Couldn't miss the chance to do it that day."

"It's the day I would've picked, too." Mia loved how cute a couple they were.

When the stewardess came by with drinks, she dropped off a tiny bottle of whiskey for her and a pop for Ruth from the guys in front of them. Mia happily drank it. This was actually the most exciting day of the year. She was getting out of Landstad. She may have to go back in a few days, but for today, she was free. And she was getting to see one of her best friends get married in a secret ceremony to her long time crush. What a vacation it was going to be.

CHAPTER 13

Once the plane landed, Mia's mind was blown. She had never been to Las Vegas, and it was fascinating, busy as sin. She had never seen so many people in the same place at once, and they were just at the airport. Anderson took charge and led the group to the rental car area, and soon they were driving around the city with everyone else who had ever lived. Mentally, she checked Las Vegas off her preferred cities to live in. Too many people.

Anderson weaved in and out of traffic with ease, but after two little bottles of whiskey on the flight, Mia wasn't enjoying the swaying of the car. Not at all. Once they stopped, she was quick to get out of the car. Maybe too quick because she landed hard on the cement of the parking lot.

Rafferty climbed out of the front seat and helped her up as he accused, "Are you tipsy already?"

"No, I'm just done with the car," she said, looking into his blue eyes as he continued to hold her hand after she was on her feet again.

Shaking it off, she turned to look at the actual building from Ruth's printout. Here it was in person, and it looked even cuter. Ruth and Anderson had picked the perfect spot to get married. If Mia had to get married in Vegas, this was exactly where she would pick, too.

The happy couple went inside and said that Mia and Rafferty could stay outside, but not wanting to be alone with him in sin city. So, Mia followed them in. Rafferty followed her. Inside, the air was cool but not cold—the perfect temperature for Ruth and Anderson.

While the happy couple talked to the receptionist, Mia looked around the chapel. She was excited for the next day and was happy Ruth had chosen her to be there. The only one there for her.

Rafferty came up behind her and asked, "Do you like it?"

"Yes, it's perfect. I can't believe how perfect it is," she whispered, trying not to interrupt Anderson as he talked.

"That's what I thought. When Anderson first said they were going to Vegas, I didn't really think it would be like this." Rafferty looked around the building and the upscale decorations.

"More tacky?" she asked. It was what she had thought also.

"More Elvisy," he confirmed with a nod. "So, what are you doing the rest of the day?"

"I want to see a show and gamble. And you?" That was just the beginning. She was going to do Vegas in two days if it was the last thing she did.

"Maybe that. I hadn't thought of anything I really want to do," he confessed.

"If you promise to be good, you can see a show with me. But I gamble alone," she stated firmly. Then laughed at his reaction of sadness.

By the time Anderson and Ruth were ready to leave, Mia was still a bit wobbly on her feet. As Mia followed the rest outside, she wasn't excited to get back in the car, not yet. So, when they got to the car, Mia hesitated. "How far is the hotel?"

"It's not far," Anderson replied, looking at her.

"Close enough to walk?"

"No, it's like a mile." Anderson leaned on the car, looking at her over the top of it.

"I'll walk the mile," Mia stated. "Which way?"

Anderson just pointed down the busy street.

Smiling at him, Mia turned in that direction and started walking.

No way was she getting back in that car with the way he drove in a city. It was bad enough that she would have to get back in there in a few days. On top of that, the weather was perfect. It was October, but she already missed summer. Today, she could enjoy it for a mile or so.

Before she made it out of the parking lot, Rafferty had caught up to her and was following her. But she didn't acknowledge he was there. Just walked ahead, looking straight, her eyes trying to take everything in. But in her mind's eye she saw him walking behind her in his gray slacks and white polo shirt, no tie or jacket anymore.

"Really, Mia. You couldn't ride for another two minutes?" Rafferty demanded.

"None of your business." She wasn't going to explain it to him; he wouldn't understand.

"Are you drunk already? You can't take a car ride?" he asked from behind her.

Spinning around, she glared at him. "I'm *not* drunk. I had one drink on the plane. One!"

Cocking his head, he said, "Two."

"Two drinks on the plane, two!" Correcting herself, she hadn't thought he saw both.

Spinning back around, she started walking again. Hopefully, he left her alone until they got to the hotel. Looking in front of her, she wondered which hotel it was. She counted seven from where she was. Okay, she should have asked which hotel, that would have been smart.

"Do you know which hotel?" he asked from behind her, like he could read her mind.

"I know which hotel it is," she lied.

"Which one?" He sped up, so he could walk beside her.

"That one." She pointed down the road, not at any particular one.

"So, you're blindly walking down the Vegas Strip, looking for a hotel?" he asked.

"No, I'm having a nice walk in the warm afternoon before I look for the hotel," she countered, because she was enjoying the heat, something that had been lacking in her regular life for a few months now.

"I love how stubborn you can be." He took her hand in his.

"Excuse me?" she asked, but she must have been a little drunk because she liked his hand in hers. It was warm and comforting. Or maybe it was the way he said the L word so casually about her.

"You're stubborn, Mia Lawson."

"I am not."

She knew she was.

"How about calling Ruth to find out which hotel it is?" he suggested.

It was a great idea, but she had left her phone in the car. So, maybe the walk had been a bad idea. But she would never admit it. She just continued to walk in silence, holding his hand.

"How about I tell you which hotel it is if you promise to spend the night with me?" he asked, squeezing her hand lightly.

"In your dreams, Rafferty Brooks. I'm not that drunk," she hissed at him.

"I don't mean that. You with the dirty mind. Just in public, a show, gambling, or whatever. We do it together."

"What about Anderson and Ruth? Don't you want to be with them?"

"I believe they're starting their honeymoon early. Without me."

"Maybe if you ask, they'll let you in," she bit back a smile.

"I would rather see the town with my favorite waitress." He turned on the charm.

"Hey, I'm not a waitress; I'm a business owner," she corrected.

He turned up the charm. "Okay, my favorite business owner."

She knew she was drunk because she found herself agreeing, and he happily pointed at the hotel they had just passed. Entering the lobby, Rafferty checked in for them both since Mia didn't have her purse on her. To her luck, her and Rafferty's separate rooms were across the hallway from Ruth and Anderson's room. So, when they finally made it to the floor, they would grab their luggage from the other couple.

Mia laughed at Ruth from her door. "Just like at home. You guys are across from me."

"Yes, but there's less weather happening between us," Ruth agreed.

"So, what are you guys doing tonight?" Rafferty asked. It was already close to seven local time.

"Nothing," Ruth said with a shy smile, leaning into her fiancé.

"Good enough for me," Rafferty stated. He wasn't pushing the other couple to spend time with them, it seemed.

"When is tomorrow going to happen? Did you pick a time?" Mia asked the couple.

"Yep. We'll leave here at a little before four, unless someone walks. Then she has to be there by four." Anderson was looking at her.

"So says the crazy driver," Mia mumbled.

"Okay. See you tomorrow at four," Rafferty said, letting the couple get to doing nothing.

When their door closed, both Mia and Rafferty went into their respective rooms. Mia took her time unpacking, hanging the dress she was going to wear the next day. She had forgotten to ask if Ruth had a particular color in mind. Maybe she would text her and see if lavender was okay, it was all she had in her closet that she thought looked nice this morning..

Pulling out her phone to text her in case she needed to do a little shopping. Stopping when there was a knock on her door, she hoped it was Ruth, so she could just ask. Mia quickly opened the door and saw it was only Rafferty. But now he was in jeans and a soft gray T-shirt that stretched nicely across his broad shoulders. She so rarely saw him in anything but slacks and button-up shirts that it was a shock to see him in actual casual clothes.

"Are you ready?" he asked.

"One second." She turned from him and his crazy-sexy outfit. Taking a picture of her dress for tomorrow, she sent a text about it to Ruth, then grabbed her purse and phone. She was ready to go.

Rafferty had followed her into her room and was looking at the dress. "You're going to look gorgeous in that. Are you sure you're not getting married?"

"Nobody gets married in lavender, Rafferty." She rolled her eyes at the mere thought.

Turning from the dress to her as she looked through her purse to make sure she had everything, he said, "How about we stay here, and I can see what you look like in the dress. Then we'll see what you look like when I peel it off you tomorrow after a few toasts to the happy couple."

Her eyes snapped up to his, and she saw him looking her up and down with desire. Was she seriously still drunk? Because she wanted to say yes? Yes, please. But instead, she stammered out, "N-no, thank you."

Slowly, he walked over to her, not breaking eye contact. His blue eyes were boring into hers until he was inches from her. Unable to tear herself away, she watched as he lowered his head, but not to kiss her, to whisper in her ear. "Liar."

His breath on her ear made her shiver. How could he read her mind again?

The sensible part of her mind finally took over and pushed him away. Surprisingly, he went willingly. Because if he had pushed it, she would definitely have given in. No way could she say no to sober sex with Rafferty Brooks in Vegas. Maybe she should see if she was missing out by always being drunk.

CHAPTER 14

THE SUN WAS STREAMING into the bedroom, making Rafferty realize he hadn't closed the curtains before he went to bed. Looking across the room at them, he wondered when had he gotten such tacky curtains? When had he gotten curtains at all?

His window looked out at the wall of his neighbor's house, which was so close, he didn't need curtains. Rolling onto his back, he wondered how much he had drunk last night. Too much was the obvious answer.

Wait, his mind finally caught up with him, he was in Vegas with Ruth and Anderson and, of course, sexy Mia. The last thing he remembered was Mia drunkenly almost getting hit by a car outside the hotel. The car had stopped just in time, and she started cursing and pounding on the hood until Rafferty dragged her off and back into the hotel.

Smiling at the cute, angry Mia Lawson, turning her anger on him until he stopped her with a kiss. The memory of the steamy kiss made him realize he was naked beneath the thin sheet he had slept under. Turning to see whose hand had just landed on his chest, he knew before his eyes saw the brunette beside him.

There she was, the cutest girl in Landstad. Today, she was even cuter than normal because her brown hair was back. He had been shocked to see it when she climbed into Anderson's pickup yesterday. She hadn't had brown hair since he'd moved back years ago, always having a weird color instead.

Sighing, he decided he had better get out of there before she woke up and was mad at him for having drunk sex with her. Except he couldn't remember the drunk sex at all. Maybe they were too drunk to do anything but sleep.

Gently, he lifted her hand from his chest and was about to put it down next to him when her hazel eyes popped open, and she looked right at him. She was about to say something when she bolted out of the bed and ran into the bathroom, not even able to close the door before she started throwing up last night's drinks.

Getting up, he put on his boxers then dug through her bag. Taking out a pair of her panties and a T-shirt, he went into the bathroom. No longer was she throwing up. Instead, she was sitting against the wall, knees up with a towel between them and her head resting on it.

Slowly, he slid down the adjacent wall and admitted, "I have no idea what happened last night."

"Me, neither," her towel-muffled voice answered quietly.

"What do you remember?" he asked, holding out the clothing to her.

"We saw that show, and I lost all my money at the poker table." Her head came up, and she grabbed her clothes.

"Poker isn't your game." He remembered that.

"The house was against me." Angrily, she pulled her T-shirt on.

"I remember you almost getting hit by a car." Picking up the panties she had dropped, he held them to her again.

"I don't remember that." Frowning, she grabbed them before shimmying them on.

"Why were we outside?" he asked. They hadn't left the hotel, even the show had been there.

"What time is it?" she asked.

"I'll look," he said, in case she was going to be sick again. Heading out to the main room, he grabbed his phone. It was 2:00 p.m. They still had two hours before the wedding.

She must have been feeling better because she followed him into the bedroom and picked up her phone. "Two."

"I see that. We have time to get ready."

Getting up, he picked up his jeans so he could go back to his room to shower and shave. At least she wasn't mad at him this morning. She was sharing the blame for getting wasted.

On her side of the bed, Mia screamed and flopped back on the bed like she passed out. He was worried until he saw her hand clenching a piece of paper. With her eyes closed, she flung the paper at him and demanded, "What is this?"

Grabbing the paper out of her hand, he sat heavy on the bed. What she had handed him was a marriage certificate. For them. For Rafferty Lee Brooks and Mia Autumn Lawson.

"Your middle name is Autumn?" he asked. He had never known.

"That is *not* the important thing on that paper."

"Well, Mrs. Brooks, this means you love me enough to spend forever with me," he teased her, looking at the paper.

She rolled over faster than he thought possible and was on him in a heartbeat. Maybe he had gone too far. He was as shocked as she was about this.

Married?

Her nails dug eight nice trenches in his chest before he could get her flipped on her back and pinned to the bed. He brought her hands with those sharp nails above her head. Her glorious body beneath his.

"Mia, I don't remember it anymore then you do. I was kidding." He looked into her anger-filled hazel eyes, but they were more brown today.

"I don't believe you," she hissed.

"Why would I want to be married to you?" Rafferty stated, though he couldn't really think of someone he would rather be married to.

"Thanks, Brooks. You know how to make a wife feel loved." She mocked his earlier statement.

"If I let you go, will you not scratch me?" he asked and watched her eyes look at his chest. They flew back to his when they saw the damage she had done to him.

"I guess, unless you act like a jerk again," Mia conceded.

Slowly, he let go of her hands and watched her closely to see if she had been lying about being nice. But she left her arms above her head until he had picked up his phone. Rolling over, he saw her pick up hers from the bed where it had landed. They both quietly scrolled through their pictures.

"Looks like you got married in the purple dress." He showed her his phone with the photos.

"Lavender," she corrected. "But at least it was classy. You wore jeans."

"And a suit jacket." He grinned at her.

"That doesn't fit at all." She giggled a little.

"Hey, I put forth the effort." Shrugging, he looked through the photos painfully slow as if he was looking for something that would explain why they were getting married. There were only ten, and most were out of focus, and not one had a good reason as far as he knew.

Her eyes swept the room, and she was off the bed in an instant. He watched her pick up the dress from the middle of the floor, where it had been in a pile for who knows how long. Hurrying, she took it into the bathroom and turned on the shower, and came back out. "I hope there's enough time to get some of the wrinkles out."

"Are you still going to wear it to Angel's wedding?" He sat up, not knowing how to help her with the dress.

"I have to; I don't have another one. And there's no time to find a new one. And I already sent her a picture of it. What am I going to tell her? That I married her brother in it already?" She looked at the license again. "Yesterday."

"What?" he asked, grabbing it from her.

"We got married yesterday. At least it's not the same day. God knows how it would look if two siblings got married the same day. I always thought that was creepy. Well, sort of cute, but mostly creepy." She went into the bathroom with the dress.

"Looks like the same place, though," he said.

She stuck her head out of the bathroom door. "Do you think they'll remember us?"

He picked up the license again and looked at it, loving their names together on the paper. Mia Autumn Brooks, he liked it.

She came out of the bathroom empty-handed, and he put the paper on the nightstand again. "I would think there's probably a different staff late at night than during the day."

"Thank god." She flopped back onto the bed.

"What, not planning the reception when we get home?" he asked, looking down at her.

"No. Planning the divorce," she admitted.

Oddly, her words kind of hurt. Maybe they should give it a try, see if it worked. They seemed to get along well when they were drunk; in fact, she usually had to be drunk for them to get along.

Both their phones dinged with texts at the same time. Both looked at their respective phones, and both groaned. One hour until the wedding.

Grabbing his jeans and shirt from the floor, he said, "I have to go get ready I'll see you in an hour. We'll talk about this later."

"I'm walking. I need fresh air today." She didn't get up from the bed, just said the words to the ceiling.

"Then you have even less time. I'll see you in a half an hour, and I'll walk with you. No way am I letting you walk alone down the Strip in that dress."

"What's wrong with my dress?"

"Nothing, it's perfect. You would be kidnapped in a heartbeat for your sexy body." He smiled as her head lifted and looked at him. Turning, he poked his head out in the hallway. It was empty, so he rushed to his own room next door.

After tossing his clothes on the bed, he headed for the shower, where he climbed under the hot spray and couldn't stop smiling. He was married to Mia Lawson, Mia Brooks. He had no idea whose idea that was, but he didn't care. It was a great idea. Now he just had to figure out how to stay married to her. That was going to be harder than keeping her in Landstad for the next three months.

CHAPTER 15

A MILE WASN'T a long enough walk to clear Mia's mind. Maybe it was because the object of her thoughts was with her the entire time. How could she plan their impending separation and divorce if he was right there? All handsome in his suit. The same suit he always wore to work, but he still was handsome in it. She wished he had worn it last night for their wedding. He was far sexier in jeans, but it was a wedding, after all.

During the ceremony, she wondered if it was the same words she and Rafferty heard last night. Probably. Looking across the happy couple to see if he was paying attention, she saw he was looking at her. Her dress wasn't as wrinkled as she thought it would be. She could only hope Ruth would think it was because of the plane ride.

Ruth looked beautiful in her off-white, form-fitting dress. It was stunning with her white hair and blue eyes. But it was the look on Anderson's face when he saw her in it for the first time. It took his breath away, and Mia saw it happen. He was so in love with her. Mia loved that she was a part of this little moment of their lives.

After the ceremony, Mia and Rafferty signed a marriage certificate that was a copy of theirs, but this time, their names were on the witness line The group went out for a fancy supper that lasted longer than any of them actually thought it would. Or maybe it was just longer than Mia thought it would be. She needed alone time to think.

By the time she made it back to her hotel room, it was close to nine p.m. The previous day was catching up with her, and all she wanted to do was climb into bed. So, after taking off her wedding dress, literally, she threw on the T-shirt she had worn that morning, or afternoon, and started to flip through the TV channels for something good. Something that would take her mind off weddings and grooms and sexy guys in jeans.

She never found anything good on since she fell asleep so fast that she woke up to the weather channel the next morning. Her phone was ringing. Rolling over, she saw it was her cousin Mandy from next door. Well, she would be next door if she was in Landstad, but instead, she was in Las Vegas, which Mandy didn't need to know, so she ignored the call.

With a start, she realized she had about twenty minutes before the car left for the airport. Jumping from bed, she hurried through changing and packing and was only five minutes late meeting Mr. and Mrs. Miles in the lobby. There they were, looking just as much in love as when they had parted the night before. Of course, Rafferty was there too, but he looked anything but in love this morning.

"How is everyone today?" she asked carefully as Rafferty angrily grabbed her bag from her and headed to the car. At his actions, she answered for them. "Grouchy."

Once at the airport, they could relax since they had over an hour to wait for the plane. Sitting next to Ruth while the guys went to hunt down something to eat, Mia asked, "How's married life?"

"About the same as single life," Ruth answered and smiled at her. That's how Mia felt about it, too. She didn't feel any more married to Rafferty than she had last week.

"When are you going to tell the dragon?" Mia asked about Ruth's mom.

The woman was a legend in town as someone you didn't mess with—or slip anything past, though Ruth had from time to time. Mia had always applauded the woman's pluck. She never managed to get anything past her own mom, and she didn't fear her as much as Ruth's mom.

"I don't know. I'm starting to think we're not going to tell anyone. I mean, we'll get married one day. In town, that is. I mean, we did this for us. Maybe one day, we will do it for everyone else," Ruth said quietly, To quietly, like she was hiding it.

"Did you just get married so your baby would be born in wedlock? But really, you like living in sin with Anderson?" Mia questioned, wondering exactly how much money the couple had spent on this little trip for nothing.

"More like I feel bad that everyone didn't get to be there. I mean, Hazel gets married next week, and she'll have everyone there. The ceremony was beautiful, but I missed my friends being there. I really want to get married with my friends there," Ruth admitted.

Mia almost told her to try thinking about getting married and not even remembering it. That was a bigger bummer than not having people there.

"I found muffins for us." Anderson came back toward them with a bag he handed to Ruth.

"Good," Mia said, grabbing the bag from Ruth. She was starving.

Ruth looked at the guys and said, "I was telling Mia that I want to keep the wedding to ourselves. Just get married later. I want the church wedding."

Rafferty looked at her. "So, nobody will know you're actually married?"

"Yes. Can you guys do that? For me?" Ruth pleaded, looking from Mia to Rafferty.

"Are you sure, Angel?" Rafferty meet Mia's eyes as he asked. Was he thinking about telling people about their wedding? Because she wasn't. Not ever.

"Yes, Rafferty, as sure as I hate that name. Stop it. Both of you, actually," Ruth said to Mia and Rafferty.

Mia looked up in confusion from the bag of muffins with one already in her hand. "What? Me?"

"Yes, from now on, you two do not call me that. It's Ruth," she told them.

Mia took a bite of muffin and said with a full mouth, "Just not Ruth Miles?"

"Correct." Ruth nodded.

"Where are we going to say we spent the weekend?" Rafferty asked.

"Ruth and I went on a little vacation," Anderson provided.

"I was sick," Mia said, finishing her muffin.

"I went to visit a college buddy since Anderson had the day off." Rafferty made up an excuse easily, too easily as he grabbed the bag from Mia, just as she was reaching in to get another muffin.

By the time they got on the plane, Mia had to change the name she called her friend, hide her friend's marriage, lie about what she did all weekend, and hide the fact that she got married. Maybe she should have just said no to this trip.

To top it off, this time she had to sit with Rafferty instead of the bride. Apparently, the bride and groom wanted to sit together. Odd, since the other bride and groom didn't. Or at least the bride didn't. They were a few rows behind the happy couple, so they could discuss their impending divorce.

Mia took the window seat and ignored him until they were in the air. Once the seatbelt sign went off, she stated, "I want a divorce."

"Can't we just give it a try? See if we're compatible?" Rafferty joked, though it didn't sound like a joke. It was definitely a joke though.

Rolling her eyes, she leaned back into her seat, trying to get comfortable. "No, and we will also be keeping this under wraps. No need for the entire town to know my business."

When the flight attendant came by with drinks, they declined.

Rafferty crossed his arms. "We'll have to, or else we'll have to tell on those two."

"Once I move to Grand Forks after Christmas, I'll get a lawyer, and we'll get it done down there. Nobody will ever know."

"You're still leaving?" he asked.

"Yes, before the new year." Which was probably starting to not look like a reality anymore It was only a few months away, and she was nowhere near ready to leave her business yet.

"You do realize it is mid-October, right?" Rafferty reminded her.

"I do. I have some irons in the fire." Actually, she didn't. She'd tried to hire a manager for months, but with no luck. Managers for small cafés were in short supply in Landstad or anywhere close. In reality, she was having enough trouble keeping waitresses lately.

But suddenly, she had more motivation than before to move away from Landstad. She needed a new life and a divorce. At this point in her life, she could be married for a few months; she had nothing else going on. Hadn't for a long time now. And she didn't see that changing anytime soon.

CHAPTER 16

RAFFERTY'S LEG was bouncing under his desk. Time couldn't go fast enough. This morning he had woken up determined to win his wife's heart. But he couldn't do it alone.

Finally, the clock ticked to noon. Jumping up from his desk, he told Anderson he would get lunch, something Anderson almost always did. But he needed an excuse to talk to Ruth alone. Since he would drop lunch off for Ruth, it was covered. Also, he wanted to see his wife, and she was, as always, where the food was.

Today was their one-week anniversary, and he hadn't seen her since Tuesday. That was two long days ago to be without his bride.

Heading out the door, he walked down the block to the café. He was sure she would ignore him—she always did when he went in. He had gotten used to it now. He just enjoyed looking at her and making sure she was alright.

Pushing his way into the café, he saw her right away as always, down at the end of the booths, taking someone's order. Actually, it was her mom and aunt she was talking to, so maybe she wasn't taking their orders. She mostly just talked to them for a while when they were in the café.

Turning to the waitress at the counter, he placed his order: the special for Ruth, and sandwiches for him and Anderson. As he waited, he watched his wife talk to her mother. After a week, he still liked calling her that, not that he had been able to say it out loud to anyone. But he said it all the time in his mind.

So far, he had done well at not telling anybody about where he had been for three days, and sadly, no one had even asked. Though he had friends, none cared what he did from day to day, except Anderson, and he knew where he was. Neither had mentioned the trip week, not even when they were alone. It was like it never happened.

When his order was ready, Mia was still talking to her mom, but she had glanced over at him at least once. As he left, he waved at his wife, and to his delight, she waved back at him and smiled. Maybe it wasn't love, but it wasn't hate either.

Across the street, he pushed into Ruth's office. Since it was close to lunch time, she was sitting in the outer office, still with her headphones on, listening to music while she did something on the computer that was up front. Since she was looking out the window and saw him approaching, she took off her headphones as he let the door close behind him.

"Rafferty. Is Anderson busy today?" she asked, looking out the window probably in hopes her husband was coming also.

"Nope, I just wanted to see my sister." It was still weird saying it out loud after all these years, and he wouldn't say it out loud if there was anyone around.

He handed it her the white box, and she opened it to see what it was. She looked at him. "No, really. Is he busy?"

Sitting in the chair that one of her earlier visitors had left in front of her desk, he chuckled. "Do you remember when you always sat out here?"

This had been Anderson's insurance office, and Ruth had been his secretary for years. Then one day, Anderson had noticed her. Now he worked across the street, and she ran her rental office from this location. But she didn't do much business in her rental properties. Mostly, she wrote books in the inner office away from the distractions of town.

"You mean six months ago?" She started to eat and looked at him. Their relationship was still strained from the years she disliked him.

"No, it was more like eight. You should keep track of this stuff. You're a girl." He opened his box and started to eat the chips beside his sandwich.

"I'll write it down," Ruth said, not writing anything down, just eating her potatoes. "What do you want, Rafferty?"

"Are you buying the Baker house?" he asked. He needed to know if he even had a shot at it. Because if Ruth wanted it, Ruth would get it. But since it was still on the market, he didn't think she was all that interested.

Since Mia had talked about it months before, he'd kept an eye on it and the for-sale sign in the yard. So far, it hadn't been sold. On his first day back as a married man in town, he drove past it and knew it being still for sale was a sign. He was going to buy it and show Mia that they could build a life together in that house.

His only hurdle was that he didn't have the money for it, and his sister did. Once she knew he wanted it, she was sure to buy it out of spite. Maybe she already had bought it, and this was a wasted exercise.

"On The Hill?" she asked in surprise, looking out the window as if she could see it from her there. She couldn't.

"Yes, that one." He ate another chip, hoping he didn't just show his hand.

"No, well, maybe. It's still for sale, so I could buy it." She shrugged and poked at her meal.

"I thought maybe with the baby coming, you would want to move to a house," he said, then regretted it. There were other houses in the town, so why was he pushing that one? The only thing Mia wanted.

Slowly she closed her food container and set it on her desk. "Can't kids be raised downtown?"

"They can. You were. But Anderson isn't as keen on the idea of living downtown forever." Rafferty knew he shouldn't bring it up. Anderson had said it once, and that was months ago.

"Anderson is used to it now. I don't think he would be interested in starting a car to get to work anymore." She pointed her fork at him.

"That house is a block away. He wouldn't have to start his car; he could still walk."

"Just saying. Is he talking about it?" she asked.

"No, he hasn't said anything." He tried to put her at ease.

"I'll talk to him tonight since I don't trust you," she said with a brittle smile.

"I went to your wedding!" he joked.

"Anderson wanted you there. I took Mia," she pointed out.

The room fell silent for a moment. At the time, Anderson had asked him if he was sure that his sister had thawed a little toward him. But he could see that wasn't going to happen. Not anytime soon anyway.

Taking a deep breath, he asked, "How is it priced? Is there wiggle room?"

"I think it is, but I have little experience with buying property," she lied to him, but she couldn't even keep a poker face as she did it because she was smirking. The woman owned half the properties on Main Street and a few more throughout town.

"By how much?" he pushed, because he knew she had an opinion on it.

"I would offer about 20 percent off and meet them as close to 10 percent as possible." She spoke with confidence.

"How much of a down payment do you think?"

"I don't do loans, but if I did, I would say 20 percent as well, unless there's more available."

Rafferty closed his box and leaned back in his chair. "I don't have that."

"I didn't think you did. How much do you have?" She gave him a smile, obviously still enjoying his misery. Old habits died hard.

"Maybe close to ten grand, and then my house. I own it and would have to sell it. But besides you, not many people are buying in town." It was a sad truth. It usually took months for anything to sell ... unless Ruth was buying.

Ruth shuffled a few pieces of paper around on her nearly empty desk, not meeting his eyes. "If you sold your house, would you have enough for the 20 percent? Because if you still don't have it, we don't need to be talking."

Doing the numbers quickly in his head, he knew he would. "Yes, but who's going to buy my house? It'll take time to get it sold before I can make an offer on that house, and then I might lose it."

"Why do you want this particular house? It's far bigger than what you have, and you're just you."

"I want a place to raise a family. I'm getting to that point in my life. Seeing everyone in town start to settle down. I want that, too." He wanted to tell her it was for his wife and making her dreams come true.

"Or is it because Mia said she wanted it, and you're buying it so that she doesn't?" Ruth accused him.

A few years ago, that would be exactly why he would buy the house. But not anymore.

"That's not why I'm doing this. I looked at the house, and I fell in love with it." Or he had planned on looking at it. But if Mia loved it, he did, too.

"So, it has nothing to do with Mia at all? That she likes that house." She raised an eyebrow.

"Not a thing," he insisted as he felt his face heat up.

"Not a thing," she mocked him, "You can't even lie well. What do you even hope to accomplish by buying this house? That she will fall madly in love with you, because of a house?"

"No!" he denied, maybe a little too quickly.

Ruth smirked and snapped her fingers. "That's it. You want her to fall for you. I can't even believe you think it would work. Why are you suddenly turning your attention on Mia? Have you made your way through every other woman around?"

"What the hell, Ruth? Is that how you think of me?"

"That's how everyone thinks of you, Rafferty. You don't exactly hide your dating habits." Ruth stopped talking and analyzed him for a few moments. "That's why you need to change. That's why I wouldn't help you before. If you want Mia to fall for you, then you need to change and change right now."

"I'm trying." Suddenly, he saw a glimmer of hope that Ruth would help him. Both with the house and with Mia.

"You haven't been trying very hard," Ruth stated flatly.

"Will you help? I'm trying to buy her a house."

"I will, for Mia. But I'll have you fired if you mess up and break her heart. If you're the reason she ends up leaving town …" Ruth glared at him in challenge.

"You can't fire me."

"I sleep with your boss; I can do anything." Frowning, she pointed at him.

"He's my brother-in-law. I'm family," he reminded her.

"Doesn't matter. I'm giving you until the baby's baptism to get this all straightened up. I want you two idiots to be the godparents, but I want a couple. If you can make it happen, the job is yours." Ruth set out her timeline.

"But you'll help?" He needed to make sure, to hear her say it one more time.

"Reluctantly, I'm saying yes. Now get back to work before I call your boss and tell him your lunch has run long." Ruth picked up her headphones.

He had been dismissed, but he had what he wanted. Actually, he had more then he wanted. He wanted help with the buying process and the local market, and what he got was her help to actually buy the house. Mia's dream house.

CHAPTER 17

THE TURKEY SMELLED marvelous when Mia opened the door to her parents' house on Thanksgiving morning. But she knew it was going to be dry. Her mom had never made a good turkey. Even so, she always showed up and ate, and she always complimented her mom's cooking as any good daughter did.

Her mom, Dotty, was busy in the kitchen with two of her sisters, Darcy and Kelsey. Both sisters' husbands were in the living room with her father, watching some sport. Both sisters now lived in Fargo and liked to talk about all the stuff they did all the time. Mostly just to annoy Mia. This year, her sisters, Bianca and Faith, weren't coming. They were going to see their husbands' families for the holidays. Kipling, the baby, was probably in her room, avoiding everyone. Mia wondered if her little sister wanted company.

Waving at her dad, Roger, as she passed the doorway to the living room, she walked into the room with all the food. It was her favorite room, even when there were too many cooks in it, like today. Her parents still lived in the old farm house they had raised their girls in. And even if her old room now contained her mom's sewing stuff, it also had half the stuff she had left in it when she moved to town.

But she would leave it there. It was nice to know where it was when she needed it, if she needed it. So far, she hadn't, but you never know. Besides, then she didn't have to have it in her small apartment.

"Happy Thanksgiving, Mia," Dotty called to her. Her mom's cheeks were red from the heat of the kitchen and the activity of getting the meal ready. Mia hadn't been blessed with her mom's blonde hair or blue eyes, but she got her mom's wide hips and her red cheeks. Most of her sisters got the better qualities of their mom while Mia and Kipling were stuck as the brunettes like their dad.

"Happy Turkeyday, Mom." Smiling, she put her bag of wine bottles on the table. She brought four, but they would be gone before the turkey made it to the table.

"Mia, you came," Darcy said, as if Mia, who lived closest to their parents, would not be here.

"I did. No other offers," Mia half-joked.

"No boyfriend this year either?" Darcy said from behind the bowl she was mixing something in. Like every other year, her married sisters liked to point it out if she wasn't dating someone for the holidays, and she usually wasn't.

"No, no boyfriend," Mia stated, biting her tongue to stop herself from saying that she did have a husband, he just wasn't there because they weren't exactly talking right now. Every few days she saw him, but she didn't talk to him. Their relationship was the exact same as before they got married.

So far, she had been able to keep every secret she had to keep from everyone. Even during book club after their trip when Mandy had commented that she looked tan—curse her ability to tan easy—after being sick in bed for days. She actually broke down and said she took an impromptu visit alone to Las Vegas, saying she just needed to get away from it all for a day or two. Everyone seemed to buy it, even if she didn't. After swearing everyone at book club to secrecy, she hadn't slipped again.

"Maybe next year," Kelsey stated, and then she gave Darcy the look. You know the one that said how pathetic she was to not have a boyfriend or husband at almost thirty.

Mia ignored the comment and started arranging place settings around the big table. It took some time with all the people who would be there for the meal, even if some of the sisters were missing. Over the years, the once-close sisters were getting more distant. Or maybe it was just her who was feeling the distance. The others all had husbands and offspring, but she was single still. Only her baby sister Kipling was also single, but she was in college, so she was forgiven by the middle four. But Mia knew Kipling's day would come.

Mia felt closer to her cousins, Dotty's kids, than her sisters. She had always been close to Julia because they were the same age, but these days, she was way closer to Mandy, who was a part of book club and lived next door. Even if Mandy was six years older than her, it didn't feel like it.

"Mia, did you hear who bought the Baker place?" her mom asked from across the room.

"No, I hadn't heard it was sold." Mia's heart sank a little. Her house was gone. Her old wish was that Ruth bought it to live in. Then she could visit, probably every two weeks. But now it was in someone else's hands, and she would never see the inside.

"I heard it was Rafferty Brooks," her mom said in a whisper. It must have been heard from a secret source, which was probably her sister.

"Why would he buy it? Doesn't he have a house in town?" Mia asked her mom. His house was a little ranch on the edge of town. Mia had driven by it a few times over the years just to see. And maybe once or twice during the last few weeks—not to check up on her spouse, though.

"He sold his house to buy this one. Maybe he wanted a nicer one. He just had a little one on Kinley. Maybe he met someone, someone special this time," her mom told Mia's sisters.

Mia arranged the silverware on the place setting she was working on a little too long. Rafferty had stolen her house. Or the house she wanted Ruth to raise her baby in. How could he? He didn't even know which one it was when they talked about it. This was crazy.

"Wasn't that your favorite house in town, Mia?" Darcy asked.

"When I was a kid, it was. I like newer houses now," Mia lied and continued to lay out the silverware.

"Are there any new houses in town?" Kelsey wrinkled her nose as she asked from by the stove.

"Yes, Kelsey, there are. Not many, but there are some. And the thing about new houses is that you can just build one," Mia stated to her sister, who was a year younger than her, and she still liked to put her in her place when need be.

Everyone let the conversation drop with Mia's argument. It turned to babies, always babies. Each of her sisters, except Kipling, had at least one. Her mom was a grandma twelve times over, the same number as her sister. Mia wanted to point out that Dotty had two more kids than Dolly. And if her cousin Kit didn't have five children of her own, Dolly would never have gotten to the lofty number she had. But instead, she stayed silent.

When the meal was over, and dessert had been served, so Mia felt she could head out. As with every holiday, she was the only one able to leave her parents' house. The rest stayed for a few days, but Mia lived in town and could leave, so she did. With leftovers in hand, she said goodbye to everyone, stopping herself from running to her Jeep to get away from these people. A few hours were all she could take with them.

Sure, she loved her family, but four hours was more than enough time with them. Way more. Apparently, her sister Kelsey was going to have a baby by summer, putting her mom in ahead in the grand baby race again. She would have to tell Mandy when she saw her. Maybe she could get Kit to have a few more, even without a husband. Before today, the number had at been dead even with Math's new baby, but her mom was pulling ahead again. And Mia was sure that Dolly's run was over.

Parking in front of her apartment, she saw Mandy's car in the street but decided her information could wait. Mia needed a nap more than a gossip session right now. Heading up to her apartment, she was happy to be home early enough to get some movies and a nap in before she had to work in the morning. She could maybe even get some online shopping in.

Changing into orange lounge pants and a Landstad Tiger's T-shirt, she sat down to look through the movie offerings on the TV. Christmas movies started today, so she was thinking about watching one of those. Get the season started right.

Before the TV couple had even met, there was a knock on her door. It was probably Mandy coming to spend the evening discussing their family's holidays and remembering holidays past when they spent them together. Mia could tell her about the new development in the baby race.

But instead of her cousin on the other side of the door, it was her husband. Today, he was wearing gray sweatpants and his fall jacket—black with his name in white stitching.

"Rafferty." She hated how her heart skipped a beat at the sight of him.

"Beautiful wife." His eyes ran up and down her body with a sexy grin as if she wasn't in the most unsexy clothing known to man.

Her eyes darted to her neighbor's door. "Shut up. Someone will hear you."

"Who? The school teacher who lives across the hall is probably gone for the weekend. She doesn't know you anyway."

"She does too." Not much, but they've talked … once maybe.

"We need to talk." Rafferty let it drop.

Mia agreed with the house stealer. "Yes, we do."

"Can I come in, in case your neighbor is still here?" He looked at the neighbor's door again.

She opened the door wider and let him in. Once inside, she closed the door and watched him slide off his jacket to reveal a white Landstad Tigers shirt stretched tight over his muscles. Muscles she wished she could remember feeling.

Turning to her as he kicked off his shoes, he said, "We've been married so long we're starting to dress the same."

"Which is why I'm still divorcing you the first chance I get." She shut the door and leaned against it.

"Admit it, Mia, you're madly in love with me," he teased her.

"You have me figured out." Still leaning against the door, she wondered why his words made her stomach drop a little. Love wasn't a part of their relationship. It never was, and it was never going to be. "Now what do you want?"

"What are you watching?" He changed the subject as he walked towards the TV.

"A movie. You wouldn't be interested." She followed.

"A Christmas movie, Mrs. Brooks?" he asked as he sat down on the couch.

"Don't call me that," she hissed.

He ignored what she said and kept talking. "Isn't it a little early to be watching these?"

Still standing, she folded her arms. "Once turkey has been eaten, Christmas season is here."

"Good thing I didn't eat turkey. The season won't be able to start for me yet," Rafferty said, looking at the screen.

Mia's eyes followed his to the TV and saw that the couple had met, and she had missed it. Now she had missed the best part. "If you missed turkey, that's on you. The season starts anyway."

He leaned back into the cushions.

"So, the season comes no matter what?"

"Yes." Her attention was on the screen. Now she realized that she had watched this one last year.

"Sit down, Mia. You can't watch it from there." He patted the couch next to him.

Glancing over at him, she reluctantly sat down on the other end of the couch and pulled the blanket already there over her, deciding she could watch the movie and ignore him at the same time. After all, she was a good multitasker. Even when he pulled her closer to him, stating he was cold and wanted to share her blanket, she ignored him.

But the movie had captured her attention, and his arm was nice around her. Far too nice. Perfect, in fact.

CHAPTER 18

Pulling out his phone, Rafferty looked at the time. It was just after six in the evening, and he was starving. He'd missed lunch. But he didn't move. No way was he moving. Mia was sleeping in his arms. Not really expecting her to even let him into her apartment, he was surprised when she fell asleep within minutes of sitting down.

In reality, he had no reason to be here. He was bluffing when he said he had something he needed to talk to her about. He had just wanted to see her. It was a holiday, and he wanted to see his wife. Her hair was still brown, but when he was this close, he could see her real brown was showing at the roots, and it was a richer color than the brown she had now. So far, she hadn't dyed it since they got married.

The only thing he could've told her was that he bought her a house, but that wasn't final, and he was waiting to surprise her with it. Once he got the key, he was going to show her around. And he was going to tell her he bought it for her, for them. Her choice of movies indicated that she would fall in love with him in that moment.

She had slept through the entire first movie as well as the credits, and he watched her sleep. Rafferty enjoyed sleeping with this woman, even if he wasn't sleeping. The little sounds she had in her sleep made him want to carry her to her bedroom and make her make those sounds for him. But he stayed right there, just watching her sleep.

Since their wedding, he hadn't seen her much, mostly just talked to her a few times. Never about anything, and mostly about the weather and what he was going to eat. Waitress stuff. But she had stopped ignoring him completely during the last two weeks. One day, he saw her and her cousin Mandy walking together from the grocery store as he drove through town. If one hadn't been blonde and the other a brunette, they could've been twins since they were shaped the same way. But only one made his mouth water just looking at her.

Shifting a little since his arm was asleep, she mumbled something but didn't wake up. So he shifted again, and again, and again until she was lying between his legs with her head on his chest. His arm wasn't tingly anymore, but other parts of him were well aware she was there.

Glancing at the TV, he realized the movie was a cartoon, not the romantic comedy he knew she preferred. Not seeing the remote, he had no way of turning to another channel. So instead of focusing on the TV, he watched her sleep.

"Did they get together?" came a groggy voice from his chest.

"Yes, at the tree lighting at the end," he told her, hating that she was waking up.

"We should do that?" she said dreamily.

"Get together in the end?" he asked hopefully.

He felt her laugh as she said, "No, have a tree in the middle of town. Really get into the season. Make a celebration of it."

"You can organize that," he suggested. His hands were on her back, half holding her in place with him.

"Maybe I will." She had started organizing things around town a few years ago. This year, she had taken on the auction in the spring and a lot of the Fourth of July parade stuff. He wouldn't be surprised to see a tree in the empty lot down the block by morning.

"I think you should make it big. Something for the whole town. Raise money for something."

"Oh, it's going to be big. I don't go small." So far, she hadn't lifted her head or moved her body, she just laid in his arms, her eyes on the TV.

"That's what makes you perfect for this town. Landstad needs something big once in a while. Without you here, who would make the big stuff happen?"

He felt her laughing on his chest again. Not hearing her, but feeling her. "Did you really not get any turkey?"

"Nope. Mom's in Fargo now and didn't want to do anything." He ran a hand tentatively down her back, not quite to her butt, then back up.

"What about Ruth?" she asked. She was now using her given name and not the nickname they always used for her. Just like the woman asked them to.

"She and Anderson went to his parents. I wouldn't be invited if they had something alone anyway. We're not holidays-close." He remembered his conversation with her about buying the house. Not exactly warm and fuzzy family moments.

Lifting her head she met his eyes. "Do you want turkey, Raff?"

His heart stopped. She had never, ever called him a nickname. Quickly, he said, "Yes."

Sadly, she climbed off his body, throwing off the blanket, and walked to the kitchen. Instantly missing her body on his, he got up to follow her. In the kitchen, she had dug out some containers from the fridge and grabbed two plates.

"Anything you don't like?" she asked, then continued. "It is going to be dry. My mom hasn't mastered turkey yet, and at this point, I don't think it will happen. So I'm just going to enjoy eating dry turkey."

"You could make the turkey," he suggested, leaning against the counter next to her.

"No way. For one thing, I have this little apartment. For another, I would have to invite all my sisters and their families. And then I would miss my favorite part of Thanksgiving." She had the plates nearly loaded with food.

"What's that?" he asked when she wasn't going to answer.

"Leaving," With a grin as she took one plate and put it in the microwave.

"Leaving is the best part?" he asked in confusion.

"Oh, yeah. They all have to stay because they're staying with Mom and Dad, but I get to leave. They can spend the entire time bragging about their husbands, jobs, kids, and big-town living, but I get to walk out the door after a few hours," The microwave went off, and Mia took out the hot plate and put the cold one in.

"But when you move, you'll have to stay, too," His stomach growled at the smell of the holiday, dry or not he was eating everything on the plate.

It was down to nearly a month now before her self-imposed deadline. And he had no idea how close she was to making her dream come true.

"No, that's the beauty of living not in Landstad. Mom doesn't know whether you're really busy or not. I can say I'm busy, and she won't be able to question it. I don't have to go to holidays at all unless I wanted to." Mia put the hot plate on the table, indicating him to sit down.

Sitting, he said, "Holidays without family aren't as much fun as you think."

He should know, he had spent most holidays without family. To tell the truth, his parents hadn't even tried to keep those types of traditions going. This wasn't his first year alone, and it wouldn't be his last.

"Having to put up with your sisters rubbing your nose in the fact that you live here and have no boyfriend or life is not fun." Her plate complete, she carried it to the table.

"But your life is fun. You're busy all the time, and you have book club, and everybody goes to the café to see you,"

"But I don't belong to a *gym* And according to Darcy, I should join a gym. And there are no coffee shops."

"First off, you don't need a gym. But if you do want to join one, there is one here in town." He had been there today after all, because what else do you do when you are alone.

"I'm not going to stand in line for the treadmill."

"There are two, smarty pants. And Ruth has that fancy coffee machine, so you can go see her anytime for a fancy coffee. Or you could even get one of those machines for the café." Anderson sometimes went over to see Ruth and brought back coffees. They were amazing, but Rafferty knew how much that machine had cost. It wasn't that amazing.

"Ha, her coffee machine cost a fortune," Mia told him with a pout.

"Everything of Ruth's costs a fortune. But as for a boyfriend, you don't need one. You have a husband," he said, pointing at himself.

"That doesn't count. We're not really married."

"Just say the word, Mrs. Brooks, and we'll make this thing real."

Laughing, she asked, "What's the word?"

He looked at her closely. Was she joking, or was she serious? He couldn't tell. "Make it real. Just say, 'make it real.'"

Her head jerked up and she caught his eye, but didn't say the word. Instead, she shook her head before setting down her fork, "You bought the Baker house. At least, that's what Mom says. Is it true?"

Dang it.

So much for the surprise and the happy ending he had planned. When will he realize he can't hide anything in this town? Especially from the biggest gossip in it. "Yes, I really liked it after seeing it."

"Why couldn't you just let Ruth and Anderson buy it?" She picked at her food now. He was sure she was either still full from lunch, or she wasn't in the mood for the same meal again.

He shrugged. "Ruth didn't want it."

"Anderson might have talked her into it."

"You do know that Ruth wears the pants in that relationship, right? Maybe they'll move when the baby comes, but right now, she wants to stay downtown." Rafferty finished his plate, the turkey not as dry as Mia indicated, or maybe it was the conversation that made the meal so delicious.

"What are you going to do with it?" she asked with interest.

"Live there," He stole a small piece of turkey from her plate, if she wasn't going to eat it he didn't want it to go to waste.

She slapped at his fork but missed. "You don't even like it. You couldn't even say which one it was this last summer," she argued, as if she hadn't just indicated she remembered the conversation.

"I walked through it and loved it. It was exactly what I was looking for." He didn't say that he had almost bought it sight unseen. All because Mia wanted it.

"When do you move in?" she asked, pushing her plate away from her and towards him.

Pulling it to him he tucked into the potatoes, "In two weeks. Are you going to help me move in?"

"I'm busy that day," she stated quickly with a grin.

"I can change it to when you're not busy."

"I'm busy that day, too. My days are pretty packed."

"If I have a party, will you come?" He would do just about anything to get her there. Actually, he would do anything.

She shook her head. "Nope. I think you're going to trap me into helping you move."

"I might've been planning that." He stabbed the last piece of uneaten turkey from her plate and ate it.

Getting up, she took their empty plates into the kitchen. "I'm on to your traps, Brooks. I won't help you move."

"I would help you move." He followed her into the kitchen with the glasses. Just like the married couple that they were.

"Okay." She turned quickly and was almost in his arms, but then she took a step back and bumped into the cabinets. "How about this? I'll help you move, but you have to help me move to Grand Forks when I finally blow this town."

Putting his hands on the counter on either side of her, trapping her, he said, "You have a deal. But what if you don't move?"

"I'm moving," she stated firmly, looking into his eyes, but she didn't move to get out of his trap. "No way am I not moving."

Slowly, his hand moved along the counter until they touched each other, then he dropped one to her back and then the other until they were both touching her. Slowly, because he didn't want to spook her. He wanted his wife in his arms, sober and willing.

Just as slowly, he lowered his lips to her upturned face.

At the first touch, her hands went around his waist and pulled him to her. Instantly, the hesitation was over, and he deepened the kiss. Her response was just as instant, and she met his tongue as it plunged into her mouth. In that moment, he couldn't remember kissing her in months, wanting to and dreaming of it, but not actually doing it.

Continuing to kiss her, he felt her hands slide under his shirt and skitter across his stomach, moving up his chest. His instantly went up her back, under her shirt, and up her smooth, warm skin, pulling her closer to him as he went. He needed her as close to him as he could get her.

Far off in the distance, a phone was ringing, but he could care less. Mia was finally in his arms. Until she pushed out of them, ending the kiss. Watching her take a step away from him, then grab her phone from the counter. She looked at the display and answered it.

From less than a foot from her, he listened to her make plans with Natalie to make a quick run to Grand Forks for some Black Friday shopping. Right now—she was leaving right now. As if they weren't in the middle of something.

Ending the call, she said, "Natalie wants me to go Black Friday shopping."

"Could you have said no?" he asked, touching her cheek.

"Um, no. We needed to stop anyway. We can't just sleep together every time the mood hits us." Not meeting his eyes, she walked away from him.

"Except we can. Legally," he followed her through the apartment.

"We're getting a divorce as soon as possible, Rafferty," she reminded him as she went into her bedroom.

Stopping just outside the open door, he stated, "We could just give it a try, Mia."

She turned and glared at him. "No, Rafferty. I'm getting out of this town. You're willing to be trapped here, but I'm not."

"Come on Mia, you're as much a Tiger as I am." He pointed at his shirt and her shirt. Once a Landstad Tiger, always a Tiger. It had been a joke around town forever.

She shook her head. "No way. I'm not a Tiger. I'm getting out of here."

"You own and run the café in town. You're just going to leave that?" She was already a part of the town; she couldn't leave that.

"I'm hiring a manager,"

"People like the place because you're there. No manager can be you." He wouldn't go in there four times a week if she wasn't there.

"Yes, the right one can." She walked away from him in a huff, and opened her closet.

"Dream on, Mia."

Still angry, she turned on him, "No, Rafferty, you don't get it. You got to spent years out of this town. I've been here the entire time. I want out before it kills me."

"Quit being overdramatic. The rest of the world is nothing special."

"I want to find that out for myself. I want—"

Her words stopped when there was a loud knock on the front door.

Rafferty almost laughed at the panic that spread across her face. Rushing past him, she slammed the door shut as she left it, leaving him alone in her bedroom as she let her friend into the apartment. He should have been offended that she didn't want her friend to even know he was there, but he didn't want her any more upset with him so he let it slide.

Sitting on the bed, he waited for her. No way was she going to town in that outfit, and he knew for sure she had no bra on. She was coming back in here. He could wait.

Which was why he was still on the bed when she came rushing in, closing the door behind her. Turning to him, she stated in a whisper, "I have to change."

"Okay, I'll watch." He leaned back on the headboard, grinning.

"No, you won't." Turning from him, she pulled out a shirt from the closet.

"I'll go out and keep Natalie company then," he quietly suggested as she picked up a pair of jeans from the chair in the corner.

Her dark eyes went wide at the idea, and she looked at the closed door in panic. "No."

"Then I guess I'll watch." Sitting down on the bed he nodded at her indicating she should be changing. Rolling her eyes, she pushed off her sweatpants and shimmied on the jeans. He was happy he was forced to be there.

"You will shut your eyes, Rafferty Brooks," she hissed as she grabbed a bra from the same chair the pants were on.

"Nope." He barely said the word loud enough to be heard as he turned to see her better.

"I hate you." Shooting him an angry look, she pulled her shirt off.

"A husband can enjoy his wife's strip tease if he wants." Forcing himself to stay put with her breasts on full display for him. All he wanted to do was jump up and take them in his hands, taste them.

"No, you're a pervert." Hooking her bra, she covered the beauties from his view.

"Just because I enjoy your body?" he asked.

She pulled her shirt on and said, "No, because a gentleman would haven't watched."

"Then I'm a pervert, because I like to watch you," he admitted as she grabbed a pair of socks form a drawer.

"At least you admit it." Slamming the drawer closed she turned to him as she headed toward the door. "You don't have to lock up on your way out. It's Landstad."

"Love you," he said quietly to the already closed door since she was gone.

He sat there for another few minutes until he heard her front door close. Knowing she was gone, he got up and picked up the outfit she had left on the floor and tossed them into the dirty clothes hamper, then he went out to the main room of the apartment. Quickly, he washed the dishes from supper and left them in the sink to dry.

She had turned off the TV on her way out, but he folded the blanket they had laid under. As he did, he wished they were back under that blanket, watching some Christmas show. Or better yet, in her bedroom not watching some Christmas show.

When the apartment looked clean, he found his shoes and coat. They were stuffed between the couch and the wall. Must have been the first place she thought of when she had to open the door. Chuckling, he wondered how much fast talking she had to do with her friend.

So maybe he didn't end up sleeping with her, but he got to spend a few hours on a holiday with his wife. It was a start. And he had a month to get her to stay in town and with him.

CHAPTER 19

Winter

ALL MIA COULD SAY WAS that Rafferty owed her big time after today. She had just spent the entirety of her Tuesday off moving his stuff from one place to another. It was only six blocks, but it seemed like it was across the country. On top of moving, he hadn't packed many of his things beforehand, so she had to do that, too.

Fortunately, she had Ruth's help for some of it since Anderson had volunteered her. She wasn't happy about it and made everyone know it. Most of the comments made Mia laugh at her friend. The woman wasn't Rafferty's biggest fan, but Mia was sure she was just doing it out of habit.

The guys were getting the last load of stuff as Mia and Ruth unpacked boxes in the kitchen. Ruth was taking stuff out of boxes and putting them on the counter, and Mia was finding homes for the items in the recently cleaned cabinets. It was up to Mia because she owned a café. Ruth promised she would set up his office. Which she wouldn't—he didn't have one in the old house or in the new one.

"Do you wish you had bought the house?" Mia asked Ruth.

Ruth looked around and said, "No, I like my place. It's more airy. Less confined."

Mia looked around. Ruth was right, her apartment was open concept, but this place had a room for every individual space, making it seem smaller. But Mia loved it, you could close off the mess when people came over. Unlike her own place that had no good hiding place for boots and coats when guest come and you don't want them to know you already have a guest.

She wondered how Rafferty had found his things after she had left on Thanksgiving night. Not that she had asked him. She didn't care that much.

"I like it. And I love the woodwork." She looked at the dark wainscoting on the walls. It was in almost every room. She wondered if Rafferty was going to paint since he hadn't had time before he moved in.

"It's really dark in here," her friend said, looking around herself.

"I guess," Mia said, but she loved it. It was everything she had always imagined the inside would look like. She had always loved the outside, and now she loved the inside even more. She just wished there was less Rafferty in it.

"How is the Christmas thing coming?" Ruth asked.

"It's called the Winter Carnival, and you know it. We're raising money for a new gym floor, and it's going better than expected for the first year." Mia had started planning this event in September, and it was coming together wonderfully. And she had added the tree lighting since Rafferty had suggested it. In fact, the high school choir had taken over, and they sang carols every night as the lights came on. It was simply amazing.

Not that she was giving Rafferty all the credit, but it was a good idea. If she had stayed awake to watch the end of the movie, it would've been her idea anyway. And now she was paying for it by finding a home for all his two spatulas. How does a person live with only two spatulas? She had close to a dozen, which is maybe more than a single person needs, but she had yet to not have one when she needed it.

"The gym does need a new floor. Do you think you'll get enough money?" Ruth asked.

"I think we'll come close," Mia said, adding the one broken wooden spoon to the spatula's lonely drawer.

"We'll have to visit when you have the numbers. See what can be done." Ruth said innocently.

Mia smiled at her friend. She was always willing to donate as much as she could for anything happening around town. But she never made a fuss about it and never wanted people to know it was her. Mia knew for a fact that if she had just gone into the rental office and asked for the full amount, Ruth would've written the check. But she didn't want to take advantage of her friend like that.

"I'll do that," Mia said, putting the plates in a cabinet that seemed right for them. Rafferty could move them later if he wanted to.

"So, Mia, why are you helping Rafferty today?" Ruth asked.

"Because he's going to help me move when I go." It was, after all, the reason. Not that she had wanted to see Rafferty again, and not at her workplace. "I'm moving a few hours away and need his pickup. My car will only hold so much."

Ruth chuckled quietly. "You mean in three weeks or so? How's that going?"

"I might have it figured out," Mia hedged, hating that Ruth was seeing her plans to leave as a joke. An unobtainable joke.

She knew she would never be out of this town on her timetable and would have to move her exit date. She just hadn't figured out when her new date was going to be. Not another year, that was for sure. Just another few months.

"I think he got the better part of this bargain. You had to pack and unpack for him," Ruth said, adding a few more glasswares to the counter. What he lacked in utensils he made up for in glasses.

"I think so too." She put the new glasses with the others. "How are you doing?"

Ruth stopped working completely and sat down on the loan barstool. "Good, I had my appointment with Mandy this morning. I wasn't just avoiding this project, but I was a little."

"And?" Mia grabbed another box from the floor.

Shrugging, Ruth said, "Things are going as expected. But I think something is up with Mandy."

"Me too. She hadn't been herself for a few months. I'm going to dig into it after the holidays. She's always had a hard time with the holidays." Mia didn't want to go into her cousin's past since, in reality, Mia didn't know all of it. Some things the sisters kept to themselves about their kids. Mandy's issues were one of them.

"I don't know her all that well, but I just feel she's not the same as she was a few months ago when book club started." Ruth tossed the newly emptied box and tossed it toward the corner.

"I know. I've known her forever." She picked up a pile of straws, looked at them, and added them to the spoon drawer, then moved them to the cabinet with the cups. In reality, she had no idea where straws went. "What are you and Anderson going to do for Christmas? It's your first one."

Ruth nodded. "Yes, it is. We are going to go to his parents and stay overnight with them. Then come back and spend the day with my mom."

"Are you going to get together with Rafferty?" Mia added another pile of plates to the other set. How many plates does a single man need? But then again, if he wanted a plate for every glass at a party, he was covered. On the other hand, if all his guests wanted to eat, they would have to share forks.

"No," was all Ruth said.

"Why? He's family," Mia pointed out since they were alone.

"Because we're not really a family. We're just related." It seemed Ruth didn't want to talk about it.

Mia grabbed a stack of pans from the counter and found a lower drawer to put them in. From her position on the ground, she looked up at her friend, who was actually her secret sister-in-law. Sometimes, Ruth was a little mean to her secret brother. If she would just let the past be the past, she could be friends with the man. Her husband was already friends with him, so it seemed like it would be easy to Mia.

"Fine." Putting her hands up in surrender, she wasn't going to push it. She didn't need Ruth to get suspicious of her feelings for Rafferty.

"So, how are things going with you and Rafferty?" Ruth handed Mia more pans.

"What does that mean?" Mia asked. Did she know? Had she known the entire time? Why didn't she ever say anything?

"Here you are, helping him for no reason,"

"He's helping me later," Mia focusing on putting the pans away.

"We all know he'll back out of that," Ruth stated with authority, as if she knew Rafferty better then Mia did.

"No, he won't." She shook her head There was no way he was getting out of helping her. No way.

"He's Rafferty. He doesn't change."

It was the truth. It was Mia's biggest issue with him and the reason she had been avoiding him for months. Because he was a playboy, just playing with her. And when he was done playing, she would be heart-broken. Even if kissing him made her insides turn to jelly.

"I know. Rafferty is … Rafferty," Mia stated as the man in question came in the front door, yelling about having gotten it all.

Mia's eyes met Ruth's, and they laughed as they went out to see what the excitement was about. The guys were lugging in Rafferty's couch. It looked heavy, but not heavy enough to where Mia thought she should help. Instead, she directed them to put it facing the fireplace.

"No, I want it looking at the TV stand," Rafferty said, pulling it the other way.

"No, looking at the fireplace. Anderson, turn it this way," Mia said sternly.

"Mia," Rafferty grunted, still holding up the couch.

"Rafferty." She stared him down, not caring.

"I'm just going to move it when you leave," he told her, reminding her whose house they were at.

"Then maybe I'll never leave, so you can't ever move it!" she yelled as Anderson set his end down and Rafferty pulled his end a foot, and then dropped it in anger.

Turning his anger on his friend, he said, "Anderson, why did you drop it?"

Anderson took a step away from the couch and held up his hands, "I'm not carrying around a couch while you two fight about it."

"Anderson's on my side," Mia stated smugly.

"I'm not on anyone's side, and I'm not carrying that thing any further." Anderson said.

Mia walked over to it and pushed it so that it was facing the fireplace, then sat down. When she had envisioned the room the first time she walked into the house, the couch was facing the fireplace. So, while she was there, this is how it was going to be.

"I can move it with you on it." Rafferty flicked her ear from behind her.

"No, you can't. I'm too fat." She covered her ears, so he couldn't do it again.

"Okay, love. Time for us to go," Anderson said to his wife.

"No, we're not done yet," Mia said from the couch, not getting up.

"We decided this morning that when you two started fighting, we'd leave," Ruth stated as she walked toward the door.

"Anderson thought we would be done by noon. It's almost five, so you two lasted way longer than we thought you would."

"Ruth owes me money. I said you would last longer than noon, but seriously. I'm surprised you too lasted this long." Anderson took his wife's hand and headed to the door.

"You can't abandon me! You still have stuff in your pickup," Rafferty argued as he follow them out the door.

Once they were gone, she laid down on the couch. It had been a long day of lifting and carrying. Tomorrow, her body was going to be sore. And since Rafferty was trying to keep his help here, she was going to rest. Maybe when he came in, he would get her something to drink.

A few minutes later, he came stomping in, carrying a box. Mia didn't open her eyes when he dropped it on the floor in a huff. Nor did she for the next five loads. She heard them, but that was all.

"Are you going to help anymore?" he asked on the sixth load.

"Sorry, holding down the couch," she answered, not opening her eyes but hearing him leave again.

"What if I promise not to move the couch today?" he asked on the seventh load.

"Still a no-go, but you need to shut the door between loads. It's getting chilly in here."

He was again gone.

"Are you awake?" he asked, but this time, he wasn't by the door. He was very near her.

Opening her eyes, she saw he was standing behind the couch, looking down at her. His blue eyes ran up and down her body. "No, I'm not sleeping."

"Yes, you were."

"No, just relaxing. I've been worked to the bone today." She muffled a yawn.

"Thank you for helping me."

"Just remember, you owe me now. Any day, any time," Mia stated with a smile.

"Who can forget?"

"You can. Can you get me something to drink?" She waved her hand at the kitchen, not telling him where she had put the glasses. He needed to figure that out himself.

"What do you want?"

"A beer. The expensive stuff; not what you served at lunch. You should be ashamed, Rafferty. We all know that you have good beer," Mia complained.

Smirking, he said, "I always keep the good stuff for myself."

"Are you going to paint in here?" she asked, letting that statement go.

"Yes, wife. What color do you want?" he asked, heading for the kitchen.

"Stop that. "She said, but then gave her opinion anyway, after all he probably had no idea what colors to go with, and the walls were right now a bizarre greenish-yellow color, "I would go light. Mostly some shade of off-white."

"Are you going to help me pick out paint?" he asked as he set her beer down on a box he'd moved close to the couch.

"I don't have time. Through Friday night, I'm busy with the carnival," she explained as she sat up and took a drink of the beer, then held it so she could lean back into the couch again.

"How about Saturday?" He sat down next to her.

"Can't, I have a date in Grand Forks," she said. Shit, she wasn't going to tell him that.

"A date or a *date*?" he asked with a frown.

"Kind of blind date," she admitted as he took her beer from her hand.

"Who is my wife blind dating?" he asked, taking a drink of her beer —a big one.

"A friend of Ruston's. They've been trying for weeks to make this happen, and I've been putting it off." She took her beer back and held it away from him. Wondering why he was so upset with her dating. It wasn't like their marriage was real.

"Because you're married?" he asked, still angry.

"No, because I really didn't feel like it. I met the guy a few weeks ago, and Hazel said he's interested in dating, but I'm just not feeling it." Maybe the connection wasn't there because she had been married for over a month now, and it was feeling more real than she'd liked to admit. Or at least real enough that dating seemed like something she shouldn't be doing.

"So, you're going on a date as a married woman?" He wouldn't let it drop.

"Yup. It'll get Hazel off my back for a while at least." She admitted the real reason for saying yes as she finished the beer and put it back on the box at her feet. Who knew Hazel could be such a nag? And what was she supposed to say? I can't go out with this guy because I'm married and it feels weird?

"So, you don't want to date him? Because you're madly in love with your husband?" He held out his arms wide for a big hug.

"God, no, I just spent eight hours as his slave and only got a cardboard pizza and cheap beer for my efforts," she said with a laugh.

"You just drank the best beer in the house." He pointed to it, but it was empty.

"But only one. The least you could do was have two in the house. If this were my house I would have two."

Taking the hint, he got up to get her another one. By the time he got back, she was once again lying out on the couch with her eyes closed. She heard him leave the room again, then come back, half expecting him to throw a blanket on her. But instead, she felt his hands slide under her body and pull her into his arms. Then he lifted her into the air.

Her eyes popped open, and she grabbed him around the neck in case he was going to drop her. "What are you doing?"

"If you're going to sleep, you might as well do it in a bed," he told her, shifting her slightly.

"You're not carrying me to bed! Your bed?" she exclaimed.

"Yes I am. You seem tired." He started up the stairs.

Mia grabbed on to him tighter, knowing he was going to drop her on the stairway. "You're going to drop me."

"I'm not." He tightened his grip on her.

"Yes, you are. I'm fat." She silently prayed he didn't drop her on the steps.

"You're not fat, Mia. You're perfect." He made it to the landing with ease.

"I need you to call my mom and tell her that," Mia whispered, letting go of her worries as they made it to the top of the stairs.

"Any time." He kissed her head. "I'll tell anyone and everyone how perfect you are."

Ignoring how his words made her heart sing, she also ignored how him carrying her made other parts of her come to life.

All the way to the master bedroom, he carried her. It was stacked with boxes, and the bed was set up, but there were no sheets or blankets on it, not even a pillow.

"You think I can just sleep on a mattress? No blankets or anything?" she asked, looking around the room, hating that this moment was ruined by a bare mattress.

"Nope, I've changed my mind." He slowly lowered her to the ground, but he held her close to him. "No nap," he whispered as his head lowered, and his lips slid from her cheek to her neck.

"What then?" she asked as if she didn't already know.

"I'm going to make love to my wife so that she'll remember me when she's on her date." His lips moved to hers.

Sighing, she let it happen and slid her arms around his neck. She had wanted Rafferty back in her bed since he'd crawled out of it when she was sixteen. Suddenly, her defenses were lowering, and he had just made it through the walls.

But she needed to think this through before she slept with him again, because sleeping with him back then had been a mistake, and sleeping with him now would be even worse.

Yes, she wanted to sleep with him, but she knew that when she did, she would lose the rest of her heart to him—that little sliver she had been able to hold on to until now would be gone. And then what?

Pushing him away from her, she got herself together. "Rafferty, I'm disgusting. I'm sweaty and dirty and just gross."

"I happen to like you sweaty and dirty." He nuzzled her neck.

"I don't." She pushed him away.

"Okay, how about you go take a shower, and I'll make the bed a bit more inviting?"

"Or I could just run home?" she asked, hoping he would just tell her to leave, taking the decision out of her hands completely. Because she didn't want to leave, not anymore.

"Shower, Mia," he stated gruffly, and she rushed toward the bathroom, no arguing. But happy for the stall for time. She needed it.

CHAPTER 20

RAFFERTY HAD NEVER MADE a bed so quickly in his life. He just wished he'd had the foresight to put sheets on it before carrying her up the stairs. Because he was damn sure that her seeing a bare mattress had reminded her of their very unromantic first time together. Back when any bed would do … or couch, as the case had been.

Once the crisp new sheets were on and the pillows stuffed into cases. He added a quilt and grinned. It was perfect. After shutting down the lights in the house and heading back to his room, he turned off the overhead lights and lit two candles he had found during the course of the day. Those he had thought to put in here.

The shower was still running as he pulled off his T-shirt and socks, tossing them toward where the hamper was going to go. The hamper was someplace else, and he wasn't going looking for it now. Not with Mia in his shower.

He was starting to worry a little about her, so he stuck his head in the bathroom. The steam assaulted him with her scent, the same one that always got to him.

"Are you about clean?"

"Oh, uhm, just about. Do you happen to have shampoo someplace?" she asked through the shower curtain. Right now he deeply regretted not getting the clear one.

"I do, but I don't think it's the same kind you use." He stepped into the bathroom, dug through the box, and pulled out the shampoo and conditioner. Then he stuck them through the end of the shower curtain and held them until she took them.

"Thank you. This one's fine," she said, her voice a little unsure, and he decided the next time he was at her place he would see what kind she bought and order some for their bathroom in case this happened again. He hoped it would happen all the time after tonight.

"Do you need some help with that? I happen to be an expert at using that kind. It might work different from yours." He lingered in the bathroom, not wanting to leave.

"I think I can manage," she said quickly, maybe too quickly.

"I was thinking I should shower as well. I might be too dirty for you once you're clean, you know?" he teased as he unbuttoned his pants. Seeing his wife wet was suddenly going to be the high point of his day.

"You didn't seem dirty, Rafferty. You just go back to the bedroom, okay?"

"Okay, sure." He changed his tactics. "I'll just find you a towel first."

"Thanks."

"How's the water pressure?" he asked, digging through a box for his fluffiest towel, the new ones he had bought a few weeks before with her in mind.

"Good. Actually, it's better than my apartment's. But you knew it was good because you checked it before buying the house. Or at least, that's what you're supposed to do."

"I might have forgotten to do that. But at least I got lucky, and it's good."

She stuck her head out and looked at him, her brown hair wet against her head and water droplets still clinging to her eyelashes.

Instead of handing her the towel, he unfolded it and held it open for her. For a moment, he thought she would ignore him and stay in the shower, wet forever. But then he closed his eyes to encourage her into his arms.

A few seconds later, she was in the towel, in his arms, lecturing, "Did you at least have the roof and foundation checked? Maybe that was why Ruth wasn't interested in the house. Bad foundation."

He opened his eyes as he ran the towel over her "pink from the shower" back and arms and argued with her. "The foundation looked fine. And the roof was new not that long ago."

"But you didn't hire someone? You just bought a house that might fall into the ground?"

With subtle hand movements, he turned her in his arms until she was facing him, then ran the towel over her stomach, chest, and arms. Lingering maybe a little longer than he had in the back. "There hasn't been one house in this town that has ever just fallen to the ground." He dried her face and then used the towel to dry her hair, leaving her entire body naked for his eyes to enjoy.

"The one next door is gone," she said when the towel was finally off her face and head.

"Other issues, I'm sure." Taking her in, he wasn't about to admit not having any idea about why it was torn down.

"You forgot my legs." She reached for the towel.

Not letting her have it, he sank to his knees in front of her, looking up at her as he ran the towel over her left leg. Her breathing was rigid, and she had stopped talking. "Have I ever told you how much I love your legs?" He ran the towel over the right one, then lifted her foot so that it was resting on his thigh.

Her head just shook as she watched him caress the towel up her inner thigh. As he slid it over her core to run down the other leg, he felt her toe curl into his leg. His heart was beating faster because she was as turned on as he was.

"Rafferty, are you going to shower?" Her voice was husky as she leaned back slightly and braced her hands on the vanity behind her. Her foot didn't move from his thigh. The action just exposed more of her to him.

Dropping the towel, he didn't answer; instead, he kissed a water droplet he had missed from her inner thigh, making her suck in a breath sharply. But she didn't move.

Tracing the path of water with his tongue, he ran his hands from her ankles up her legs. His own body was screaming for release, but he had waited so long for Mia that he would go at a snail's pace in order not to scare her.

His tongue slid to her inner thigh and headed to where he wanted to be. Dreamed of being. But just as he was about to hit home, he paused and looked up at her. Her pupils were dilated to the point he couldn't tell their color anymore, and her lower lip was firmly between her teeth.

Knowing she wanted him too was heady, and though he knew she was interested on some level, he hadn't been as sure that she wanted to be here. Being drunk and wanting sex with him was one thing, but she was most definitely sober right now. And she still wanted him.

But he wanted her begging.

Skipping over her core to her other inner thigh, she actually growled deep in her throat, something he had never heard before.

"Are you dry yet, Mia?" he asked, his eyes on her swollen sex that was soaking wet and just at eye level.

"No," she said on exhale.

"Do you want me to finish?" he asked, needing to hear her say it.

"Please, Rafferty, please," she begged him.

That was all he needed before he turned all his attention to her beautiful pussy. Running his tongue from back to front made her moan, so he did it again, causing the same reaction, only she included a few choice curse words during her prayer to the lord.

Hands on her thighs, he continued until after the fifth time, where he ended by focusing all his concentration on her clit, running his tongue over and around it as her body started to shake more and more under his hands, and she became more vocal.

Rafferty knew she was on the edge of her orgasm. She was far more vocal than she had been at sixteen, and he loved the new dirty talk. It was turning him on far more than he should be letting it.

Slipping two fingers into her hot center was all it took to take her over the edge. Her mouth didn't stop as her body pulsed around his fingers, and he continued to use his tongue and lips to keep her orgasm going until she was begging him to stop.

Kissing his way up her body, he stopped to spend a few moments at each breast. Still amazing. He swore he would spend more time with them later. But for now, he waited for her breathing to slow before he kissed her.

Her arms instantly snaked around him as their tongues met and bodies pressed together tightly, her breasts pressed to his chest.

Lifting her into his arms, their kiss didn't break as her legs wrapped around him, and he carried her from the bathroom. In the bedroom, the candles provided the only light into the room. Mia stopped kissing him and looked around.

"Sheets? Have you grown up, Raff?" she teased.

"I try to be an adult sometimes." Setting her on the bed, he hoped she wouldn't get cold feet again.

When she laughed he relaxed. He had started to realize the trick to relaxing her was letting her talk.

"You sure had some adult moves in there." She nodded at the bathroom.

"I had my suspicions you'd like them." He grinned, loving that even here now, they could joke around with each other.

"And I tried so hard to not let my feelings show." She laughed at her own joke. "Take off those jeans and show me what else you've picked up while being the ladies' man of Landstad."

"I haven't been with that many women since coming back," he argued as he pushed off his jeans. If she said to, he would. How could he denigh her anything?

"Which is why you have a one hundred-count condom package that's open?" Not shy in the least, she crawled up the bed and opened his night stand.

"How do you know that?" he asked, getting on the bed and following her.

"Your sister even knows, Raff. Next time you move, pack what you don't want your helpers to see." She pulled out the package, which he had left in the drawer, thinking they could just move it without looking. But it seemed they had looked.

"Did you count how many were missing?"

"I don't have time to count everything you have, Rafferty Brooks. I know you only have two spatulas, and that's concerning enough. I'm not counting your condoms." She opened the packet and pulled one out, and pushed him on his back.

"I'll save you time, then. There are ninety-seven, now six. One is in your hand, one is in my wallet, and two are, or were, at your apartment," he said and watched her tap the condom wrapper on her chin as she thought.

"I don't want to know tonight. Tonight is about other things." Shimmying up his body, she took his cock in her hot hand, her fingers running over it a few times before rolling the condom on him far slower than he thought necessary.

"Like what?" He barely choked out as he fought the urge to just come on her hands.

"Like making up for the last time we were together." She straddled him and rubbed her core over his hard cock, and her sly smile said she knew exactly what she was doing.

"You were drunk." He grinned at the sight of her breasts above him.

"Not then." She slapped his chest lightly, stopping her movements. "In high school. I don't even think I came that night. Well, maybe I did, but not like in the bathroom. You have skills I want to take advantage of."

"Take advantage of me then, Mia. As long as you want." He cupped her breasts. How could he not? They were so perfect and so *right there*.

"I plan to," she said and laughed, which continued as he rolled them over and, in one motion, slipped into her hot folds.

Instantly, her laughing turned to murmurs of pleasure again. But as he drove into her time and time again, he was afraid she wasn't taking advantage of him, and he was the one in charge.

Except he knew he wasn't going to last. He held out as long as he could, but when her orgasm hit, and her inner walls constricted around his cock, he was lost. Of course, he was always lost when it involved Mia Lawson Brooks.

Always would be.

"We should do this sober more often." She giggled under him.

Her breathing was still off as he rolled off her and pulled her into his arms. Holding her close, he felt her relax and sigh. It had been a long day for them both, and it was catching up with them.

Now wasn't the time to talk about their future, because they had one. The morning would be soon enough to tell her he bought the house for her. That he didn't want her going on a blind date. That he wanted a future with her. That he loved her. Still and forever.

CHAPTER 21

OFFICIALLY, she had failed.

It was New Year's Eve, and she was still in Landstad, North Dakota. She knew she would never get out of here. She was trapped. Sadly, she had even worked a full shift today, just to show the world she wasn't leaving anytime soon. But she had grabbed a bottle of whiskey to help her forget. Alone.

It had been three weeks since she had crawled out of Rafferty's bed in the middle of the night, scared of her feelings for him. She hadn't been back. Not that she hadn't wanted to, but she knew that if she crawled back in, she would probably stay and accidentally tell him she was in love with him. He would dump her, and she would be humiliated, heartbroken, and sexless. Instead, she was sexless and heartbroken. But at least her humility was intact—whatever good that did her.

Her Christmas Carnival had been a huge success. Next summer, the high school gym would have a new floor. And she hadn't even had to ask Ruth for any extra. She had made that floor happen. Her. Mia Brooks. Shaking her head at that thought, she chanted, *Mia Lawson, Mia Lawson, Mia Lawson.* Not that she needed to be reminded of it.

Of course, now that she was staying in Landstad, she had no idea how she was going to get divorced. The plan was so easy before, but now she had to either stay married to him, or it would be in the paper.

Yes, Landstad still listed when divorces were finalized.

So, there was the need for a stiff drink or two today. At the last moment, she decided to check to see if her cousin was still at work. Mandy was always up for spending some time with Mia, and getting drunk together seemed like it was going to be a blast.

Mia smiled when she saw her cousin sitting at the reception desk, daydreaming. Maybe she was thinking about having a receptionist to fill the desk. Not having one was a pain in butt for her cousin. Pushing open the door, Mia was surprised that her cousin didn't hear the noise the door made, making her even more nervous about what was happening in Mandy's life.

An hour later, she was still nervous about her cousin, but now she knew that she needed to be. Her cousin had a secret, too. And now, Mia knew her secret. Well, two secrets, but one was way bigger.

One was that she had the hots for her neighbor. That wasn't a big one; Mia had heard something about that a few weeks ago. The big one was that she was pregnant and wasn't telling anyone. Not because she was ashamed that she was unwed and pregnant, but because with her history of miscarriages, she was sure she was going to lose it. Mia made her promise to call when it happened. Mandy didn't need to be alone. Sadly, Mia didn't think Mandy would call her.

So now Mia carried another secret with her. Over the last few months, everyone in this town had secrets she had to hide. Well, not everyone, just her friends, because everyone else's were available for discussion. But what if there were more things that happened in this town without her knowing? What were others hiding from her?

Though she had downed a few glasses of whiskey with Mandy— Mandy didn't drink any, of course—she wasn't drunk. She really wished she was. And she wished she wasn't going home alone. But she didn't want to go to the bar—too many people. Going to the Landing to see who was around used to be her favorite time, but not anymore. She didn't even care today.

Heading back to her apartment after leaving Mandy's clinic she missed her turn. Missed it by two blocks. Looking at the big house that needed to be painted again, she walked up the eight steps to the front door.

Do you knock on your husband's door, or do you just walk in? What was the etiquette on that? Deciding that if he had a date, she needed to know so that she could file for the divorce with good reason.

Opening the door, she was surprised it wasn't locked. Inside she saw that all the walls had been painted since she had last been here. They were now a soft, warm white, and it made the woodwork shine just like she thought it would. Kicking off her shoes, she wandered around the main floor and saw he had bought some more stuff, trying to fill the mostly empty house.

But he wasn't around, not in the kitchen or the dining room or the living room. Up the stairs she went. On the top step, she heard the shower running somewhere on this floor. As she walked to the master bedroom, she saw it wasn't the hallway bathroom but the master bathroom. Which she should have guessed since he would use that one the most.

Putting the bottle of whiskey on the bedside table, she slipped off her jacket and hung it on the door knob to the bedroom. As she pulled out her phone to kill time while she waited for him to come out of the shower, she wished she had taken off her work clothes. Black jeans and a pink T-shirt with her logo on it was now feeling uncomfortable and dirty since she had put it on close to twelve hours before.

Quickly, she dug through his drawers until she found a T-shirt she could replace the pink one with. Slipping her shirt and bra off, she pulled on his Landstad Tigers shirt from Thanksgiving. It looked way better on him, but had to do.

Looking at the bed, then down at herself, she suddenly wondered what was really on her pants. Quickly, she shimmied out of them and climbed into the bed. Sitting against the pillows, she started to look at what she had missed on Facebook that day. She wasn't surprised that it was nothing. Nothing ever really happened there just like in town, usually.

Closing her eyes, she tried not to think about all that Mandy had said earlier. Why did she think it was better for her to suffer in silence? Everybody who loved her saw that something was up and were worried about her.

She smiled at the thought that the two of them should move in together. They would be fun maiden aunts to all their nieces and nephews. It would always be a fun place. They would get along as well as their moms did. Maybe, they would even fight over who had more nieces and nephews.

"Sleeping?" Rafferty asked quietly.

"Not sleeping; just thinking." Opening her eyes she wished she hadn't. He was only in a towel, and he was still very wet. Did he even try using the towel?

"She's just as cute thinking as she is sleeping." He sat down on the bed. Still in the towel.

"Raff, you're getting the bed all wet," she said, watching to see if the towel was going to fall off. Sadly, it didn't.

"Are you scared of water, Mia?" he asked, grabbing at her.

"No, but you need to learn how to use a towel on yourself. You obviously know how to use one on someone else."

He stood up and pulled it off his waist and handed it to her. Naked. "Show me how to use it."

Her gaze raked that splendid, sexy, naked body. Sitting up, she couldn't take her eye off his chiseled chest and the fact that he was there, standing at attention. Full attention. Grabbing the towel, she slid it down his still-damp chest and then down his back, pulling him closer as she did.

Taking the towel, she started to stand up on the bed to dry his hair. As she did, he pulled her to him, knocking the towel from her hands. But she didn't care. His mouth was kissing her neck, and his hands were already under her shirt, making her forget everyone's secrets. Even her own.

CHAPTER 22

RAFFERTY COULDN'T BELIEVE that he was going to ring in the New Year in bed with his wife. This morning, he couldn't even have dreamed that this could be a possibility. Why she was here, he didn't ask. He didn't care. She was there. He walked out of the shower, and she was in his bed, as if she had been there forever. Sure, he was pretty sure she was sleeping, but she was there.

Over this last year, he had come to the realization that she pushed herself too much. Almost every morning, she woke up at five a.m. to get to work by six, then spent the next nine or so hours on her feet. Afterward, she would make time for family and friends and staying out late. She had to be exhausted. He was exhausted for her.

Running a hand over her still-brown hair as she slept, he just watched her. After they had made love, she had almost instantly fallen asleep and had been sleeping since. He had slept for a little while, but her groaning in her sleep had woken him. It was then that he had went down and made them some sandwiches. He hadn't eaten, and he was sure she hadn't either. Back in the bedroom, he didn't have the heart to wake her, so he climbed back into bed.

He wondered what she had thought of the paint. He had taken her suggestion, even if she hadn't help pick it out with him since she had been on a date that day. Not that he was worried about it, or worried now. If the date had gone well, she wouldn't be here two weeks later.

Okay, so he had spent two weeks worrying about it, but he had thought he would've heard if it had gone well. He listened to gossip as much as the next guy.

Her winter carnival had been a huge success, Anderson had said, but he had known she would put on a great show. He had been proud of her.

Leaning down, he kissed her forehead and whispered, "Mia, wake up."

He was rewarded by her mumbling and groaning and rolling over onto her stomach. So, he got to kiss his way from the middle of her back up her spine until it disappeared in her hairline. At that point, she rolled back onto her back and looked at him with her hazel eyes.

"It's almost midnight. Want to ring in the New Year?" he kissed her neck and shoulder.

"No," she answered, pushing his face away.

"You want to stay in this year?" Kissing her hand that covered his mouth, he then lightly bit it.

"If at all possible." With a frown, she pulled her hand away at the nip.

"It's been a great year." It was the truth. He had few complaints.

"Speak for yourself, Brooks," she rolled away from him.

Pulling her close to him, he asked, "What's wrong? Is it that you wanted to not be in Landstad anymore?"

"Yes and no."

He kissed her shoulder that was in the air. "Which one is making you sad?"

She sighed. "The no."

"Can you tell me?"

"No, it's a secret," she said to the wall.

"I think you can tell your secret husband. He can keep a secret, too."

"It's been a long year of secrets."

"Tell me?" He pulled at her shoulder until she rolled onto her back, so he could see her face.

"First, it was all that stuff with Ruth and Anderson, but mostly Ruth's stuff, though. Then it was that Tess was pregnant. Then it was that Hazel had hooked up with Ruston. Then also that summer, Natalie had a secret mom, and Mandy had a secret lover. Then this fall, there was all the Ruth and Anderson secrets." Mia shut her eyes.

"But most of those are out in the open. Even the Ruth one, where she owned all the buildings in town." Rafferty was confused why all these secrets would still bother her.

"I knew that years ago," she smiled at him. Of course, she knew that one before anyone else did.

"So, the only ones left are Ruth and Anderson's marriage and ours. And nobody knows about that one." Though he wished that one was in the open. Of all the secrets she listed, he wanted the entire town to know that one.

"Mandy told me one tonight that I can't tell anyone, and I don't know if I should keep it or tell. It's not like the rest; those were little. They would all come out eventually, except of course ours. But this one might stay hidden forever, and I think it needs to be told. There are people who need to know, should know." Mia rubbed her hands over her face.

"Can you tell me, so I can maybe help?"

"You can't help. I can't help, either." She leaned over and buried her face in his chest.

Holding her while she let the tears for her cousin fall, he watched as the clock struck midnight, just letting her get her emotions out as he murmured in her ear about how special she was. When her tears finally were gone, she looked up at him. "Thank you for keeping my secrets."

"I don't even know this one, but I will never tell a soul." He kissed her nose.

"Mandy is pregnant but won't tell anyone because she thinks she's going to lose it. She doesn't plan to ever tell anyone," she whispered into his chest.

Rafferty hid his shock. That was the last thing he thought it was going to be about. He didn't know the woman well, but his heart broke for her just the same. Maybe it was because Mia's heart was broken already for her.

"Does she have a good reason?"

She shook her head. "She thinks so, but she's really, really depressed."

"I would be, too." If Mia was going to lose his baby, he would be barely hanging on.

"Do you even want kids?" she asked him.

"Of course, I do, one day." Suddenly, with the new year ringing in, that day seemed closer than ever.

"You just don't seem the type."

"Are you going to have six like your mom?" Maybe one day, she would see him as father material.

"No, never. Maybe two. But with the way my life is going, it will probably be none."

"What's wrong with your life? You run a successful business and are married to an amazing guy who sells insurance. Seems like you have it all." He ran his thumbs over her cheeks, wiping away the tears.

"Married," she said with a grunt.

Rafferty rolled onto his back, taking her with him so that she was half laying on top of him. "Okay, back to Mandy. I think you have to respect her wishes. But keep a close eye on her. Maybe check in more often."

"You're right. I just needed to tell someone. I just can't keep some secrets to myself. But you can't tell anyone. Ever," she said from above him, her hazel eyes boring into him.

Wrapping his arms around her, he whispered, "I'll keep your secrets forever, Mia. Till death do us part."

Sliding his hands down her body, he loved that he could touch her. It had taken him so long to get her here that he wasn't going to miss a chance to just touch her gorgeous body. When she didn't push him away but responded to his touch, he pulled her closer and rolled her over.

As he kissed her, he knew the New Year was going to be even better than the year he married her. Maybe this was the year she would became his wife.

CHAPTER 23

BEING Rafferty Brooks's wife was amazing!

Mia had been playing the part for two weeks, since New Year's Eve. She started the New Year in his arms and had woken up there each and every morning thereafter.

At 4:45 in the morning the alarm would go off, and she would rush back to her apartment, shower, and then go to work. After work, she would just head straight over to his place and make supper for him. He would get home, and they would eat and discuss their day. After they washed the dishes together, they would watch TV in the living room and then go to bed. And going to bed was her favorite part of the day.

The only break in the routine had been when she had Sunday off, and they had just stayed in bed until it was time for her to leave for book club. It had been the first time she had wanted to skip book club since it started nearly a year before. And she loved book club.

When she had left, she had been certain she would tell the girls about Rafferty. Not about the wedding thing of course but the fact that they were sleeping together. But after they had argued through whether Charles Manson should be considered a serial killer, the group quickly disbanded. Way faster than any other time. Mandy took off first, even before Mia could talk to her. Then Hazel and Natalie had left since Hazel's son was sick, and they had ridden together. That left Mia and Ruth, and Mia wasn't ready to tell Ruth alone without everyone else there. And anyway, Mia had wanted to get back to Rafferty, so she made her excuses as well.

Now she was happy she didn't share last weekend. She had gotten another week of them just getting to be together without the outside world intruding. Mia knew the book club wouldn't say anything since what happened at book club stayed at book club, but she decided to just give it two more weeks; until the next meeting. She could do two more glorious weeks of secrets.

So, as far as she knew, nobody knew about her relationship with Rafferty. She was lucky it was freezing out, and nobody was just wandering around the streets to see her walking to his place. Double lucky since she had to bundle up so much to fight off the freezing cold. Nobody could tell it was her, since she had to stop using her pink jacket and was wearing her older black one now.

Not that she was really trying to hide their relationship from people, because it *wasn't* a relationship. Rafferty Brooks didn't do relationships. He was a playboy who had sex with a woman until he grew tired of her and then dumped her. Mia was determined that nobody found out she was dumb enough to fall into bed with him and get dumped.

Which is what made their conversation that morning so bizarre. It was Sunday, and not just any Sunday—it was the Sunday of her cousin Math and book club member Tess's baby's baptism. Everybody in the Nordskov and Lawson families would be in attendance. Well, not all her sisters, as they were busy. Or so they told their mother.

As she was leaving to go get ready at her apartment, he had surprised her by asking, "Can I go with?"

Laughing at his question, she asked, "Imagine all the old biddies talking about us if we showed up in church together. Why would you want to do that?"

"Because it's important to you." He frowned.

Rafferty didn't attend church at the same place her family did. In fact, she had no idea where he went. That had been a topic that hadn't come up. But now was not the time to talk about it.

"But how would I explain you to my family?" She zipped up her jacket and looked at him. He was still in pajama pants and a T-shirt, super sexy as he watched her.

"You could tell them we're seeing each other,"

"Why would I do that?"

He looked at her quizzically. "Because we are."

"No, Rafferty, we're having sex. That's different." She was running short on time as it was and didn't need him distracting her. Mia gently pushed him away.

His arms dropped as he said, "Oh, is that how you see us?"

"Rafferty, I don't have time to do this now." She turned to the door.

"Are you coming back here after?"

"Yes, but I don't know when that will be." And she left for her short bitter walk to her apartment.

Now Mia was sitting in a pew listening to the pastor talk as she tried to decide if she had been wrong to not let Rafferty come. But what would everyone have thought? That Mia was just his next conquest? Most likely.

When it was time for the actual baptism, she pushed him from her mind and watched Mandy in front of the church. When she had first seen her today, Mandy had looked good and was in a better mood than she had been in months. But now, standing in front of the congregation, she was starting to lose that new good mood. Was it because her ex was right next to her, or something else? Something with her pregnancy?

She would corner her in the back room of the basement during the reception and get her to talk. Not that they hadn't just been in there when the book club had toasted the baby before the service began. Mia hoped the book club would always get together whenever there was a special event in each other's lives, in their little room in the basement. Or wherever since maybe all the events wouldn't take place in this church. Just, so far, they had.

"I thought Mandy wanted to be the godmother?" Ruth leaned over and asked her.

"She does." Whispering back, Mia leaned toward her friend.

"Doesn't really look like it."

"I know," Mia agreed.

What she didn't tell her friend was that she had an idea of what her cousin's issue was. Biting her lip as she watched her cousin looking at the baby in her ex's arms, Mia realized she hadn't checked on her cousin as much as she should have since she had confided in her two weeks before. No extra calls, no visits, nothing. All her time had been consumed by Rafferty.

After the service, Mia followed Ruth and Anderson into the basement for the small family gathering that was happening there. As she filled a paper plate with food, she watched as pictures were taken of the baby. Mandy was there and looked paler than she had during the service.

Sitting down next to her mom, she watched Ruth and Anderson sit by the other members of book club and their boyfriends. But since it was her family event, she decided she should sit by her parents. As soon as she was done eating, she would go back with them. Taking a bite of her ham bun, she realized she had lost track of Mandy.

Looking around, she didn't see her anywhere. Her eyes were still scanning the church basement when she heard Rafferty's name mentioned. Snapping back to the conversation, she heard her mom tell her sister Darcy, who had come for the event. "… and since then, Rafferty has worked for Anderson at his insurance office. But they're in Rafferty and his dad's old building. Very confusing."

"Who is Rafferty dating now?" Darcy asked. Everyone knew he didn't date any one woman for long.

"I heard a blonde from Campbell, but nobody has confirmed it," her mom, Dotty, said.

"I heard it's been going on for almost a month, but who knows with that boy." her aunt Dolly stated from across the table.

Mia stopped eating and stopped looking for her cousin. Of course, Rafferty was seeing someone. She was just a side piece for him. Why had she even trusted him? What was two weeks when you have a blonde over in Norden eight miles away? Just far enough to where gossip takes a long time to get between the towns.

"Have you heard anything?" Darcy asked her, with her mom and aunt looking on interestedly. Why did everyone think she knew everything?

"I, ah …" she stammered.

She was reprieved when Tess tapped her on the shoulder and asked in a whisper, "Have you seen Mandy?"

Glad to have an excuse to leave, Mia jumped out of her chair leaving her meal behind. "No. I'll look around."

Immediately, she headed upstairs to check the bathrooms and the sanctuary. Both were empty; no Mandy. Then she checked the pastor's office and a few meeting rooms around the church, but still no Mandy. Coming back to the entryway, she poked her head out into the sunny, freezing parking lot. Nothing.

Turning around, she decided to check the room they had met in before the service, though it was right in the middle of the crowd now eating, so maybe she hadn't managed to go in there. But before she could make it too far, she saw Tess and Hazel coming up the stairs.

Shaking her head at them, she bit her lip to stop the tears. Mandy was gone, and Mia was pretty sure what was happening. And she couldn't tell anyone.

"Where could she be?" Hazel asked as Natalie and Ruth came up the stairs toward them.

"It doesn't matter," Tess stated to the group. "I asked her to be there for this one event. She promised she would. I guess I shouldn't have taken her word for it."

With that, Tess turned and stormed back into the basement. Mia knew that the two of them were close, especially now that Tess was dating Mandy's brother. Trying to stop her tears, she hoped Mandy would one day tell Tess the reason for her vanishing act.

"I would be just as mad if it were me," Ruth added, watching Tess leave.

"I think I'll go check her apartment. Maybe I can get her to come back if she's there," Mia left the group to get her jacket. Needing to find her cousin, and try to be the friend she was supposed to be.

All three of the others insisted they should go instead of Mia, who was a relative, but Mia assured them she was the best to talk to her cousin if she happened to be at her apartment, muttering something about them being related. But in truth, she owed it to her cousin to be there for her now. When she hadn't in the past.

With a quick goodbye, she headed out to her Jeep and drove the cold car the four blocks to her apartment. Parking behind Mandy's car, she knew she couldn't have gotten too far. Her Jeep said it was fifteen below, so she couldn't be outside.

Quickly, she headed up the stairs to Mandy's apartment, and her heart sank when she got there. The silence in the apartment had Mia more scared than she had been at the church. She had been so sure her cousin would be hiding here.

Sinking into Mandy's couch, she tried to come up with another location her cousin would've gone. Maybe the clinic downstairs? But Mia couldn't get in there if Mandy had locked the door.

Pulling out her phone, she sent Mandy a text, asking her to call or text so she knew she was okay. But even as she typed it, she knew her cousin wouldn't reach out until it was all over. And she probably wouldn't then, either.

After texting Ruth that Mandy wasn't at her apartment, Mia stayed there. She would wait for her to return. No matter what was happening, Mandy would come home eventually, and Mia was going to be there when she did.

CHAPTER 24

IT WAS ALMOST four in the afternoon. when Rafferty gave up on Mia coming over and called her, but she didn't answer. By five, he was worried enough to go out in the freezing cold to look for her. As he waited for his car to warm up, he called her again and sent a text in hopes that she would respond. But there was no answer, and the text went unanswered before he got into his car and drove to the church.

But when he got there, the parking lot was completely empty with no Jeep in the lot, or any other vehicle either. Next, he drove past her apartment, and that was where he found her Jeep parked just down the block. It was the same place it had been parked most of the week.

Parking his truck closer to her building, he went up to her place, which was unlocked. But her apartment was dark and empty. No signs of her at all. Not even her car keys were in the bowl she usually kept them in.

Trying not to panic, he wanted to text her friends, but did any of them even know they were seeing each other? He didn't think so. This morning she didn't seem too interested in telling anyone, and since she wasn't telling, neither was he. So far, he hadn't even told Anderson, who in the last year had turned into one of his closest friends.

He still couldn't believe she was in his bed on New Year's Eve. Nor could he believe that she was still in his bed two weeks later. And not only was she in his bed but also in his life every day. He loved coming home to her cooking in his kitchen. She had even rearranged it, which made him laugh since she was the one who put all his stuff away in the first place.

In the evenings, he loved to watch movies with her on the couch—he hadn't moved it since she had said it needed to be facing the fireplace. Each night, she usually fell asleep watching the movie but woke up to go upstairs to bed. At that point, they would make love and fall asleep in each other's arms. Then the next day, they would do it all over again.

The biggest issue he had with the entire setup was that she didn't seem to want to tell anyone what was going on. They hadn't talked about it, but when Anderson didn't say anything at work after book club, he knew she hadn't told her friends.

He hated that she didn't want anyone to know. Why didn't she want anyone to know? The marriage thing was okay to keep secret, but they were dating. What was wrong with them dating?

With her apartment empty, he drove through the streets, aimlessly looking for her. But he didn't even know what he was looking for since her Jeep was on Main Street. Torn between angry and worried, he kept calling her, kept texting her.

Circling back to Main Street, he parked in front of her building to wait. Once again, he texted her and called her, but there was still no response to either one. Sitting in his pickup, he saw lights on at Ruth and Anderson's apartment, but not Mia's. Next door, the TV was on at her cousin Mandy's place next to Mia's, and though the lights were out, he could see the flickering of the TV in the window.

He tried telling himself that she was just visiting someone and not looking at her phone. But it had been close to three hours since he had first texted her. Three of the longest hours of his life.

It was full dark now, and his truck was getting cold, but he didn't want to attract attention by letting it run. Every once in a while, he would leave and drive past his place to see if she showed up. She never did.

At close to eight, he looked from one occupied apartment to the other. Ruth and Anderson or Mandy? Deciding that since it was Mandy's apartment and Mia had been so concerned about on New Year's, he would see if she knew where Mia was.

Getting out of his truck, he went up the stairs and knocked on Mandy Nordskov's door. He knew the nurse, but he didn't know her very well since she was years older than him, and she had only recently returned to town. As far as he could remember, they had only had a conversation or two since then. And he knew trying to explain why he was looking for Mia would be awkward.

To his disbelief, it was Mia who opened the door, and the words out of her mouth were, "Mandy?"

"Nope," he said with relief. Mia was safe; she wasn't frozen somewhere. Then relief turned to anger. "Where have you been?"

"I've been waiting for Mandy. Nobody can find her," Mia explained, her eyes darting behind him in case Mandy was in the hallway as well.

"She's not the only one. Why didn't you answer my texts?" He pushed into the dark apartment.

"I was waiting for Mandy," She waved at the room behind her.

"There isn't enough extra time in waiting to tell me you're alive?" he questioned as he rubbed his hands together to warm them up.

"I can't let you distract me. I let her down. I wasn't there when she needed me." Mia sat heavily on the kitchen chair as tears started to fall.

"How am I a distraction?" he asked in confusion.

"Because I was supposed to keep an eye on her, check on her, but I was too busy with you. Wasting my time with you." She buried her face in her hands .

"Wasting your time?" he asked in disbelief. Had she really said that? The happiest time of his life had been a waste of her time?

"Just leave, Rafferty." She dropped her hands and glared at him.

"What?" He had finally found her, and she was sending him away.

"Just leave. Go to your blonde and leave me alone." She waved at the door, dismissing him.

"What blonde? What are you talking about?" He had lost the focus of this entire conversation.

She just glared at him, "Everybody knows you're dating a blonde from Norden."

"I am not." He defended himself from the rumors that even he had heard. But Mia should know better since he had been spending all his time with her. Every moment he wasn't working, he was with her.

"Liar," she hissed at him, not being rational.

"I haven't dated anyone since we got married. Hell, even months before that." Rafferty told her the truth. Hell, not since this time last year, when he decided he wanted Mia and that he needed to stop wasting time on women who don't mean anything to him.

"Bull," she barked and turned her back on him.

"You're the one who has been dating, Mia, not me!" he yelled, because he was still pissed about her going on that date.

His words rang though the room as her phone went off in her hand.

She looked at the screen and immediately answered the call. "Mandy, where are you? I've been trying to call, and you don't answer …" He couldn't hear what Mandy said on the other end of the call, but Mia's face showed lines of concern. "Mandy, really. I'm not taking that for an answer. I'm calling your mom." Mia turned away from Rafferty.

Again, Mia was silent as her cousin spoke on the other end.

"Okay. I'll try." Mia's voice was calmer than before.

Maybe her concern for Mandy had equaled his concern for Mia. And now that Mandy had been found, Mia will relax.

Mia listened for a few more seconds, then dropped the phone from her ear. Turning back to him, she stated calmly. "I have to organize a group phone call now. I'd like you to leave and stay away from me. Enjoy your blonde."

With her words, she rushed out of the apartment, only taking a moment to grab her jacket. Watching her leave, he stood there, stunned. Had she said that? Couldn't she see this rumor for what it was?

Turning off the TV she had left on in her haste to leave, he followed her down the stairs and across the street. Today, she was quick, and he couldn't catch her before she went up the stairs to Ruth and Anderson's apartment.

Cursing, he turned and went to his pickup and took off. Driving the short few blocks to his place, he wondered why she was willing to believe he was cheating on her, even when he was with her every minute.

What was it going to take to get her to trust him? How could a rumor be enough to kick him out of her life without letting him defend himself? Why couldn't she see that he was madly in love with her? And had been for a long time.

CHAPTER 25

Nora Andrews was the eighth person today to tell Mia that Joe Johnson was having his annual "over the donut" party today. Mia knew it the moment the radio DJ said that they had finally hit zero degrees after weeks of not seeing it that warm in Landstad.

Looking out at the falling snow, she wondered how many people would show up this year. It was snowing, and it just happened to be Valentine's Day. Not that it was her favorite holiday, but those in love went all-out for it.

Even on this most romantic of days, she wouldn't even admit the fact to herself that she was married to Rafferty Brooks. Nor did she admit to herself that she was in love with him. And she was never going to. She wasn't stupid enough to fall for him.

She had finally made it back home after Mandy's requested conference call, which Mia had turned into a full-on meeting with all book club members present. Mandy had finally revealed to everyone that she had been pregnant for months, and instead of it ending in the miscarriage she had predicted, she had given birth to a live, healthy baby. Which had made Mia especially happy for her cousin.

By the time she had climbed into bed after the worry and excitement from the day, she was suddenly swamped with emotions of how she had treated Rafferty. Admittedly, she had spent seven hours on her cousin's couch, just letting the guilt overwhelm her. By the time Rafferty had knocked on the door, everything was his fault, and she had let him have it. Inaccurately.

It had all been *her* fault. Mia, herself, should have just admitted that she had been consumed by their relationship and had let everything else take second place, or maybe last place. If she hadn't hidden it from everyone, she could've been there for her cousin and anyone else she hadn't had time for over the last two weeks instead of avoiding everyone.

Looking back, she knew she should have just asked about the rumors about the blonde, but at the time, all she could feel was embarrassed. Embarrassed that she wasn't enough to keep him happy, embarrassed that she had let herself be with him when she knew how it would end, embarrassed that she had let herself believe she was the kind of woman he would want. Mousy, plain Mia Lawson.

For hours that day, she had let herself dwell on that spring day almost half a lifetime ago when for one brief night, she had let herself believe that Rafferty Brooks would be interested in her. Her, who worked at the café every day after school to earn much needed money. The same Mia Lawson who got straight As without even trying and wore the big glasses because her parents couldn't afford a nicer pair. Plain Mia Lawson, who was overweight and unpopular.

It was prom night, she had no date, and he had gone with Gaby McIntosh. Gaby was a senior and active with the boys in school, so it was no surprise when her date was a recent graduate from Landstad High. It had broken Mia's heart a little since she'd had a crush on Rafferty since the eighth grade.

So, when the girls started to make fun of Mia and her not quite sexy hand-me-down dress, she decided she'd had enough and would just go home early. Leaving the school during prom was against the rules, but Mia didn't care. She was done. It was the last school dance she would attend.

On her way to her car, Rafferty had caught up to her and talked to her for the first time. They had spent almost an hour leaning against her car, talking about the school and shared memories. Future plans of getting out of Landstad and being adults.

How they went from talking to kissing, Mia still didn't know, and how they made it to the nearly empty apartment above his dad's insurance office was also lost to passion and time. The rest of the night was seared into her memory, not to be replaced until she was back in his bed all these years later.

Back then, when she had woken up, she was alone. He was gone without a trace, and she wouldn't hear from him for six years. Not until he came back to town to work with his dad. Then he didn't acknowledge that he had taken her virginity that night or spent a moment with her.

And she never acknowledged that he took her heart that night and never gave that back. Even now, he carried it around, not even caring that he had it. And no matter what she did, she never got it back.

But she had stopped trying over the last year, only admitting to herself deep in the lonely night that she would never need it again anyway. It was his for the keeping. And she had messed it all up.

As he paid for his cheeseburger and onion rings, Lane Hanson became the ninth person to tell her of the party that she would not attend this year. This was one of her favorite parties, but this year, she didn't have the heart for it. Rafferty had that.

Valentine's Day was her most hated holiday in her perpetual singlehood. This year it seemed everyone was paired up. Not only were Ruth and Anderson out of town, but Natalie and Hazel and their men were going to Grand Forks for supper. Mandy was still in the hospital with her premature baby, and Tess and Math were spending the night with their kids, leaving Mia alone. Not that any of them noticed. They never did.

In fact, nobody ever noticed. Everyone always just assumed she was doing something with someone else. But she rarely was. Her nights were mostly spent in front of the TV and going to bed early so that she could get up early for work. All alone.

It was late afternoon, and she was trying to get her aunt Dolly off her back about finding a nice boy to settle down with, like Mandy and her sister Kit had done recently. Though Mia was surprised that neither sister pointed out that the Nordskov sisters had found love for the second time this time around, they usually did.

Dotty was sitting across from her, agreeing completely with her big sister about the state of Mia's love life. Or lack of love life, which was more true.

"You just have to put yourself out there," Dolly told her with an authority she didn't deserve since she had no part in any of her kids finding love.

"How much more out there should I be? I work here," Mia pointed out.

"I guess more. This isn't working, Mia. Look at Mandy. She looked a little and found Hue," Dolly gloated.

She rolled her eyes at her aunt's words. Since Mandy and Hue had always known each other and lived across the hall from each other when they fell in love, that meant Mandy had only looked a little. Not that she begrudged her cousin even a little, but it was not the same.

"Have you looked online? I hear that's how the young people are finding each other these days," her own mother stated.

"No, Mom, I have not," Mia said, as if Landstad and its surrounding towns had some hidden bachelors who were only on the internet. Besides, Mia had checked out the popular site, and there wasn't anyone worth joining for.

"You should try it," Dolly said.

At the front of the restaurant, the door opened, and her husband walked in, right in the middle of her mom trying to find her a man. What would her mom say if she told her she didn't need a husband because she already had one? But instead, she bit her lip and watched him talk to another waitress.

"I'll pay for it, Mia. If you don't want to," her mom was saying about online dating as she watched Rafferty give the waitress a pink bag. Her new young waitress, who wasn't even nineteen yet. Was he dating her? She hadn't heard he was seeing anyone, not that she was paying attention. But her own waitress?

She watched him smile his sexy smile at her as he handed her the bag. Today, he was wearing his bulky coat that hid all his hard muscles that Mia loved to touch. Or used to, back when she could touch them.

"No, Mom," she stated firmly, maybe too firmly.

"Okay, Mia, but you will never get married if you don't try," Dotty said as Mia walked away from them.

Mia didn't care that the conversation with the sisters had ended early she walked to the front of the café as he walked out the door, taking the last of her desire to stay at work with him. He hadn't even ordered anything while he was there. Not even the heart-shaped meatloaf, and everyone was ordering that today.

"Mia, Rafferty dropped this off for you. He said it was from Ruth and Anderson for Valentine's Day." Paige held out the bag Rafferty had given her.

"Paige, I know you haven't worked here long, but you can't flirt with the customers." Mia chastised her for no reason. But he was still her husband, and so far, she hadn't come up with a plan to make him her ex-husband, nor had she tried.

"I'm sorry, Mia, I haven't flirted with anyone. I swear," Paige said with her innocent eyes as she looked around the café, as if the man she had flirted with was still there.

"Rafferty," was all she said to the younger woman.

The face the young woman gave her said she didn't see Rafferty worth flirting with. Mia just waved her away as she took the bag from her hand. Looking down at it, she remembered his gift from last year. Funny how she had forgotten the pregnancy test of the previous year. She wondered how her life would've changed if the test had come back positive back then. That was the night Tess's daughter was conceived. Would she and Rafferty be as happy as Tess and Math were these days? Or would they be just as separated as they were now, but with a baby to shuffle between them?

But the present hadn't been from him anyway, it was from Ruth. But really what would Ruth give her for Valentine's Day? Resisting the temptation to look, she went back to her mom and aunt's table and steered the conversation to their grandbabies. Mandy's surprise baby had ticked off Dotty a little, as if Dolly had been hiding the pregnancy instead of her daughter to spite her sister. And to Mia's delight, that made her put pressure on her married daughters to produce more children. Her sisters deserved a little of their mom's pressure.

By the time three and the end of her day rolled around, Mia was more than ready to leave behind the meatloaf special and go home. Happily, she shed her work clothes and put on pajama pants and a Landstad Tigers sweatshirt to watch a few Valentine's movies. As she found a good one, she picked up the pink bag to see what Ruth had gotten her.

Inside the bag was the movie Sleepless in Seattle and a post-it note that said:

If you want to watch You've Got Mail, it starts at eight. If you want to watch them both together, I'm home at five. Pizza will be served. Rafferty

Was he asking her out? On Valentine's Day? Was he luring her to his house with Meg Ryan and Tom Hanks?

Was it working?

The movie on the screen had lost her interest. Staring at the DVD in her hand, she wondered what it meant. And what would happen if she actually went over there. Well, she knew what would happen, but what would happen tomorrow.

Looking at the clock, she saw she had just over an hour to figure it out. But the more she thought, the more she knew what she should do. What she needed to do. Going into her bedroom, she looked through the boxes on the floor in her closet where she kept her movie collection, the collection that she already had both the movies mentioned. Grabbing what she was looking for, she slid it into the pink bag and put on her coat, hat, and mittens for the short walk. Before she left the apartment, she grabbed her half-empty bottle of whiskey, and out the door she went.

Her feet still knew the way to his place, so she didn't have to think about the walk, just the destination in the falling snow. Once there, she let herself in; the door was unlocked. She took off her outerwear, hanging everything in the coat closet next to the front door. He wasn't there, but it was before five, so she assumed he was still working.

Putting the bag of DVDs on the coffee table, she saw the movie he had mentioned already there. Still in plastic and a price tag on it from a big box store, meaning he had planned this entire thing out. That made Mia feel a little special.

Going into the kitchen, she looked around for a while and then decided on what to make him for supper. She wasn't up for frozen pizza. By the time he walked in the door at 5:05 p.m., the house smelled of baked chicken and roasted potatoes.

"You didn't have to cook," Rafferty said from the kitchen doorway, not mentioning she hadn't been there in a month.

"I didn't want frozen pizza." She didn't mention it either. Or that their last conversation was a huge fight.

"Thank you It smells great."

"Thanks, it was nothing. It's almost ready. You can get the movie ready, and I'll bring the food out. Eating on the couch, right?"

"Sure. Which did you want to start with?" He didn't apologize.

"You forgot the first one in the collection, so I brought that one. We have to start there." Neither did she.

By the time they sat down to eat, he had changed into sweatpants and a T-shirt to match her lounge pants and sweatshirt. Even his shirt had a tiger on it. Once the movie started, they talked about everything from the plot to the characters to the actors who played them. But nothing about anything that had happened in Landstad, North Dakota, ever. Once the second movie started, they had settled into a pleasant silence that was comforting to them both, bringing back memories of their short two weeks together.

Before that movie had finished, Mia was sleeping in Rafferty's arms. It had been so comfortable to be there that she had let it happen. She didn't even try to stay awake, just let herself be with him one more time. Just be exactly where she wanted to be, one more time.

CHAPTER 26

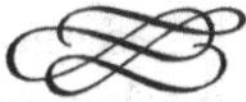

Spring

HOLDING the invitation made it real. This time, Rafferty was invited to Natalie Beckett's wedding, so he didn't have to crash it like he had the year before. Not that he would've this time. Since Valentine's Day, every Friday he dropped off a movie outside of her apartment door in the afternoon, and that night she would bring it to him and add one of her own. She would make them supper, and they would watch the movies.

In the morning, as with on Valentine's Day, she would leave at five in the morning to get to work. She even tried not waking him when she left, but he would wake up anyway and walk her to the door, kissing her one last time. It was only on Fridays, and she didn't tell anyone. He didn't either. He was just happy she kept coming back, even for one day a week.

But in three weeks, she would not come since it would be the rehearsal dinner, and the girls would have a sleepover before the big day. They had a tradition now.

Rafferty knew the invitation was for the office since they handled her dad's insurance, but it didn't matter. Natalie's last wedding had been one of the best days of his summer, even if Mia had gotten trashed. He had gotten to dance with the brunette, even if just a few times.

"What are you grinning about?" Anderson said from his office door.

Rafferty dropped the invitation at his boss's voice. "Nothing really. Just wondering if Natalie will run again."

At her last wedding, she had taken off before the ceremony could start. Now she was marrying a different guy nine months later. That seemed quick to Rafferty, but he had been trying to win his girl for so long, he couldn't imagine how that would be.

"No, she'll marry this one." Anderson knew the couple, so he would know better than Rafferty.

"What can I do for you?" Rafferty asked. Anderson usually didn't come to his office. It was usually the other way around.

"Just wanted to talk to you about Ruth."

"Is there something wrong? Her pregnancy?" Rafferty asked in concern. She had to be around six months along. Maybe a little less.

"No, nothing like that. I just want to ask you a question." Anderson sat in the chair across from him.

"I don't know what kind of help I can give. You know her better than I do." Rafferty wished he had a better relationship with his sister, but she didn't want that. So they didn't.

"As you know, tomorrow night is the Red River Flood auction. We're going, but Ruth has told Mia she would work the tables at the auction to make sure everything is going well. But I don't want her to be on her feet all night. And if I do it, she'll just be there anyway. I was wondering if you could do it instead?" Anderson asked.

"Sure, just give me a time to be there," Rafferty said. Of course, he knew the auction was tomorrow. It was one of Mia's projects and she had been talking about it for a month. So far, she hadn't asked him to be there and he hadn't pushed to be there. But this gave him an excuse.

"Thanks. Ruth doesn't need to be on her feet all night long." Anderson didn't get up.

"How is pregnancy treating her?" Rafferty hadn't seen her in a few months, even if she worked across the street and was dating/married to his boss. They didn't run into each other all that often without one of them going out of their way. And lately Rafferty hadn't went out of his way at all.

"It's going okay. Her mom is on her about being a single mom, as if she didn't raise Ruth alone," Anderson said.

"That's the dragon for you. Are you going to really marry her one day?" Rafferty asked.

"I don't know. She never talks about it anymore. I think she kind of likes the town thinking she's an independent woman who keeps me because she wants to, not because she has to." Anderson leaned back in his chair and smiled.

"How do you feel about that?" Rafferty asked. Because all he wanted to do was take out an ad in the newspaper and announce that he and Mia had been married for months. But that was sure to get him murdered by his lovely bride, and he had learned months ago that antagonizing her just made her pull away even further.

"I'm okay with it. I know that I have her pinned down, even if nobody else does. I love having this little secret. And I know she does, too. Since word got out that she owns all these buildings and that she's a writer, she hasn't had the secrets she likes to have." Anderson grinned at him. It was true—Ruth loved a good secret, so if people found out about the wedding, she would be almost completely out of secrets. Almost. But that one remaining wasn't one she relished keeping.

Rafferty nodded. "She does like a good secret. So, you think you'll just live like this?"

"Yes, I think we'll just be secretly married and openly living in sin. Maybe things will change later, but for now, we are here."

"Well, congratulations," Rafferty said with a sinking heart.

Anderson left his office, and Rafferty wanted to yell at the man. If he and Ruth didn't reveal that they were married in Las Vegas, he and

Mia couldn't reveal that they were also married in Las Vegas that weekend, leaving them in limbo forever.

At this rate, Mia would find a way to secretly divorce him before he was able to tell anyone about their marriage. He would lose her before he could even tell anyone she was his.

This one-day-a-week marriage wasn't what he wanted. He wanted her every day and in every way. Be by her side for every event in their lives, big and small. He wanted her not to ask him to help her at the auction that night because she didn't have to ask, not because she didn't want him there. Did she even want him there?

Shaking off the thought of her getting angry at him being there, he vowed he would make her see that he wanted to be there and wanted to help. That by her side was where he wanted to be. Where he belonged.

CHAPTER 27

THE AUCTION HAD GONE EVEN BETTER than last year's. If the numbers floating around her head were correct, she had raised more money this year. But this year, she had gotten more people to donate their time instead of items. Last year, she had twelve people from around town who volunteered to give a day to charity, whereas this year, she had twenty-four. And everyone was finally getting into the spirit of it.

Now that part of the auction was done, so she could concentrate on the donated items. Ruth was supposed to be in charge of it, but since she was pregnant, she had asked Rafferty to do it. Not that Mia was worried about Rafferty's ability to organize, she just knew he hadn't done it before.

When Ruth had called to tell her that she was making Rafferty do it, Mia had been slightly mad at her friend. Ruth had known Rafferty wouldn't say no to his sister. He would do anything for her. But Mia had made sure not to include him in her auction. She wasn't ready to have that part of her life mix with this part yet.

Yes, they spent every Friday night together, all night. But that was all. Neither had pushed for a relationship, and neither had pushed for more time together. It had been a month and a half, and they hadn't talked about them or the future. And they had told nobody.

Her reasoning had been that she didn't want to rock the boat—she enjoyed their time together too much to have people talking about them—but in reality, she was scared that once everyone knew, it would be over. And she never wanted it to end, even if it was just one day a week.

Sadly, she was looking toward a month where she would be unable to see him on Friday night. April was going to be busy. Natalie and Tess were both getting married on two separate weekends, so two Friday nights would be the bachelorette sleepovers. Then tonight, they were missing their movie night because of the auction. That left one Friday of the month free, and that was Easter weekend, which meant her sisters were going to be coming up, and her mom was talking about a family meal to greet them. Her whole April too busy for her once a week night with her husband.

As she walked through the school hallways toward Rafferty's auction area, she was deciding what day during the week would be best to change Friday to. Maybe Tuesday? Or Thursday? Would he even agree to a change? Maybe he was busy other days ... she had never asked.

"How's it going?" Mandy asked from behind her.

Stopping, she turned to her cousin. "Good, looks like it's a success."

Mandy was holding her tiny son in her arms. He was close to four months now. After spending two months in the NICU, he was happy and healthy now that he was home. And so was his mother, who was glowing. Maybe because she was already pregnant again So far, that was a secret only the book club knew. But Mia knew it was more because she was madly in love and had every one of her dreams come true by being a mom to the baby in her arms.

"I'm so glad it's working out again. But I wasn't too worried; everything you do works out. I saw you talking to Nick Nelson. Is there something I should know about? Is romance in the air?" her cousin hinted, bouncing the baby in her arms.

"No, we were just reminiscing about high school," Mia stated the truth.

"He's divorced now," Mandy informed her. Though she hadn't

heard officially, it had been the rumor going around. But she wasn't interested. She was busy this month.

"Oh, that's nice. But I have to make sure Rafferty isn't messing up the donated items auction. Ruth bailed on me." Mia pointed toward the school wing the auction was happening in, just out of her sight.

"I was the one who mentioned that she shouldn't spend the night on her feet." Mandy was a nurse practitioner, and Ruth was her patient.

"Well, she shouldn't have made Rafferty do it," Mia tried to keep the annoyance at their friend from her voice.

"I think he was happy to," Mandy said, looking down that hallway also.

"Still, she never has time for him unless she wants something. And he does it," Mia grumbled. She had known that they were siblings for a year now, and she saw it all the time, but nobody else probably did.

"I've never noticed." Mandy looked at Mia with a puzzled expression.

"I'm sorry, Mandy, I have to go." Mia turned to make sure he was doing okay. And she was too busy to have Mandy distracting her right now.

Leaving her cousin, she walked into the auction area and saw him right away. He was talking to her little sister, Kipling, who had volunteered to fill in the gaps during the event. And here she was, just flirting with Rafferty instead of doing actual work.

Deep breaths, she commanded herself as she walked up to them. He was wearing gray slacks and a black polo shirt today. Rafferty was the first to notice her and smiled his sexy smile at her. But had he used that sexy smile on her little sister?

"How's the auction going, Mia?" he asked, still smiling.

"Fine," she hissed at him before turning to her sister. "Don't you have something else to do, Kipling?"

Her baby sister gave her an odd look and shrugged. Without a word, she walked away, disappearing into the crowd, looking at the items that would be bid on.

"Are you a little stressed?" Rafferty asked with a look of concern.

"No, I'm not!" she growled at him, then added, "I just don't need you flirting with my eightteen-year-old sister."

"I was talking to your sister, not flirting with her."

"Just remember, she's eightteen," Mia hissed and turned away from him.

Grabbing her arm, he stopped her in her tracks, leaned in, and whispered into her ear, "You're the only Lawson I want in my bed."

He let her go.

She was stunned. Had he just said that in public? Looking around, she tried to see if anyone was watching them. Nobody was watching them, so she hurried back out of the area. Going to check on something else, anything else.

What was happening to her? Was she actually jealous of her sister, who was just talking to the man? The man she was sleeping with? Maybe if their relationship was public, she wouldn't be so jealous of everyone he talked to. Every time she saw him with another woman, she wanted to push the woman aside and yell that he was her husband and to get her mitts off him. Instead, she just fumed about it.

For the rest of the evening, she ignored both Rafferty and the silent auction area until she couldn't anymore, then it was so busy, she didn't have time to think about him or talk to him. After ten, she didn't see him anymore. He must have left. Though she should be more relaxed with him gone, she wasn't. Had he left alone?

Over the next two hours, she couldn't stop wondering who he could've left with while she worked to get the school clean. That and getting the auction items handed out or put to the side until Monday when she would meet people who couldn't make it back tonight.

At midnight, she was exhausted and just wanted to crawl into bed and sleep. Forget her jealousy and anger. Parking in her usual spot, she turned off her Jeep and went up to her apartment. Her quiet, lonely apartment. She slipped out of the dress she had worn and put on leggings and a sweatshirt. At the door, she stepped out of her pink winter boots and shut off her light.

The two-block walk was short. It was a warm night for the first week of April, and it made her excited for summer. Kicking off her shoes inside his door, she went up the stairs and into his bedroom, where she slipped off her clothes and slid into bed with him. It was Friday night after all.

Her side of the bed was freezing against her naked skin, but when he pulled her into his arms, she was instantly warmed by his body. Sighing, she nestled into him.

"Goodnight, Mia," he whispered into her hair. Not mentioning their fight.

"Goodnight, Rafferty," she didn't say anything about it either.

CHAPTER 28

IT WAS THURSDAY BEFORE EASTER, not a day they had ever had book club. This was their first midweek get-together and would be the day set for the month of April. It was the only time they could all be there since half the group was going to be out of town this year.

Tess was going to show her daughter off to her family in Minnesota, even if it wasn't the day they celebrated the holiday. Since she was raised orthodox Christian, her Easter was the following weekend, but that was Natalie's wedding weekend, so her new little family was going down there early. Mia knew her extended family was having a small reception for their wedding in two weeks. Most of her family would not be attending, which was okay since there were over a hundred people in her immediate family. That was far more out-of-towners than Landstad could hold.

Natalie was also going to Minnesota to see her birth mother, also a week before her wedding, so that her mom's sisters wouldn't have to make the trip out to North Dakota. Ruth and Hazel were going to Grand Forks to visit their in-laws, though Hazel would be back on Sunday since her husband was the pastor and had to work that day.

That left only Mandy and her in Landstad for the weekend. And Mandy was debating going to Hue's sister's place in Fargo. Or they would stay and have the holiday with her family, minus her brother, Tess's fiancé.

Nobody even asked what Mia was planning for the holiday, because everybody assumed they knew. Except they were right, she was going to her mom's and leaving early if possible. Alone.

So here they were on a Thursday night, talking about Ed Gein, who was a creepy topic for any night of the week. Natalie and Ruth really had the best books about him, and they dominated the conversation. Mia's own book had been disappointing.

Natalie laughed at Ruth as she stopped recording. Mia pulled her headphones off and joined in as she got up to fill her glass of whiskey, her drink of choice. Turning to the group, Mia asked if anyone else wanted anything while she was up.

As she filled glasses for others and brought them to the table, she let the conversations circle around her. Sitting back down next to Mandy, she asked her cousin, "Have you guys decided if you're going south for the holiday?"

"We're staying here. Hue doesn't want to take the baby down there right now. He still doesn't do well in cars," Mandy said about her son.

"You'd think that Hue would be okay with long car rides," Mia joked to make her cousin laugh. It worked.

From across the table, Ruth joined in, stating, "Anderson and I decided to stay close to home, too. I just don't want to do the big family thing this year. Just something small with my mom on Sunday after church."

Mandy turned to her. "Maybe we should do something in the evening?"

"We should. That would be fun. Just a little dinner party," Ruth said with excitement.

"You should invite Rafferty." Mia bit her lip at the suggestion. She wished Ruth would include him in things, but Mia wasn't even invited to this particular event.

Ruth turned to her with a glare. "Why would I invite him? He's just Anderson's employee."

"And his friend," Mia pointed out. They were probably together tonight since they usually were during book club.

"But he's not my friend, so I'll pass on that," Ruth stated coldly.

"It was just a thought," Mia mumbled, trying to stop the conversation before it focused on her and Rafferty.

"Well, you can keep those thoughts to yourself," Ruth said, glaring at her still.

Mia set her glass down far away from her. Slowly, she got up and looked over at who she had thought was one of her closest friends for over a year, someone whose secrets she held close to her heart. A friend who couldn't seem to find it in her heart to forgive a man who did nothing but love her like the sister she was to him.

Looking across at Ruth, Mia just held the steel blue gaze and stated coolly, "Don't ever tell me what to do, Ruth. You know exactly what I'm asking of you. I know more about you than anyone in this room."

Waiting for Ruth to say something, she just stared into her unflinching eyes. Mia knew all eyes were on them. Silently, the moment went on without anyone saying a word, not even Ruth.

Angrily, she turned and walked out of the apartment. She grabbed her shoes on the way but didn't put them on. Today, she was tired of how Ruth treated Rafferty.

All she wanted to do was go the two blocks to his house, but she knew Anderson was there. So instead, she went up to her apartment and slammed her door shut behind her.

She didn't know how Anderson did it. How could he sleep with Ruth and be friends with Rafferty and understand how she treated him? She was his counterpart, and she was hating it more and more every day.

Half expecting someone to come and talk to her from the group, she was surprised when half an hour went by, and nobody did. Ruth must have told them something that made sense as to what they were talking about. Right now, she really didn't want to know what Ruth had told them.

What she had said was true. She didn't think anyone else at that table knew that Rafferty was her brother or that she and Anderson were married. But Mia knew. Mia also knew that nobody else in the group had any big secrets from the group anymore, just her and Ruth. And their secrets were suddenly causing friction between them.

After fuming on the couch for two hours, she decided no one from the group was coming over and that Anderson must be home by now. Locking her apartment, she headed to Rafferty's house. It was Thursday, but tomorrow, she was going to her mom's for supper and wouldn't see him until maybe late. So, she decided to go over there now.

When she got there, Rafferty was watching some kind of sports in the living room, and she curled up with him on the couch. It was only then that she had finally been able to let the tension release as he held her close.

By the time the game was over, she was asleep, and he must have carried her to bed because when her early morning alarm went off, she was in bed with him. And somehow, she had gotten all her clothes off. She still didn't know how he got her undressed so easily without her knowing how it happened. Maybe one day she would figure it out, but for now she just liked being with him.

CHAPTER 29

That was how long Mia had been ignoring that Rafferty was even at Natalie and Sam's wedding. So far, she had ignored him through the ceremony and through the reception, and it looked like he was going to be ignored through the dance.

She had made a point of talking to everyone else in the room. But she had pointedly ignored him and didn't even get close enough to him for him to say anything about it. He just watched her flit around the room.

Finishing the beer he was drinking, he set it down and watched her dance with the bride and their little book club. Or trying to dance since Hazel was currently teaching the entire group some dance move that was far beyond the skills of most of them.

He was sitting with most of the husbands and boyfriends, none of which had been ignored as much as he had been. They at least got to sit by their women during the wedding, and most even held hands. Mia had made sure that Ruth and Anderson were between them, as if they needed a buffer.

Which had been totally uncomfortable since the women were not getting along at all. Anderson had told him there was a blow-up at book club between them, but not about what. As far as he could tell, it was still going on. The two seemed to be only getting along for the sake of the bride today. And he assumed they would do the same next weekend for the next bride. Though he hoped they would patch up their differences, since the strain was becoming obvious.

Mia had gone to her mom's on Friday night, so he really didn't get to talk to her that day. But to his surprise, she had come over after she got home at around eleven and crawled into bed with him. That was two nights in a row.

Saturday, she had worked her usual shift at the café and then went back to her mom's to spend more time with her sisters. They seemed to be getting along better now than in the fall, which made Rafferty happy since she was happier when the six sisters got along.

Then, to his surprise on Sunday, she had called her mom claiming she was sick, and she had spent the day with him. They had watched movies and talked all day. She had made a beef roast and potatoes, and they had eaten that all day, wearing pajamas.

It wasn't a traditional holiday, but he would take it over anything anyone would've offered him. Maybe they would start a new holiday tradition of not getting dressed or going anywhere for the holidays.

It was that day that she had finally told him why she had blown up at Ruth over her not being nice to him. Or something like that. Which had made him love her even more because she was defending him to his sister. She may not want to tell anyone about them, but she was defending him. It was a step in the right direction.

Or he had thought it was, but now he wasn't to sure. Tonight, he would rather have her by his side than defending him to his sister.

Anderson, Math Nordskov, and Hue Strong were talking about the women dancing. Since Hue was dating Math's sister, Math was mostly making fun of her to get a rise out of his friend. Except it didn't work since Hue admitted his girlfriend wasn't coordinated enough to dance, but she looked hot trying.

A look of disgust crossed Math's face before he asked Hue, "So, when are you going to ask Mandy to marry you?"

Hue turned away from watching the women with a smile, "I already did."

"Did she turn you down?" Math laughed, because everyone in town knew that Tess turned him down at least a dozen times before she ended up asking him to marry her.

Hue grinned. "Nope, she said yes."

"When were you going to tell us?" Math asked, taken aback. Hue was his best friend, and Mandy was his sister.

"After you were married." He smiled at him.

"How long have you been planning this?" Math demanded.

"Since March. And if my future wife hasn't told you yet, we're having another baby," said the man with the tiny baby already in his arms.

"And you weren't telling?" Anderson asked, eyes wide.

Rafferty looked at the men in surprise. Mia had told him at least a month before that Mandy was going to have another baby. It seemed all the other women had assumed it was a secret. Mia, it seemed, was secreted out. Or maybe she was letting him in on the secrets.

"We wanted you guys to have your day first, but you pressured me to tell," Hue said, though the pressure had been light at best.

Turning to Anderson, Math asked, "What about you? Are you secretly engaged also?"

Rafferty watched his brother-in-law with interest. The man was actually secretly married, but would he tell the men that? Would he let the cat out of the bag like Hue had? So Rafferty could finally be married to the woman he loved.

"Nope. She's not ready." Anderson laughed and dodged the question. Sinking Rafferty's heart, again.

Math suddenly turned his attention to Rafferty. "How about you, Rafferty? Got a woman hidden in that big old house you bought?"

Stopping himself from asking the man what he had heard, hoping no one had heard something, he instead plastered on a fake smile. "You know the rumors in this town are out of control. If I had a woman in my house, the entire town would know about it instantly."

"If anything was happening close to downtown, Mia would know and would've told everyone," Anderson said, his eyes going to the dancers again.

"All you have to do is tell it from Mia, and everyone knows," Math said about his cousin.

Rafferty wondered if these men knew how much Mia had known about their relationships and how she had kept them from the entire town. Or how she had manipulated information to make them look better than they really were. After all, it was Mia who had the rumors of Math and Tess's baby out while they weren't even in town. And Mandy and Hue's baby's paternity was never questioned because of Mia.

Anderson was about to say something, then stopped when he caught Rafferty's eye. Anderson knew that Mia had and was keeping every secret Ruth held close. Even before they had become friends, Mia never told a soul that Ruth owned half the town.

The song on the dance floor changed to a slow one, and as one, the men got to their feet. It was time to dance with their women. Except Mia wouldn't want to dance with him.

At that point, he got up and said to the men who were no longer paying attention to him, "Well, I'm going to go."

Without looking at the dance floor to seek out his wife, he walked out of the reception hall. He was tired of being ignored in public by her.

Walking home slowly, he wondered if she would show up in his bed tonight. Would he be good enough for her when nobody was around?

He didn't know and didn't really want her to tonight. But he didn't know how he would kick her out if she was there. All he wanted was her.

CHAPTER 30

MIA PICKED a sprig of baby's breath from Tess's hair and made sure that it was still perfect. It was. Looking at this week's bride, she wanted to hug her friend but resisted because she would then have to straighten her dress back out. Tess had opted for an off-white dress that wasn't nearly as tight as Natalie's dress had been last week, but it was gorgeous just the same.

Also in the room was Mandy and Tess's niece, Natasha, who were the bridesmaids this week. Mia was glad Mandy had chosen mid-June as her wedding date since it was getting old to have one every week.

Mia asked the same question she asked at every wedding she was the personal attendant at—which was all of them as of late. "Are you going out the window, Tess?"

Mandy laughed beside her, and Natasha looked at her niece in question.

"No, Mia. Thank you for asking," Tess said with none of the nervousness of the previous brides. Maybe it was because she was older or because she had already had a reception with her family in Minnesota, but she was calm.

"Just checking. You never know." Mia sat on the same table she always sat on.

It was at that point that something happened that had yet to happen at any of the previous wedding she had attended: the bride and her bridesmaid started to speak in a different language than they had ever spoken. Mia's eyes were wide as she listened to the exchange. Her usual slow-talking friend was talking at a speed Mia was sure she couldn't have kept up with if they had been speaking English.

Though Mia knew Tess's native language was Russian, she had rarely heard her speak it, and never in actual sentences. But with her best friend there, she was able to converse with someone in it. It was amazing.

When they stopped, Mia asked, "What did you say?"

"I told her about Natalie and her first wedding," Tess stated about their friend who went out the window last summer.

"I want you to talk like that always," Mia said as the door opened, and Natalie and Hazel came into the room.

"You sound like Mathias," Tess said with a smile to her.

"Ick. Now talk for these two," she demanded.

"No," Tess said with a wink.

Natalie looked around the room and said, "We're short one Where is Ruth?"

"You two were the ones who have been outside this room in the last half an hour." Mia was glad her former friend wasn't there yet.

Over the last few weeks, they had managed mostly to avoid one another. Not that it had been hard since Ruth didn't come into the café, and Mia didn't go to her rental office. It was only at events like this that they saw each other, and neither spoke to the other if possible.

"Fine, I'll go get her," Hazel groaned, squeezing back out the door.

"How's married life, Natalie? Any advice for Tess?" Mia asked last week's bride, who was still glowing with happiness.

This time, Natalie had married the correct man, and it showed. Mia was more than a little jealous that all her friends had found the right man for them. Or maybe it was that the correct man wanted her friends. Her own correct man wasn't the forever kind of guy like her friends had found.

"Married life is the greatest. My advice would be to wait until it's warmer to honeymoon by a Minnesota lake. The water is *cold* right now." Natalie laughed at her own private joke that nobody understood, and nobody asked any more questions about it.

Tess turned to Mia and asked, "So Mia, how's Rafferty?"

Mia froze. She had told nobody about them. Had someone seen her? Sure, this week she had been to his place nearly every day again, but she had been very careful.

"I have no idea what you're talking about," Mia squeaked.

"I heard a rumor you two have been chummy lately." Natalie jumped into the conversation.

"And after what you said at book club, it seems like the rumors are true." Tess looked at her and straightened a lock of her still brown hair. She had only colored it once, and that was to better match her natural color.

"I have no idea what you're talking about," she repeated, because she had no idea what else to say.

Knowing she should just admit that they were seeing each other and doing it were two different things. Biting her lip, she wondered if she could swear all of them to secrecy. But she worried that everyone would know within an hour if she told.

"Ruth said something was up," Mandy said from beside her.

"I wouldn't believe what Ruth says." Mia's back was up with Ruth's name. That must be how she deflected on book club night. Since they had just had a bachelorette party the week before, and Tess's family was in town, they didn't repeat it last night. The week before, Mia had stayed for a few hours and had left early, complaining of a headache, which was actually Ruth and her angry glares.

Just then, the woman in question walked in with Hazel, and the group was all there in the little room with one extra person and a ton of tension. Natalie handed out the shots to all, including Natasha, and once again it was vodka, since it was Tess's beverage of choice. There was also some sort of clear juice for those not drinking the hard stuff. Mia had no idea of that flavor since she needed the vodka.

After a toast and hugs all around, the three not in the wedding went back to sit down. Mia once again made sure that the bride was perfect, then checked the bridesmaids. Then it was time to get them upstairs. Mia walked with Mandy and Natasha while Tess walked behind them.

Mandy took her hand. "You can talk to me if you need to. I love to talk to you."

"I know, but there's nothing to talk about," Mia whispered.

"I like him; I always have," Mandy assured her with a squeeze to her hand, then let it go.

"I don't know what you're talking about." Mia looked into her blue eyes and then made sure the teal dress was perfect before nodding to her cousin to head for the front of the church.

Next, she checked over the next bridesmaid and sent her going at the proper time. Turning to the bride, she whispered, "I want to hug you, but I won't."

"Thank you for being here for me today, Mia. I can't imagine anyone else helping me through this day than you." Tess then hugged her tightly.

"Now you wrecked your dress," Mia said, making sure she didn't actually mess up her dress.

"It was worth it. I want to be the Mia at your wedding," Tess said as Mia made sure the back was perfect.

"You don't have to worry about that. I won't get married," Mia assured her.

"Maybe Rafferty?" Tess asked hopefully.

"That ship has sailed." Mia pushed her friend to the front of the church.

Watching her walk toward Math, Mia smiled at the look on his face when he saw her for the first time. That was the look she wanted to see on her husband's face. That was why she knew there would never be a husband. Not a real one. Rafferty would never look at her that way, and he was the only husband she would ever have. For as long as it lasted.

CHAPTER 31

Summer

THE FIRST WEEK of June was colder than usual in North Dakota, or maybe that was just how Rafferty felt about it. Something had happened during the Nordskov wedding that once again had Mia keeping her distance from him. In just over a month, she had been to his place twice, and she had been drunk both nights.

Both had been after book club, when she was drunk and mad at Ruth. The second time she had been mad at everyone, even her cousin. He had let her sleep in his bed, and she had been gone the next morning as usual. But they hadn't made love like she had wanted to. He wouldn't be her drunken hook-up anymore. He wanted her sober in his bed, in his life.

Not that he wasn't still mad at her for ignoring him at the wedding, because he still was. After all, she had ignored him for the entirety of the wedding the next weekend also, which was why he left early again. But he hadn't been able to confront her about it because he hadn't really spoken to her.

Over the last month, he had plenty of time alone to think about their future. It came down to the fact that she was unable to commit to him in Landstad. She was so afraid of what people would say behind her back that she couldn't make their relationship official. Afraid everyone would see her as just another of Rafferty's hook-ups. They couldn't get past who everyone in this town thought they had been.

A few weeks before, he had come up with a solution that might work. It was radical, but maybe just radical enough that it might work to keep them together. Or, in reality, get them together.

Move.

Yes, he loved this town, and when he had been away, he had wanted nothing but to be back. But she wanted out. And he wanted her more than he wanted to be in this town without her. She was his priority now.

Another positive would be that he would not have to be rejected by his sister at every turn. They could move on with their lives in separate towns and not run into each other all the time. In fact, his sister would really never have to see him at all. Mia would have to decide what to do about the café, but she had always insisted she could find a manager for it at the drop of a hat.

Gathering all his courage, he walked into Anderson's office and sat down. It was close to the end of the day. He had waited until now, so Anderson didn't have a lot of time to talk him out of it before he had to go home to Ruth. Anderson never stayed late.

Anderson looked up at him quizzically, asking, "Can I help you, Rafferty?"

"Yes, I have to talk to you about something. Something important."

He really liked working with Anderson. It was completely different from working with his dad. Every day he was happy to come to work, happy to have a boss who didn't think of him as a complete screwup. He was even happy to hear about Anderson's personal life, something he himself never talked about. Because Mia wouldn't want him to.

Anderson put his pen down and turned his attention to him. "What's so important?"

Rafferty cleared his throat and explained, "I'm going to call your dad today and see if I can get a transfer to Grand Forks. If there's nothing, I'm going to find an agency to join down there."

"Why?" Anderson asked in shock. As far as he could see, Rafferty knew this was coming out of left field. But it had to be done. It was the only way to get the woman he wanted..

"Because I want Mia, and Mia wants out of Landstad," he said simply.

Watching Anderson's face, he knew the man already knew he wanted Mia. Leaning back in his chair, Anderson crossed his arms.

"What about your house?"

"I'll sell it. I bought it for her anyway," he admitted. He couldn't live there without her as it was. Every corner reminded him of her.

"Ruth said something was up, but I didn't believe her." Rafferty had been sure Ruth wouldn't keep his secrets from her husband. And he hadn't expected her to. But he just wished Anderson had brought it up months ago; then he would've had someone to talk with.

"That's another thing. I won't have to deal with Ruth anymore," Rafferty stated bluntly. It had always bothered him that his sister and best friend couldn't accept him, couldn't be on his side. Maybe Anderson wasn't the kind of friend he needed.

"Have you talked to Mia about this?" Anderson asked.

"No, I want to get everything settled before I talk to her. If she doesn't go, I'll be going anyway. I'm ready to give up. I've tried my damnedest to win Mia's heart, and at this point, I'll have to admit defeat." His stomach churned. The wheels were in motion now, and he wasn't even sure any of his plans would turn out the way he wanted them to.

After years of loving her and months of marriage, he could be heading straight into separation and loneliness. Except they were already separate, and he was lonely when she wasn't around. Moving would just remove the possibility of seeing her at all.

"Maybe you want to talk to Mia first? I would hate for you to lose her because of not talking to her. Like I almost did with Ruth."

Ignoring his words, because he and Ruth had been in a completely different spot than he was with Mia, he told the man, "Ruth is another reason I feel leaving is for the best. So, you can tell your wife she wins. Landstad is hers." Rafferty got up and headed out of the office.

Rafferty headed for the house he had wanted to share for the rest of his life with his wife. Now he was just hoping to have that wife—who cared about the house? Without her it wasn't a home.

CHAPTER 32

THE DRUNKEN CHATTER around her was giving her a headache. Looking at the clock on the wall, she decided to give it one more hour and then head home. This year, there had been too many bachelorette parties, too many weddings, and Mia was over them. But at least this one was the last.

Ruth was the only one not married, or so everyone thought. It seemed like she wasn't going to get married again, and if she did, Mia wasn't going. At all. It had been months since they had said a civil word to each other.

Which was why next week at book club, she was going to resign. She was tired of it. She hoped to remain friends with everyone but Ruth. She would understand if they slowly drifted apart. That was what happened when your friends got married anyway, and Mia had it happen over and over again. Every time one of them asked her to be a personal attendant, she knew she was sending another friend out of her life. Tomorrow would be her cousin, Mandy.

And with her, they would all be married, though nobody knew she was. Nobody would ever know that secret.

"So, Anderson came home today and said Rafferty is moving to Grand Forks. Just like that. Rafferty's contacting Anderson's dad and getting a transfer to the office down there," Ruth told everyone from across the living room, but her eyes were on Mia.

"Really? Why?" Mandy asked, her eyes also darting to Mia.

"Anderson didn't say, but he knows. I just have to get him to tell me," Ruth said with a smile.

Mia looked at her drink and tried not to cry. He was leaving. She was supposed to leave, not him. It had been months since she had thought she would leave this town, before the new year, in fact. But it didn't hurt any less that he was the one leaving. Leaving her here alone. And soon to be friendless.

"Had you heard that, Mia?" Ruth said from across the room still, so everyone was looking at her.

Mia hated that she was hearing it from Ruth and not Rafferty. All she wanted was to rush to his house and demand he tell her why he was leaving her, but she knew she wouldn't. She had no control over him, and he was over her. He was leaving her.

"It's good that someone is getting out of this town." Trying to sound cheery and she hoped she had succeeded. It helped that most of the people there had no clue she was hung up on Rafferty.

"Are you still thinking about leaving?" Hazel asked, turning her attention to Mia. Now she wished she hadn't been so vocal about leaving for so long, because the failure hurt even more when everyone knew about it.

"No, I'm stuck here, I guess. Forever." Again, faking a cheeriness she didn't feel.

"I'm glad, I love you here." Natalie leaned over and bumped her with her shoulder.

"At least someone does," Mia said into her whiskey and drank it in one gulp, suddenly wanting to be drunk tonight. If only she could drink enough to forget about this entire conversation.

As the conversation turned to local gossip, she looked around the room at her friends who had changed during the last eighteen months. All were married or going to be tomorrow. Natalie and Hazel were friends again, as they had been able to get past that tragic day so many years before. It would always be on their minds, but it wasn't the only thing they had anymore. They were back to being close like when they were young.

Tess and Mandy were now sisters-in-law and were so close. With each having a baby, they had so much in common, and they had married best friends, so they would always be closer than the rest.

Ruth had probably changed the most. She had gone from a near hermit to an outgoing member of society. This year, she had even gotten onto the city board and was making improvements to the entire town. Nobody had said a thing about her being there for years and not contributing until now.

Only Mia was stuck in the same groove she was always in: waitress and soon to be divorced. Rafferty would start the paperwork if he was in Grand Forks. It was supposed to have been her, but now it will be him. She had to just let him go.

"So, I have an announcement," Ruth said above the small conversations happening around them. "Anderson and I have asked Tess and Math to be godparents once the baby is born. And they have said yes." Again, she was looking straight at Mia when she said it.

This announcement was at least expected. No way was she being asked. No way would Rafferty be asked either. Ruth had said months ago she wanted a married couple, and Tess and Math were that. At the time, she had told her friend she would be married by this time. And she was, Ruth just didn't know about it. Hopefully, she never would.

But what Ruth was really saying with her choice of Tess and Math was that she was rejecting Rafferty. As a friend and as a brother. There was nothing the man could do to get past her bitterness at him.

Everybody congratulated Tess, even Mia. She was happy for her friend. She remembered Tess when book club started, and she wasn't the most popular member of the group, but look at her now.

Sitting there silently for another few minutes, she decided to make her excuses. Nobody argued with her leaving. They let her go. Just like that, she saw the end of her participation in book club. She didn't think she would even attend the next meeting. There was no reason to.

* * *

THE NEXT DAY found her sitting on her usual table as she waited for the bride to come back after breast feeding her son. How much straightening would have to be performed after that?

Today, she was alone in the room. Tess was running late because her daughter was teething and in the middle of a much-needed nap. The other three members of the book club were up in the sanctuary still since it was just under an hour until the ceremony.

Mia looked around the little room that had held so many events over the last year. Ruth was the only one who hadn't gotten married in this church, and if she had another ceremony, she wouldn't have it here. Mia had always wanted her wedding here, but that wouldn't happen now. Her heart was moving to Grand Forks without her.

It had taken her over a decade to get over Rafferty the first time. And she didn't think she had it in her to do it again. She would love him forever. Even after he was long gone. Again.

Don't cry, she demanded of herself. She had cried most of the night and had to put on so much makeup today that she looked like a clown. The tears were for her relationship with Rafferty and how she had messed that one up, and they were for the end of book club. She still loved it but couldn't go anymore. She didn't belong anymore. Everyone was moving into a new phase of their lives as wives and mothers. Something she would never be.

Mandy rushed into the room with no baby. Shutting the door she stopped and looked Mia up and down in her peach dress and said, "Look at you all lonely."

"I'm here with all my friends," Mia said, feeling the truth in it.

"Then it's a good thing I came." Mandy jumped up beside her.

"Get down. You'll wrinkle your dress," Mia stated sternly. It seemed the older the bride, the more relaxed they were.

"I don't care, let it be wrinkled. I'm sitting with my favorite cousin." Mandy put her arm around her.

Mia smiled. "At least we'll always be cousins."

"Does that mean that we won't have lunch once a week when we're old?" *Like their moms did*, Mandy didn't add.

"Probably not. You'll get together with Kit and never have enough grandkids to beat her." Mia laughed.

Mandy's sister had five kids already, and no matter how close in age Mandy's were, five was a lot. And now that Kit had found love again, Mia wasn't entirely sure the couple wouldn't have a few kids together. Even if Kit was adamantly against it.

"Kit wins all day long. I'll stick with you. We'll talk about our mom hips and have a competition to see who has more grandkids." Again, like their moms.

"You'll win. No kids means no grand kids." Mia sighed. It was the truth. She would have to focus her attention on others' kids. Just like she had before.

"There's always Rafferty," Mandy said with a wink.

"No, that's over. Whatever it was," Mia admitted, wishing she could at least say they had a relationship. Instead, she was left with not knowing what they had.

"Well, then there's someone out there for you."

"No, he was the one. Ever since high school, he was the one."

"High school?"

"Yup."

"Why are you giving up so easy, then?" Mandy demanded.

"Because he's done with me he's moving," she reminded her cousin. They had just talked about it the night before. Only now she had to give up on the dream of her being a mom someday.

Mandy put her arm around Mia. "Maybe you can follow him. Finally get to Grand Forks. You always wanted out of this little town."

"No, I'm a Tiger. I'll die here." Leaning into her cousin, Mia hung her head.

"Boy, aren't you the morbid one today? On my wedding day." Mandy pulled her even closer.

"Just a little depressed. Sorry, it's your wedding day, too." Mia slammed a hand to her mouth. She should not have said that. Not to the bride.

"I know how you're feeling, you know. It hasn't always been me getting married. I've been to my share of weddings that I wanted to be happy about but couldn't," Mandy admitted. She had been single for five years after her divorce.

"It's hard," Mia said.

"I know, but look at it this way Maybe you can beat Ruth to the altar. She's in no hurry," Mandy said with a laugh at her friend. She was no longer Mia's anymore.

"Yeah, at least I beat Ruth," she admitted on a sigh.

"*Could* beat," Mandy corrected.

"Yeah, that's what I meant," Mia said quickly. Only then realizing her mistake.

Mandy slid off the table and turned to Mia, and demanded, "You're not telling me something."

"Mandy, we have no secrets."

"You know everyone's secrets. Spill."

"You were pregnant."

"Nope.

"Natalie has a secret mom."

"No."

"Hazel had sex with Ruston at a party over the summer."

Mandy's eyes went wide in surprise. "Last summer. Really?"

So maybe not everyone in the group knew that one already. "Yes."

"What's Ruth's secret?" Mandy whispered and looked around the room, as if someone else was there.

"I can't tell you." She shook her head.

"I won't say, ever." Mandy made an X over her heart with a finger.

"Rafferty and her share a father. Howard Brooks is Ruth's dad also," she said and felt a weight lift off her chest. One she hadn't even known was there.

"What?" Mandy whispered even louder.

Mia put her hand over Mandy's mouth. "You can't tell anyone ever. Ruth blames Rafferty for Howard treating her bad."

"How long have you known?" Mandy pulled off the hand and asked.

Mia shrugged. "Since Howard died."

"Is that what you two are fighting about? You and Ruth?" Mandy asked, and Mia realized that maybe some in the group noticed the tension. But wondered why nobody said anything about it?

"Yes. I just want her to be nicer to Rafferty. But she can't forgive him for something he can't change." She knew she was about to cry.

Mandy hugged her to her. "How long have you and Rafferty been a thing?"

"On and off since New Year's, maybe before," she said into her cousin's shoulder, hating how much Mandy was helping her by just talking to her. Mia should be able to handle it on her own.

"Maybe before?" Mandy questioned, patting her back.

Not pulling away, she admitted, "Well, sometimes the entire year before, we would hook up for sex when drunk."

Chuckling, Mandy pushed her away so that she could look into her eyes. "And you never said?"

Smirking, she asked, "Would you admit that? I don't even remember most of it."

"Why isn't Ruth interested in getting married? She's definitely one I thought would push for it, especially now that she's going to have a baby?" Mandy pressed.

Mia looked at the door behind her and whimpered. "No."

How Mandy knew that there was a secret there, Mia didn't know. But based on her cousin's blue glare, she knew Mia knew something.

Mandy held her gaze. "Mia?"

"They got married in Las Vegas the weekend before Hazel got married," Mia said quickly and shut her eyes. "Don't tell. Ever. The Rafferty thing either."

"How?" Mandy demanded.

"We went on a Thursday afternoon and came back on Saturday. They got married that Friday." Her eyes were still shut, so she didn't have to look into her cousin's.

"Who are *we*?"

"Rafferty and I went as witnesses."

"And?" Mandy pressed.

"Nothing else." Mia opened her eyes and saw her cousin's blue ones piercing hers. She slammed them shut again.

"And?" Mandy poked her in the boob.

"Ouch." She grabbed it into her hand, more to protect it from another poke than that it actually hurt.

"And?" Mandy pressed again.

Shutting her eyes, she sighed before admitting, "And Rafferty and I drunkenly got married Thursday night. Don't tell anyone, ever. Ever. Ever."

"You're married? For months?" Mandy exclaimed.

"Ever, not even Hue. You have to promise me. Nobody can know," she begged her cousin.

Mandy just grinned at her before touching her cheek. "You were married first, but everyone thinks you're the last holdout. You are the best secret-keeper in this town, Mia Lawson."

"Ever. We are getting a divorce. Sometime." She didn't think Mandy was even listening to her anymore.

"I don't even know what to say." Mandy suddenly giggled. "You and Rafferty are so cute together, and now you're married."

"Don't say anything. Like book club, only you can't tell them either." It was dawning on her that she might have told her secrets to the wrong person.

"So, you're in love with him, and you're married to him? I don't see what the big deal is," Mandy said, more to herself then to Mia.

"So, you can't tell. Not even my mom. Definitely not my mom! Do not ever tell my mom! My mom can never know about this!" She grabbed her cousin's hand to try to get through to her.

"I was so busy keeping my pregnancy a secret I never noticed. I wonder if anyone else noticed? Does Ruth know?"

"No, we went out on the town by ourselves. Nobody knows."

Mandy was about to say something else when the door burst open, and Tess rushed in. Shutting the door behind her, she said, "Did I miss anything?"

"We all missed so much," Mandy said to Mia and winked, and then turned to Tess. "Nothing big. Did you get the baby to sleep?"

Mia sighed with relief. Mandy was going to keep her secrets. At least for now. Hopefully, she can keep her mouth shut forever.

Before Tess could finish her story about how the baby was still sleeping with her dad, Natalie, Hazel, and Ruth showed up. Book club was assembled, drinks were handed out, and a toast was made to Mandy. Mandy, who was looking at Mia the entire time.

An hour after the toast was made, Mandy was a married woman, and everyone was in the church basement enjoying a meal. This wedding was just family and close friends, so the crowd was smaller. But most were her relatives. And those who weren't were people Mia knew, but she wasn't interested in talking to anyone. Most of them she had just seen a month and a half ago at Math's wedding, so she didn't need to speak to any of them.

Or maybe it was because Rafferty was in attendance in the small crowd, and she had to avoid him because she couldn't talk to him with people around. And she wasn't ready to talk to him anyway.

Since Mandy and Hue weren't having a wedding dance, the festivities would be over after the reception. Looking at the wall clock, she gave herself an hour before she would leave. She could make an hour.

Turning to go sit by her sisters, her way was blocked by a hard body. "Excuse me."

"Mia, we have to talk," Rafferty said in the same husky voice that made her knees weak.

"No, we don't." She looked around. Did anyone notice?

"Mia, I know you know I'm leaving." He pulled her closer to him.

"I heard that. Good luck." She pushed away from him, but he grabbed on to her.

"I want you to come with me," he said into her ear.

Trying to push him away, she gasped, "What?"

Holding fast, he repeated, "I want you to come with me. Let's try being married away from here."

"I can't. I have the restaurant, my apartment. I have things here." She shook her head in defeat.

"I'm not saying you have to leave tonight," he assured her.

"People are watching." Looking away from him, she saw eyes were on her. Too many eyes. They were causing a scene.

"I don't care. Let the town see us; I want them to see us," he said, louder than before.

With everything in her, she pushed him away. People were watching. Her family was watching. Didn't he understand? He was leaving her behind, and her only saving grace was that nobody knew about it. If she stayed in his arms, everyone would know.

Turning from him, she almost ran into Ruth on the way to the door. The woman was standing in her way on the stairs, her arms crossed, two steps above her. "You told Mandy?"

Mia looked up at her, taking another step so they were more even. "What?"

"Mandy's hinting about Vegas. What did you tell her?" Ruth stated.

Shrugging, Mia admitted that she had broken her promise. "The truth. I'm sorry. I can't keep everyone's secrets anymore."

"This means we can no longer be friends," Ruth stated as Mia stepped up to the same step she was on.

Mia looked her former friend up and down in surprise. "We haven't been friends for a while, Ruth. You of all people should know that. You can't treat Rafferty like garbage and expect me to remain your friend!"

Mia was done with Ruth and Rafferty and headed for the doors to leave. She needed to get away from everyone right now. She was going to lose control of her emotions, and she wasn't doing that in public.

"Why, Mia? Why the loyalty to Rafferty? You don't even like him," Ruth demanded, following her up the stairs.

"Because, Ruth Kennedy, I love him. I have loved him for a long time. But now I can say it out loud." She pushed out the doors of the church and into the sunshine.

"He's not worth it, Mia. Rafferty is Rafferty. There's no future with him." Ruth was still following her as she spoke. As if Mia needed to be told something she already knew.

Stopping, she turned and looked at her former friend. "That may be so, Ruth, but for right now, I'm your secret brother's secret wife. And I'm tired of keeping everyone's secrets. From here on out, I'm not keeping any for anyone!"

Turning, she saw more eyes on her as she practically ran to her Jeep in the parking lot. Now she had told two people, or more. By tomorrow, the entire town will know everything. Speeding out of the parking lot, she saw the entire book club standing outside the door of the church. Who knows how many heard what she said, but right now, she didn't care. She had to get out of there. Her secrets were coming out and she couldn't seem to stop them.

CHAPTER 33

Rafferty watched the red Jeep speed out of the parking lot away from him. Turning to Ruth, he yelled, "What did you say to her? Why can't you just leave her alone?"

"What did she mean *secret wife?*" she yelled right back at him, not answering any of his questions.

"It doesn't matter to you. You want nothing to do with me. Well, the feeling is mutual. I'm done with trying to be nice to you, trying to be a family with you. Mia is my family now, and she's what's important." He rushed off toward his pickup to follow her. As he started the engine, he realized how much better he felt telling Ruth off. She was practically the only family he had, but she had just driven off the most important member of his family. His wife.

By the time he made it down Main Street, he had already lost her. He realized she could be anywhere. For a second, he thought about going back to the church to see if everyone would help look for her, but thought better of it. At this point, she wasn't getting along with any of them. So he would look alone.

Six hours later, he was no closer to finding her than he had been two minutes after she had left. Just like in January, he had looked everywhere: her parents', Math's place, Math's parents. He had even knocked on Mandy's door because that was where she had been in January. But this time, she wasn't there. Mandy had told him she hadn't heard from her and would keep an eye on Main Street for him, call him if she saw something. No call came in.

It was late when he finally decided he had to give up. She was gone. When she wanted to be found, she would be found. That was how Mia was.

Walking into his house, he heard the TV and wondered why he had left it on. Going over, he shut it off and turned and saw her. She was sound asleep on his couch. She must have turned on the TV before she had fallen asleep. Had she been here the entire time? At that point, he realized he hadn't even checked here, but why would he? She was mad at him.

Picking her up off the couch, he carried her to bed like he always did. While he had been in the bathroom getting ready for bed, he saw she had stripped out of her clothes like she usually did. Pulling her into his arms, he hoped she wouldn't be able to sneak out in the early morning hours before he woke up. But he didn't want to wake her in case that would mean she would leave now.

Someone staring at him was what woke him in the night. Hazel eyes were staring at him. Mia's hazel eyes.

"Hi," she whispered into the mostly dark room.

"Hi," he whispered back.

"Why don't I have clothes on?"

"Because you took them off." He grinned.

"You didn't? I always assumed you took them off somehow."

"No, it's always been you. You're pretty good at stripping." He smiled at her shocked face.

"I'm sorry, Rafferty." She bit her lip.

"For stripping?" he asked in confusion.

"For everything. I want you to know I'm sorry before you leave. That I messed up everything." Her chin quivered as she said it.

"Not everything, Mia. I want you to come with me. I think we can make it work somewhere elsee, not in Landstad. Somewhere else, where we can just be Mia and Rafferty." He tucked a hair behind her ear.

"But I can't leave. I've tried and tried, but I can't. I'm a Tiger." She grinned, even as she held back her tears.

"We'll make it work. You and me, together." He ran his fingers over her cheek.

"But we can't leave; we're both Tigers, and tigers don't leave."

"They do when there's nothing for them here. We can't get over the past and who people think we are here. Our future is elsewhere, where we can be the couple we want to be." It was why he knew they had to leave here.

"But what about when you get tired of me and start flirting with everyone? What do I do then if I'm not here?" A tear slipped from her eye and soaked into the pillow below her head.

"I haven't gotten tired of you ever, Mia. I regret that I didn't call you after the transplant. At the time, I was a scared kid who had no idea what I was losing by losing you. I'd spent months watching you at the café before I got enough courage up to talk to you. Then I'd go on to blow it so bad I couldn't really talk to you for another fourteen years." He kissed her nose.

"You didn't see me back then," she stated.

"Of course, I did. You used to have the tables one, two, five, six, ten, and eleven. Those were the only tables I would sit at. Your hair used to be really long, and you always had it in a ponytail. When I came back, you were coloring it I missed the chestnut color it used to be, but it's back now." Sitting up, he touched her hair, loving it was back to that chestnut color again.

"It's just plain brown," she stated.

"Not to me," he said. "Why did you come here?"

"I always come here, to you. This is our home. No matter how bad my day gets, I always feel better when I'm here. With you."

"I love it when you're here, but I love you, so it doesn't matter where we are." He kissed her forehead.

"You love me?" she asked in surprise.

He just chuckled. "Mia, I bought you this house."

"I thought you fell in love with it and had to have it?" She sat up a little and looked down at him.

Shaking his head, he admitted, "I wanted to give you the house you wanted—then maybe you would want me."

"Rafferty Brooks, you bought this house for me?" she asked again, sitting all the way up. Holding the sheet to her bare chest, she looked around the dark bedroom as if for the first time.

He sat up and hugged her to him, kissing her bare shoulder. "Yes, Mrs. Brooks, I knew I had to when we got back from getting married. I had a small hold on you then, but I needed it to be bigger."

"Do you remember getting married?"

"No, but I know why I married you. For the same reason I would marry you again tomorrow." He kissed her shoulder again. "I love you."

"Me too," she admitted. "Because I've loved you for so long but only let myself act on it when I was drunk."

Cupping her breast, he felt her inhale sharply. He loved how her body always responded to his. "Me too, though I would've preferred to marry you sober."

"Let's get married," she said with a giggle.

Pulling her body close, he nuzzled her neck. "We're already married, silly."

She sighed. "Let's get married here. In Landstad. Sober and in front of everyone."

"When?" he asked, because he would do it anytime, any day.

"It doesn't matter. We're already married." She turned in his arms.

"Before or after we move?" he asked, hoping for sooner rather than later. But he also knew that she would probably want a big wedding, and those took time.

"Either, I guess." She shrugged, and her smile slipped off her face when she admitted, "I don't want to move, but I can't stay here with Ruth."

"I told her off after you left. I told her I'm no longer interested in being family. And it's true. After watching her treat you so badly these last few months, I realized I didn't want to have a relationship with her if she could treat my wife like that." He hugged her close to him, protecting her now when he couldn't before.

"That's how I feel about her treating you. I just couldn't take it anymore," Mia said into his chest.

Kissing her hair, he said, "That's why I love you. You're my defender."

Pushing herself up on her arm, she told him, "Do you realize that we could have an eight-month-old baby now if I had gotten pregnant the night we hooked up after the bar?"

"No, we couldn't have. We never had sex that night." He smirked.

"What? No, we did. I know we did."

"Nope. We didn't have sex before the day you helped me move in, either. Although I remember giving you a fantastic orgasm before you passed out, though. The rest was staged. You were too drunk to do anything. I don't take advantage of drunk women, even super sexy Mia Lawson Brooks," he admitted, though he had mostly forgotten about how he had staged her apartment back then. Now he wished he hadn't.

"How dare you!" she yelled. "I thought I was pregnant!"

"Didn't you take the test?"

"Of course, but they are not accurate and I couldn't just go into the drug store and buy another one. Jackie and my mom are friends you know."

"Sorry, love. I did it because you're so cute when you're mad. Like now." Quickly, he rolled her onto her back and pinned her to the bed.

"Don't do it again," she pinched his side in anger. "What about the wedding night?"

"That I don't know. I don't remember that one." He kissed her, though he was sure they hadn't since he always remembered making love to Mia. Those were his happiest memories.

"Me neither." She smirked and wiggled under him, reminding him how naked she was and how long it had been since he had made love to her. "But I really like to remember making love to you."

"Let's make some more memories, Mrs. Brooks." He kissed her once on the lips, then made a trail down her body.

"Can we make them without a condom this time?" she asked as she wrapped her legs around him.

His heart stopped. Was she saying she wanted to start a family with him? Forever was one thing, but a baby was another. Not that he didn't want her to carry his babies, all of them, but he had wanted to be married for a while before that. Except he had been married a while already.

Looking up at her from her breasts to her eyes, he grinned. "But I have like a hundred condoms."

"Think again, Brooks. I think you're well below fifty." She pulled open the drawer and took out a packet. After all their times together, it was almost always her who pulled out the package and usually make some type of comment about it. Even if getting that many had been a blessing.

Stopping and resting his chin on her stomach, he asked, "Are you ready to have our baby?"

She blinked twice and blushed. "I, um, was just thinking. I mean, no pressure. There are still a lot of condoms, and I know where to get more. Not the drug store of course, online. No big—"

Her words were stopped as his tongue slid through her folds. As usual, it didn't take long before she was writhing in his arms. With her words of encouragement, he slipped his demanding cock into her, making her gasp.

It was only after they were sated and cuddling did he find the unused condom in the bed. Holding it up, he asked, "Do you really want to have my baby?"

Her eyes went to the package and then to him in shock. "I thought you used it."

Smirking, he kissed her nose, "My wife wants a family, so who am I to say no?"

"Are you sure?" she asked, because she needed his assurance he hadn't made a mistake. That he wouldn't regret this in morning.

"I'm sure of everything with you, Mia Lawson Brooks. From now until forever," he promised.

CHAPTER 34

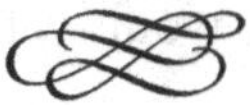

WHAT WAS Mia's favorite part of married life? Waking up late in the morning with her husband.

Okay, it had happened only once, but it had been amazing. They had made love most of the night, barely sleeping, making up for lost time. The condom had gone unused, and she had put it back in the drawer at some point, but she couldn't tell you when.

Since it was Sunday after Mandy's wedding, she didn't need to go to the café that morning, so they slept in well past six, then she woke him up like she had dreamed of doing every morning when her alarm had gone off at five for her to get to work.

It wasn't until after eight that they had made it downstairs to eat breakfast. Since she didn't have clothes at his place, she wore one of his T-shirts and a pair of basketball shorts that seemed to fit okay for eating breakfast. And since she was in such a good mood, she made him her favorite. Well, she made him pancakes because he had no waffle iron.

Over breakfast, they planned their move. He would have to go first, because she would have to hire a manager and get them settled before she could follow him. She just hoped that wouldn't take long. She was already thinking of a few waitresses who might be ready for the task, something she hadn't thought of before. But then before she didn't want to be separated from her husband for months to find an oursider.

But as soon as they could, they would need to see about finding a place to live. Mia thought they should rent an apartment until the house in Landstad sold, but Rafferty's argument was that finding an apartment in Grand Forks was different than here. Neither had given in, but in time, Mia knew she would let him win. But until then, she liked the argument.

After breakfast and a long goodbye, Mia walked home to shower and change. It was Sunday, and that meant church. Mandy's wedding or not, it was Sunday, and she was expected to attend.

She was just tossing some clothes into a suitcase when Rafferty strolled into the apartment, looking sexy in gray slacks and a white button-up shirt. How he had showered and gotten ready so quickly, she didn't know.

"You're going to be hot in that," Mia commented when she saw him.

"Thanks, beautiful. You're pretty hot yourself." Rafferty pulled her into his arms for a kiss as if it had been months instead of minutes since they had last touched.

"I mean in church. There's no air conditioning." Mia laughed a nervous laugh, pulling out of his arms. Today, she was bringing him to church. Just putting it all out in the open in one swoop. Let people talk.

"I'll be okay. Nice dress." His eyes roamed her body, from her white sandals to pink sundress, making her want to stay home completely. And not because she was nervous.

"Are you ready?" Mia said, though she wasn't.

"Yes, I am." Rafferty took her hand to led her from the apartment. "Are we taking your suitcase?"

"No, we can get it later." She wasn't completely packed yet anyway. But in reality, she wanted to tell her mom that she was moving in with a man before she actually did it. Even if she was thirty and only moving a block away.

Since it was a nice summer morning, they walked the four blocks. As they walked, they talked, and Mia felt like they were on display. Every car that drove by was another voice talking about her life. But there was no turning back now.

"Don't be nervous, Mia," Rafferty said from beside her as Mandy and Hue drove by them, waving and grinning.

"I'm not," she lied to him as she waved at her cousin, not grinning.

"It'll be done with soon, and then nobody will be talking about it anymore. You know that. You didn't have a secret baby or run off on your wedding, and both of those blew over pretty quickly," Rafferty said of her friends.

"I've been married for months," she pointed out.

"I thought you weren't going to tell anyone about that one."

"I told Mandy yesterday, and I think that she has loose lips."

"Maybe it won't be so bad, Mrs. Brooks." He bumped her shoulder with his as they saw Natalie and her husband getting out of their car in the parking lot. All waved at each other.

"We'll just roll with it." Mia tried to sound like it was going to be easy.

Inside the church, she acted like she brought Rafferty there every week. In reality, she had no idea how to act. She didn't have to introduce him to anyone; they all knew him. They both said hellos to those around them as Mia led him into the sanctuary to sit down, getting them away from the crowd by the door. Away from people talking.

She slid into the pew with her parents, who were already there. Her mom's eyebrow went up in question when she saw Rafferty. But she didn't say anything but a nice hello to him, like he always came with her. Was a part of her.

"Morning, Rafferty," her cousin Math said from the pew behind them without the usual tease in his voice. Did he know how nerve-wracking this was? Maybe, since he and Tess hadn't had a smooth time getting together.

"Morning, Math, Tess." Rafferty turned to the couple in the pew behind them and smiled his sexy smile.

Then it was over, and nobody said anything. Nobody whispered or whispered loud enough for Mia to hear. There were looks, but mostly from her family and the book club members who were there. Which was all of them except Ruth, who Mia was mostly still avoiding.

As people started to leave the sanctuary, her mom leaned over Mia and said to Rafferty, "You two must come over for lunch today. I'll whip something up for you."

Before Mia could respond, Mandy interrupted from behind her mom, "Sorry, Aunt Dottie, the book club is having a luncheon for my wedding. I have so much leftover food from the wedding."

"Oh, I hadn't heard. Where at?" Dottie asked, hedging for an invitation to the brunch.

"Actually, at Rafferty's. He has the biggest place." Mandy didn't take the bait as she explained, not even looking at the man whose house she was inviting people to. "But I bet Mia would bring Rafferty out during the week, then you can have something ready when they get there. Not be so rushed."

"That would work out better," her mom agreed, then turned to Mia and Rafferty and said, "Tomorrow night."

"We will be there, Mrs. Lawson." Rafferty grinned at her.

"Don't be so formal. Call me Dottie." Her mom giggled under the intense sexy grin.

"I will, Dottie. Now, I have to get my house in order since the book club is coming," Rafferty said, but he didn't sound mad.

"We'll drive you two since you walked," Natalie said from the aisle as they waited to shake the pastor's hand.

"That would be great." Rafferty had completely taken over the conversation, but Mia was lost in the entire thing.

Everything was a blur until Rafferty led her to Natalie's SUV, and the people around her stopped talking. Because there were no people around her finally. Breathing deep, she closed her eyes.

"Church, Mia, with your mom there? I guess that's one way to shut her up." Natalie shook her head as the short drive came to an end at Rafferty's house. "Why didn't you just let the town talk for the weekend. Monday they would've already forgotten you were never a couple. Church."

"Come on in," Rafferty said to his guests.

"I haven't been in here for ages. Okay, maybe never. But I used to trick-n-treat here, and it always seemed haunted." Natalie was making up for the fact that the other two weren't talking at all.

"It's not," Rafferty finally said, though Natalie didn't seem to believe it.

Before they even made it inside, Math and Tess pulled up behind Natalie's SUV and clambered out with just the baby today. Math's other children must have gone home with his parents since they had been at church.

In the house, Rafferty showed Natalie and Sam around and then also Math and Tess when they came in. Mia went to the kitchen to see what Rafferty had for serving almost a dozen people. No paper plates or plastic silverware and not enough regular silverware as it was. She should've stopped at her place to grab some. She couldn't host a party under these conditions.

As Rafferty led the tour through the kitchen working towards the backyard, both Tess and Natalie stayed behind.

"Your house is beautiful, Mia," Tess said.

"Thank you." Mia loved her house, and loved that it was hers. When they left, she was going to miss it. But it would be worth it to have Rafferty to herself.

"Food is here," Mandy said, but she wasn't carrying any when she walked into the room, just a baby boy in a car seat.

"Is it invisible?" Mia asked as she started to relax with everyone in her house.

"Ha ha," Mandy said as the men came in and dropped off more food than the group was going to be able to eat at this impromptu get together.

Natalie looked at all the containers of food and asked, "What's the plan, Mia?"

Mia sighed and smiled as she put the meat in the stove to heat up, "Rafferty and I are moving to Grand Forks. Together."

It wasn't what they had been asking, but it was what was on her mind. She had no idea how to feed a dozen people, and she had no idea how she was going to leave this town. Right now, leaving was foremost in her mind.

"What? No. You can't leave." Natalie looked at her.

Looking up, Mandy stopped taking her son from his car seat. "What about book club?"

"When did you decide this?" Tess pushed her sister-in-law away and took the baby from the car seat herself.

It was then that Hazel walked into the room, asking, "What are we talking about?"

"Mia thinks she's leaving town," Natalie explained to her friend as she gave Mia a side hug.

"You can't leave, Mia. We need to have an emergency book club to talk you out of it." Hazel looked around the room at the others, who were nodding.

"I was going to quit anyway. I can't be around Ruth anymore," Mia admitted as she looked for big bowls to put salads in.

Tess found some first and said, "There's no quitting book club."

"Why not? Ruth can't stand me, and the feeling is mutual." Mia slammed the cabinet door closed.

HAZEL JUMPED at the noise and said. "You two have always gotten along."

"No, not in months," Mia said, wondering how she hadn't noticed.

"Then I shouldn't have called her and invited her over? Sorry." Opening a bag of chips to far, Tess looked confused as they fell onto the floor.

"I don't really think she'll come anyway." Not after yesterday. They had said the words that had ended their friendship. There was no coming back from that.

"When are you leaving?" Mandy started picking up the chips, her focus on that and not on Mia—which meant she was more upset than she was letting on about Mia moving.

"Rafferty is leaving in a week or so, but I have to find a manager for the restaurant. Then I will follow. We were hoping to go look at places to live sometime this week." Mia tried to sound excited.

"You're finally getting out of here," Natalie said. "Who's going to do the winter carnival and the auction now?"

"You and Hazel could, Natalie. It's a lot of work, but it can be fun," Mia said to her younger, outgoing friend.

Both women looked at the other, but neither said anything. Mia knew the idea had to sit with them for a while before they decided to do it. Which she was sure they would.

"What you pulled in church today, Mia, holy cow. I think both of our mothers had you married with kids by the time the first hymn was over. And your mom had you having around six," Mandy stated with a giggle.

"She's not impressed that you're having another one?" Mia asked, dodging the marriage question. They hadn't settled on what to do with that yet. "I think it's about time they gave up on that battle. I mean, Mom always has Kipling in the batter's box. She can produce kids long after you Nordskov's are completely dried up."

Mandy laughed at the description of her family. Mia knew her mom looked on her youngest as the one who would bring her numbers up in the final inning. But maybe soon, Mia would add some numbers behind her name. Now with Rafferty in her life.

"Mandy, I don't think this salad is a two-dayer," Mia said, looking at one of the five salads that were brought that was a soupy mess. Looking up to see if Mandy had left, she saw Ruth standing in the doorway.

Putting the tin cover back on it, she picked it up and turned her back on everyone, and threw it in the garbage. Like Ruth had done to their friendship that had taken months to build.

"Mia," Ruth said in the silent room.

Turning around and facing her, Mia didn't hold back, not anymore, "Didn't think you would come since Rafferty would be here. Can't be in the same room as him, can you?"

Ruth ignored her words and asked, "Can we talk, Mia? In private?"

"Can you take care of this?" she asked the room of women, who all agreed that they could handle it as they looked from one to the other. How they were going to make the big meal happen with what little was in the house, she didn't know. But she was a little relieved she didn't have to worry about it for a few minutes. She just had to worry about being around Ruth.

Leading Ruth upstairs since there were very few rooms with furniture in them, she took her to the one spare room that did have a bed in it. Ruth sat on the bed and rested her arms on her stomach—her now very pregnant stomach. Mia stood with her arms crossed. There was no way she could relax.

"I'm sorry, Mia. You were right. I have been cruel to Rafferty over the last few months. And in turn, I was mean to you. I had given up on him actually doing something about how he said he felt for you. When he first asked me to help him win you over, it was just after we started book club, a long time ago. I wanted to protect you from him, from what the rumors about him were. I had assumed he would break your heart and not look back. I didn't want that for you. I didn't think he would change, not even for you. I admit I never got over that feeling." Ruth didn't look at Mia at all.

"We both had some issues to get over. I think we might have finally done that." She shrugged. They may not be over every issue, but the major ones were behind them, she was sure.

"No thanks to me. I should have just forgiven him when Howard died. We were both treated badly by that man. But instead, I kept punishing him for something he couldn't change. It was more of a habit than anything. Some injustice I clung to even when Rafferty asked me to forgive him." Ruth didn't move, but she did look up at Mia.

"He's all alone, you know. His mom has shut him out completely since Howard died, maybe even before that. Well, not anymore. He'll have me and my family now." Mia paced.

"But you're leaving? Moving with him?" Ruth asked, rubbing her huge stomach.

"Yes, as soon as I find a manager for the café. I hope I find someone soon. We've lost a lot of time together. I regret losing that time." She stopped and looked out the window at the plain back yard. She had so many plans for that space, and she wouldn't get to achieve any of them.

"What about book club?" Ruth asked.

Turning back to Ruth, Mia said, "I was done with book club weeks ago, Ruth. It used to be the best part of my week, but now I dread what you will say, what jabs you will poke me with. It seemed your dislike of Rafferty had turned on me."

"I'm sorry. I took it too far. It's just that everyone in book club is happy, and you seemed to be stuck on Rafferty. I wanted you to move on and be happy."

"I'm happy with him. When we're actually together, it's great. He makes me feel pretty and smart, and I love him for it." Mia smiled.

"But you're all those things without him," Ruth told her, getting up from the bed with more difficulty than Mia expected, but she wasn't going to offer to help.

"No, I'm Mia at the café without him. He makes me a better person. He's the one who put my name up for organizing the auction, which led to the Christmas carnival. He thought I would be good at it. He believed in me, even before I thought he cared about me." At the time, she hadn't even known it was him behind it.

"You are. But you will leave all that behind when you leave Landstad."

"Yes, because I want to be with him. We have too much of a past in this town, and people are always talking. I don't want to be talked about." Ruth should be the first to understand because she hated when she was talked about.

"I think you took that away from everyone today. I got a phone call that you were in church holding hands with Rafferty before it was even half over. What were you thinking? Were there no billboards just outside of town available?" Ruth grinned.

Mia just shrugged. "I wanted the town to know that he's mine. Stop the rumors before they even started."

Ruth clapped her hands slowly a few times. "Success. Remember back when we went out for drinks with Tess, when Rafferty and

Anderson brought us drinks? Tess said that night we had a thing for the guys. I guess we did."

"I remember being friends that night. I miss being friends. It seems I can't be friends with you and be in love with Rafferty at the same time. The more I fell for him, the worse our relationship became." Mia looked at her hands, lost in the past and how much she had enjoyed that night with her friends so long ago.

"I hate that I have lost you as a friend over this. Yesterday, Rafferty said that I won, but I lost you, and you were my best friend. You were my first choice to take with me when I got married. I pretended you weren't. I should have just told you at the time. But I was still clinging to the past when we were too different, we couldn't get along. I couldn't see how important you were to me." Ruth wiped a tear from her eye.

"Thanks for bringing us along. I have to say it was a huge turning point in our relationship. The turn we really needed to take. I wish I had noticed it earlier. Are you ever going to tell anyone or just get married again?" Mia asked, not for the first time.

"I don't know. I wanted to because I didn't want to be the unwed mother like my mom was. But Anderson isn't going anywhere; he's not Howard. I love the gossip and the speculation." Ruth grinned at her admission.

"I hate it. I want the wedding, at church like everyone else. I want to be the one fussed over and have everyone there. See my mom cry, and have Dad give me away. I want it all," she said, realizing it was true. As much as she wanted to tell the world she was married to Rafferty Brooks and had been for almost nine months, she wanted to have the wedding that would announce it to the world.

"But you are already married, right? When did you even get married?" Ruth asked in disbelief.

Walking into the room, Rafferty must have heard the question. His expression told her that he had been worried about the two women being alone together. Rafferty went instantly to Mia's side and took her hand in support. "For a day longer than you have, sister."

"I don't think so. I would've heard something if that had happened. Mia can't keep a secret to save her life," Ruth argued.

"I don't think you know my wife very well then, Ruth. She kept everyone's secrets as if they were her own. Since you made her promise to not tell anyone about your wedding, she couldn't tell anyone about her own."

Ruth sat down on the bed as the realization dawned on her. "I didn't know. Nobody knew. Where was I when you were getting married? We were together the entire time during that trip."

"Were we even on the same trip? We were never together. You and Anderson were so wrapped up in each other, Rafferty and I didn't even exist. We could have done anything without you knowing," Mia said in disbelief.

"And did, it seems," Ruth said just as Mandy came into the room, a little apprehensively.

"Did what?" Looking from Ruth to Rafferty and then to Mia, Mandy asked, "Oh, and we have to share forks unless I can borrow a key to the café for Hue to grab a few more."

"In my coat pocket," she told her cousin, hoping she would leave, so everyone didn't know her business.

"That Mia and Rafferty got married months ago." As if it wasn't something everybody knew, Ruth told her, ignoring the forks talk.

Tess walked into the room to hear the tail end of her explanation. "So we can finally talk about that? Thank god. I'm tired of keeping that secret." With that, Tess grabbed Mia and hugged her tight.

"What?" Mia asked, pushing her away in confusion. "How did you know?"

"You streamed Math and I the entire thing. I like to think it was because we were your first choice and not because Mandy wasn't answering her phone like you said. It was so romantic." Tess gushed a little.

"You knew the entire time? Why didn't you say anything?" Rafferty asked, because Mia was speechless.

"Because you told us not to, and had to we kept it secret until you got back and could tell everyone yourselves. But then you didn't. I had to drag it out of you that you were even in Vegas. So we started to think it was a joke. That you were playing us. For months we waited. Math even tried to get Rafferty to admit it at Natalie's wedding, but nothing. " Tess said and handed over her phone to Mia.

As Ruth filled them in on her wedding weekend, Rafferty looked over her shoulder as they watched the ten-minute ceremony where they said the drunken words they both were too scared to say when sober. They could've spent the last eight months happy instead of scared that the other didn't feel the same if they had just watched this.

Taking the phone, Rafferty sent the video to Mia, who was in Tess's contacts. Then handed it back to Tess. Now they had proof of that day forever.

"I wish I remember marrying you," Mia said. "It's unfair that I don't remember the happiest moment of my life."

"Let's do it again. A sequel, but sober this time. I know how much you love a sequel." Rafferty spun her in his arms and kissed her, not caring who else was in the room.

Mia lifted an eyebrow in question. "What sort of sequel? And how sober?"

He laughed at her questions. "We get married again, only this time, exactly like you want. Maybe not completely sober."

"I want everything. Church, dress, bridesmaids, whiskey, flower babies, oh, and flowers. I love flowers. Not roses, though, I don't love those. But other ones. Purple ones." She could see it already. Might as well lean into the color pallet of her first wedding, even if she only had a video of it.

"Lavender," he corrected. "My only request is that we get married on the same day as we did before."

Shaking her head, she questioned his idea. "We can't. That day is almost a year ago."

"I mean this year. How else would you want to spend your first anniversary?"

"I can't think of a better way," she admitted, grinning. There was nothing she could imagine would be better. Then she realized something. "And as a bonus, I don't have to tell my mom that I got married without her there. I would hate for her to miss out on seeing her oldest daughter get married."

"Nobody wants that to happen," Mandy said from beside them, reminding Mia they were not alone.

"I have a preacher who would be happy to marry you again," Hazel said from the doorway with that very preacher behind her nodding enthusiasticly.

"I'll help any way I can," Ruth surprised Mia by saying.

"I'll take all the help I can get. Time is short, and the wedding is going to be big." She smiled at her former friend, who might just turn back into a good friend again. Them being a family might not be so farfetched as it had been a few minutes ago. There was hope for them repairing their relationship.

"I'll take care of everything," Ruth said with confidence.

"We all will," Natalie assured her, since she was the one with the most wedding experience in the room.

Looking around the room, she saw all her friends nod. They were all willing to help her, to be there for her just like she had been there for them all. She had managed to find a great group of friends that accepted her and loved her. Even if she loved the former playboy of Landstad. Maybe because she did.

Leaning back into the man she loved, she whispered for only his ears, "I love you."

"I love you too, since forever. For forever."

She melted into him.

It was exactly what she needed to hear, that he felt the exact same as she did. She couldn't see her life without him in it, being the center of it. That hadn't changed since she was in high school, and it seemed it never would.

EPILOGUE

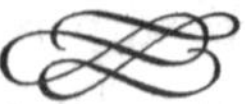

Fall

SINCE THE ENTIRE book club had been sworn to secrecy since June, nobody else in town was aware that the wedding taking place today was a sham. Especially not Mia's mom. Nobody dared tell the woman that her first born had been married in Vegas a year before without her present.

Mia was sitting on the same table she always sat on waiting for a wedding to start. Well, actually, she was waiting for her friends to show up and drink to her upcoming marriage. But she didn't know who would show up today. Book club had officially ended that day in June after Mandy got married. Though they still got together every two weeks, there was no reading involved, and no recordings were done. They just talked.

Those who could come, did. Mandy was on bed rest, so she hadn't recently been there, and Ruth had her baby soon after Mandy's wedding but had only come sporadically since then. Tess, Hazel, and Natalie were busy with their families and work and sometimes had to miss for those reasons. Mia was usually a constant since it was more often than not at her house due to the space and location, but the wedding planning sometimes got in the way of that.

After talking to Ruth and Anderson, Rafferty had decided to give it a few more months in Landstad, and it had worked out. Ruth was more accepting of him as a person. Maybe not there with the brother thing completely, but as a close friend. They had all become better friends since that day.

In the end, they had chosen Mia and Rafferty to be godparents to Mary Elizabeth Miles because they were family. Eliza ended up with the white hair of her mother, but her dad's dark eyes. She was healthy and adorable but way more work than her mother had ever expected her to be. Mia knew Ruth's writing had been suffering.

By the time July had rolled around, Mia was living with Rafferty full-time. No more apartment uptown. She had let that go. Nobody had anything bad to say about them. Not even her mother had mentioned that they were living in sin. Some asked how it was going and if she liked not living downtown, but no one said anything mean about it. Since his house had been so big, all her stuff had fit in without any problems. There was even a built-in book shelf that held all her movies cases, old and new—no more boxes taking up space in her closet. True to his word, Rafferty had helped move it all without complaining, though she had heard some grumbling because she wouldn't allow anyone else to help.

Just to upset her mother, Dottie thought Mia would not have any bridesmaids and Rafferty no groomsmen. Mia did it because she didn't want her sisters, and her friends were all busy with their families. And it was a fake wedding, all for Mia. Or so she said, but in reality it was for her mom, because she wasn't just a little afraid of the woman still.

For a personal attendant, she had chosen Ruth, but Ruth was busy getting the baby settled, so Mia was alone. And she was lonely. Maybe it was her who had kept the group together through all the big events over the past almost two years. Wedding, baptisms, even keeping the group going in the early days.

She had been there for all of their weddings, right here in this room for most of them, but they weren't here for her. She should have told them that they were all her personal attendants, then maybe someone would've shown up. Flattening out the creases in her cream dress, she wondered if she should have just said they were married and been done with it. This day wasn't turning out how she had thought it would at all.

It had started to snow and had yet to stop, though it wasn't going to stay. It was supposed to be around just long enough to make Mia's wedding a wet, sloppy mess. They had the bachelorette party at her house since Ruth had the baby, and everyone bailed on her because they had families they wanted to stay with. The only positive was that she got to sleep with her husband on the night of their wedding, but very little sleep was actually had. Her sisters had shown up at nine for hair and makeup and got to see more of the groom than they ever should have. Mia was convinced all four of her married sisters were now very envious of their big sister. Kipling now had some lofty ideas about her future spouse.

While getting to the church, she had realized getting her dress fitted a month ago was a mistake. It was tight. Remembering Hazel nearly passing out, she vowed she would take shallow breaths all day. She loved the dress. Her body apparently hated it.

At the fifteen minute mark, the door finally flung open, and Rafferty Brooks walked in, looking as sexy as always, just this time in a tux. She had insisted since he wore a suit all the time she wanted better for her wedding. This time, no jeans at all, though he looked great in those as well.

"What are you doing here? This is bad luck," she said, not moving from the table.

He shut the door behind him. "I'm going to dance with Mia Lawson one more time."

"I'm not Mia Lawson," she reminded him, and today it became legal.

"You are to me." He pulled out his phone. Tapping a few buttons, she heard Taylor Swift start singing one of her favorites—the same song they had danced to after Natalie's first failed wedding. Right here in this room.

Sliding off the table, she let him pull her into his arms. "Do you even remember dancing with me after Natalie's first wedding?"

"Yes. Some of it." It was fuzzy in some places.

"I love dancing with you, Mia Autumn Lawson Brooks." He kissed the top of her head.

"I love dancing with you to, Raff." She pulled him closer, and their steps grew smaller.

"I do wish you would've worn that purple number from the actual wedding." He kissed her temple as the moved.

"Lavender? It wasn't right for my church wedding." She wasn't going to tell him that she had almost worn it anyway. But instead had bought a sexy lingerie in the same color for tonight.

"But I want to remember getting married to you in it," he complained. The video hadn't been enough for him. Though it did show exactly how drunk they were. She couldn't believe they were even allowed to get married. There should be rules.

"Just remember this one, and remember last year's date." Resting her head against his shoulder, she smiled, she liked that they had that secret, even if others knew.

"This one is quite amazing, too. I'll spend the entire wedding planning how I'm going to tear it off you later."

"You won't; there's a zipper." She pointed to the back of the dress.

"With my teeth." He showed them. Then he kissed her, and she didn't care about her makeup or anything else when he kissed her.

"Stop it right now," Tess said from the door.

Both looked over at her and didn't even bother to look embarrassed.

"What?" Natalie asked from behind Tess.

"They were making out right before the wedding!" Tess explained as the two separated.

"As long as they're not related, to each there own, right?" Natalie asked Mia with a smile and a reference to her first wedding, where Mia was still convinced the groom made out with a bridesmaid who might or might not have been his sister after the bride left him.

"Rafferty, out. Now we have to fix her." Tess turned to Mia.

Rafferty grabbed his phone and, on the way out the door, said, "I see nothing that needs fixing. She's perfect."

Ruth passed him on his way and out and said, "She is, isn't she."

Closing the door behind Rafferty, Ruth looked around. "Where's Hazel?"

"Maybe making out with the pastor. I wouldn't put it past her." Natalie checked to make sure nothing was amiss with Mia's dress.

"Really, Natalie. I have to face the man in a few minutes," Mia argued in half outrage.

"Remember, it was you who said what you said, and I had to leave my wedding. I couldn't face the man." Natalie laughed and arranged a lock of Mia's hair. It was still brown, and she had no plans on coloring it. That is until the gray showed up, then she'd be back to coloring it every month.

"You didn't want to marry the other man. Don't put that on me," Mia said as Tess put more lipstick on her.

Hazel rushed in and asked, "Who's getting Mandy on the phone?"

"Nobody, she's here," Mandy said from the doorway. "No way would I miss my own cousin's wedding. She's my favorite."

Mia hugged her. She was supposed to be on bedrest with her second pregnancy, and had been for over a month now. This time, she hadn't hidden her pregnancy for long; she was telling everyone. And so far, the baby was staying put. The doctor wasn't even worried she would miscarry this time, but they put her on bedrest as a precaution.

"Okay, we don't have a lot of time." Hazel grabbed the tray from the shelf. "Everyone knows the rule: drink what you want, and no comments from others. Until later, then comment away."

There were twelve paper cups on the tray. Half were whiskey, Mia's favorite, and half were another beverage that was nonalcoholic for those who were abstaining from alcohol for one reason or another. Well, actually, the only reason was being pregnant.

Mandy, of course, grabbed a non-alcoholic choice. Mia watched the others grab, and of course so did everyone else. Mandy was the only one everyone knew was pregnant. Mia wanted to know who else. Ruth grabbed a whiskey, but her kid was a few months old now.

The other four eyed each other and all reached for a glass at the same time. All grabbed from the same side of the tray, and they all laughed at themselves and at each other. It seems there was going to be a baby boom in the group. A big one.

"So next time, no alcohol?" Hazel asked. She usually was in charge of the beverages. Mostly because she was married, the preacher and the old biddies in church wouldn't dare comment if she was caught.

"Looks that way, Haze." Natalie couldn't stop smiling as she hugged her friend.

"Okay, to Mia finding happiness in Rafferty 'sexy smile' Brooks, and to her staying here in Landstad forever," Ruth said.

"You mean Rafferty 'pain in the butt in a good way' Brooks," Mandy said with a wink.

"No, Rafferty 'knows better than to argue with me' Brooks," Hazel added.

"Rafferty 'looks good in jeans, but better without' Brooks." Natalie giggled.

"You mean, Rafferty 'sweetest guy ever' Brooks," Tess insisted.

"No, Rafferty 'owns my heart and soul' Brooks, ladies," Mia corrected and clinked Mandy's glass, causing everyone else to do the same.

They all drank down their drink of choice. Mia looked at all her friends who she loved and wondered what it was going to be like when all their kids were in Landstad High School. Would any of them fall in love on prom night like she did? Hopefully, if they do, they don't wait fourteen years to actually marry that person.

The group disassembled, and all but Ruth went and sat with their spouses. Ruth walked with Mia up the steps of the basement. How many times had she walked up these steps doing just this as every-thing but the bride?

Ruth leaned toward her and whispered, "So, pregnant on your wedding day? It happens."

"We weren't planning it but weren't really preventing it, either. We just felt ready. So much time had already been wasted in our relationship to put off starting a family."

It had only been a week that she had known, and Rafferty was having a hard time not telling everyone. It was like he had achieved something nobody else had by getting a woman pregnant. But she was happy he was so excited.

This morning, she had even told her mom. Not that she was already married, never that, but that she was pregnant. Because she needed the pressure to stop that her mom had started to apply the moment Mia and Rafferty had told her they were getting married. All the woman thought about was grandkids.

Mia saw her dad, Roger, waiting for her, and he smiled at her. She smiled back at him. Taking his arm, she stopped, and Ruth straightened her dress for her. Then the doors swung open to show all of Landstad had shown up for her big day, but all she could see was Rafferty in his tux, waiting for her at the end of the aisle.

As her dad walked her to him, she knew this was what she had wanted for years. Rafferty Brooks at her wedding. She still couldn't believe that Rafferty Brooks was marrying her, or was already married to her. Her. Mia Lawson from the diner with the plain brown hair and mom hips.

The End

Thank you so much for reading Irreplaceable. Was it everything you were hoping for? It would be greatly appreciated if you could drop a review so others can find and enjoy Irreplaceable and the entire Landstad series.

ALSO BY ALIE GARNETT

<u>Landstad, ND</u>

<u>Invisible</u>

<u>Irresistible</u>

<u>Impulsive</u>

<u>Insuppressible</u>

<u>Intriguing</u>

<u>Imperfect</u>

<u>Irreplaceable</u>

<u>The Great Lovely Falls</u>

Falling for the Single Mom

Falling for his Best Friends Sister

Falling for the Boss

Falling for his Step-Sister

Falling for his Fake Wife

Falling into a Second Chance

<u>Hart Series</u>

Seeing her Pain

Her Favor

Max Valentine is Looking at Me!

Keeping her Safe

<u>Stand Alone</u>

Romancing the Doctor

ABOUT THE AUTHOR

I love to read and prefer a little spice in those books. I am lucky enough to live on a small hobby farm in northern Minnesota with her husband and two kids. I enjoy spending time in the pasture with my two mini horses and one fainting goat (who doesn't actually faint). When I'm not writing, I'm busy trying to do all the things I didn't get to while writing. Or maybe I wouldn't have gotten to them anyway, because its laundry, dishes and fun things like that.

What to know more about me and my writing? You can sign up for my newsletter to get the scoop.

f